UNITIL I OWN YOU

CALLIE STEVENS

BRIDGET

The leather riding crop swipes through the air, a blurry cloud of black, and lands squarely against his open palm.

I wish I could hear the slap of the leather on his skin, but the window through which I watch the scene is soundproof.

It's erotic in its own right, the silence.

And yet, I still wish I could have the real thing, the full surround sound experience.

I tighten my thighs together as the Dom paces back and forth.

He's a specimen in his long-sleeved mesh shirt and tight leather pants. His dark, olive features are delicious to behold, and his stern countenance exudes control beyond measure. Doesn't need to bare his teeth or look angry.

He exudes the fact he's a Dom.

He keeps thwacking his palm with the riding crop.

My heart throbs in my chest.

How I would *kill* to be the sub before him on her hands

and knees with a ball gag in her mouth, waiting with breathless anticipation.

In one fell swoop, he cracks the crop against her bare backside.

She launches forward, her eyes rolling back, and I can only imagine both the pleasure and pain she is experiencing at once.

I suck in a breath. Thank god, I'm the only one in the viewing gallery today. I'm definitely enjoying the show, but I don't need that little info getting back to my dad, thank you very much.

The Dom pummels her backside, resulting in a peppering of welts across her skin. The strikes are masterfully spread, making the whole area evenly red, each welt clearly visible as if he were painter and each hit was a strike of the paintbrush.

Pain shouldn't look so pleasurable, yet here I sit, every inch of me begging for an opportunity for that to be me. Just once.

He steps away and hangs the crop on the wall with all the other toys.

The sub turns her head toward me. She's a member here.

Membership in the Lyons Club is a birth right for some, like me. For others, it's an earned honor. And considering I know her face from somewhere but not her name, I'd say she's earned the honor quite recently.

Her blonde hair, with lots of curls, and Botox job puts her somewhere between the ages of forty and sixty. She smiles around her gag at me, eyes wobbling with unshed tears.

Of pain? Of pleasure?

Probably both.

My stomach flips. That could be me. I want it to be me.

And as I yearn to be her, I don't think I could be as exposed. But truth is, no one chooses to scene in a room with a viewing gallery if they don't like being watched. The invitation is implicit to anyone who might be interested in getting a show.

The Dom grabs her by the jaw, pulls her face toward his, and seems to admonish her close yet calm.

The door to the gallery opens.

Oh crap!

My eyes fly to the door as I sit up straighter, only relaxing when I notice Sonia walking through the door. I settle back into my seat.

My best friend and member satisfaction manager of the entire Lyons Club, which, of course, also includes the underground.

"Having fun?" Sonia throws a look toward the scene taking place beyond the glass.

"You scared me." I smile.

She laughs and cozies in next to me on the luxurious chesterfield couch. "What, you thought I was your dad?"

I flush. "Dumb, I know. I'm an adult, yet I'm afraid my father catches me down here." I sigh. "And I know my dad wouldn't be caught dead down here. He's as vanilla as can be." Dad may be the CFO of the Lyons Club, but the few times he had to come down here, he got so red in the face and so uncomfortable that it was more than clear this is not his thing at all, and he is more than happy to let someone else handle things here in the Underground.

Too bad this is very much my thing.

And I hope he never finds out because the last thing I want is to disappoint him.

But I can't stop being me. I can't not come here, because

I know this is the true me that still needs to come out. The me that fights tooth and nail to make herself known while I try to hide this side from the world.Sonia giggles, rolling her eyes. "Then why are you freaked out?"

"I'm not freaked out." I huff.

"You were sitting like a meerkat! Like –" Sonia jerks her whole body upward and darts her head around.

I have to admit she does a great meerkat impression.

"Listen! Don't make fun of me!" I try my best to disguise my smile. "You just...never know."

Even with the Underground rules in place—privacy contracts that ensure that what happens in the Underground stays in the Underground—the fact that my dad is so well known by everyone here, since he is the CFO, makes this whole thing even more risky.

Sonia narrows her eyes at me. "You're an adult. You have needs, Bridget."

I try to laugh. "Yeah, of the kink variety..."

"I think you should just go for it, you know?"

My eyes widen. "Go for what? What are you talking about?" My eyes roam the place, making sure whatever comes out of her mouth stays between the two of us alone.

"You should schedule a scene for yourself," Sonia says. "You know. Instead of just sitting and watching everyone else enjoy themselves."

The Dom twists the sub's bare nipples as he spanks her clit once. Her whole body grows stiff before she collapses.

"I mean, assuming you're interested in something like that." She tilts her head to the scene that is now wrapping up.

I *am* interested. Very. I've been watching scenes since I was of age to enter the Underground. In secret, of course. Sparingly at first.

In the past few years, though, I've started coming down here a couple of times a week just to watch.

To dream, to yearn, to fantasize about something I crave but don't think I'll ever be brave enough to actually go for.

"I'm alright with just watching." Not quite a lie, but not the truth either.

"You know the rules here, so word getting around would not be a problem. Besides, I could try and schedule you under an alias if you wanted, and it would only be between the two of us. And if you are worried about your scene partner, we have some really good masks that would guarantee you anonymity." It's Sonia's job to know this stuff, and I *know* she's participated in a few scenes down here herself with her fiancé, Edwin, owner of the Lyons Club.

If only she knew how ready I am to jump off the cliff of watching into doing. How eager. But I can't.

This lifestyle is about trust, and though I have watched plenty of Doms here, and they perform amazingly, I couldn't put myself in the hands of anyone. I need someone I trust one hundred percent. And I haven't come across anyone like that yet.

I mean, I have, but that would be so forbidden and so off-limits that it is not even worth considering.

Thanks, Sonia. I really appreciate the offer."

"So, can I book you in?"

I look at Sonia and shake my head. "I'm good. But I'll let you know if things change."

She frowns. "Sure."

Sonia and I have learned a lot about each other in the short time we've been friends, just shy of two years. I'd go as far as to say she's my best friend.

There's just one thing she doesn't know about me.

I'm a virgin.

A textbook virgin.

At twenty-six, being a virgin sounds pretty pathetic. But I have my reasons.

And sure, I could "just get it over with" or hire a Dom and fulfill some of my fantasies. But every time I start to go down that path, something stops me. In my chest. A feeling that the choice I'm about to make isn't right.

So, I've never gone there. Never crossed the bridge. I'm proud of myself for staying true to what I really want.

Still, though...I can't help feeling like I'm lacking somehow. Like I'm almost immature in a sense since I've never been intimate with someone like that.

Is something wrong with me that I've never really fallen in love because I'm not lovable in that way?

If my father heard my thoughts right now about being unlovable he'd whip me right into shape, drench me in a deluge of compliments, tell me how proud he is of me.

But dads have to say that, right?

Anyway, I have to wonder, what if I never get that? What if I'm a virgin forever because I'm just too scared to take the plunge. Or what if I do and I'm not good enough? What if all I'll ever have is a Dom that makes me submit for a scene, but has no interest in *me*? In my whole *life*.

Because this, for me, is about more than the pleasure the scene would bring. Inside, this need is constant. Everlasting. All-consuming. I need this dominance in my life twenty-four-seven.

But for now, I'll just watch, and I'm okay with that because I have to hope that my time will come too and even this waiting period is part of my training process already. Teaching me patience. Teaching me to wait for my dues.

"Maybe someday," I say.

Please be someday.

Otherwise, I'm afraid I'll never know the deepest parts of me. The parts I haven't allowed anyone to see. "When my dad doesn't work at the club anymore. Maybe. Anyway, enough about me. How are *you*, Miss Bride?"

Sonia groans, putting her hands over her face. "God, don't remind me."

"It's next weekend! You're going to be reminded!"

She laughs, her amber eyes turning into mere slits as she does. "I know, I just can't believe it's real. Feels like just yesterday I was trying to avoid Edwin in the halls to keep from salivating over him."

"Okay, ew."

Edwin is the same age as my dad, and while I know some people have a taste for the much older and *maybe* wiser, that's not me.

"You know what I mean..." Sonia rolls her eyes before they drift back to the scene before us.

The blonde sub is draped over the Dom's lap as he pets her hair.

The aftercare looks like an amazing moment every time. The reward for being a good girl. I crave that too.

She sighs. "Life just changes so fast. One day, you're running across the country to leave your past behind and the next you're..."

"Marrying your boss?" I shrug.

She giggles. "Yes. Marrying my boss. Thanks for reminding me."

I smile at Sonia with love. "Well, I'm excited."

"You better be, maid of honor."

I laugh and wrap my arm around her, giving her a squeeze. "Ugh, the magic never wears off!"

She squeezes me back.

"Looks like they're wrapping up here." I nod toward the

scene. "I'm going to head out."

Sonia nods. "After you."

I get up and head out the door, but as soon as it opens, I wish I could run back inside.

At the Underground check-in desk stands Seth Carlton. My stepbrother.

His eyes shoot to me before I even get a chance to turn around.

He leans on the desk and lifts his chin, his eyes taking me in and as always finding me lacking, I'm sure. As usual, his countenance is stern and unreadable.

His clear blue eyes always give me the feeling he can read my mind. "Bridget. Didn't expect to see you here."

I try to laugh it off, but my cheeks are burning. "Yeah. Me either. I mean. Didn't expect to see you. Not me. That'd be silly."

He appraises me for a moment.

I always feel like he's judging me, thinks I'm just some silly girl who would miss her stop on the MTA. I mean, that's happened, but I've gotten better about navigating the subway since becoming friends with Sonia.

"What are you doing here?"

I shiver. He has such a deep voice. I hate how much he affects me. Partly because he's intimidating and partly because...well, he's attractive. That's an objective fact, not my opinion.

Okay, it's also my opinion, but one I keep to myself considering that we're "family."

I mean, sure I met him when he was nineteen, and we never really lived together, but our parents are married and they both deserve a happy ending that doesn't involve the girl in the family lusting after her stepbrother.

Right?

"I asked you a question." He crosses his arms over his chest. "What are you doing here?"

"At the club?"

Seth purses his lips. "In the *Underground*, Bridget."

We've never crossed paths in the Underground. I try and make extra-sure of that, only coming to the club when he's at the office unless we're getting together with our group of friends.

So, of course, he's confused as to why I'm walking out of here.

Sonia places her hands on my shoulders and pokes her head out from behind me. "She was visiting me. I'm working, so she had to come along with me on a few of my rounds. Isn't that right, Bridget?"

I try to smile. "Yeah. That's right."

Seth's frown deepens. "Hi, Sonia."

"Hi, Seth. I'd stay and chat, but I have to go check on my team," she says with a jerk toward the stairs leading upstairs to the club. "Sorry to cut this short." She is smiling at him, but I know she means it for me.

"No trouble. Good to see you." He nods.

"Bye Sonia." I don't mean to whisper the words, but all sound apparently left me along with the air on my lungs.

Sonia waltzes away, leaving me with my antagonist.

"What are...what are you doing here?"

Seth glances down at the dungeon master, a pretty redheaded sub, then back to me. "What does it look like?"

My heart drops into my stomach or my stomach leaps up into my chest. Not sure which. All I know is that my insides are in chaos. Part of me is jealous because Seth feels so free to express his sexual desires as to make appointments in the Underground. The other part of me is jealous because...

Because some other woman gets to be with Seth that way.

God, what is wrong with me? I have no right feeling like this. This is wrong on so many levels.

"Right, well, that's nice for you." I nod. "I should be going now."

I start to step past him, but his hand whips out to grab my arm.

His grip is tight but not painful, which sends my head further into a tizzy. "Bridget, were you in there alone? Did you...?" He shakes his head and takes a deep breath.

His eyes rise to glance at the door to the private viewing gallery me and Sonia just exited. "Were you watching?"

"What does it matter to you?" I jerk my arm out of his grip.

"I texted you," he says. "Didn't you get it?"

I swallow. "I haven't checked my phone."

Seth's expression betrays not a single one of his thoughts. "Because you were distracted."

"I don't owe you anything, Seth."

"I'm only trying to make sure you're safe."

"No, you're not. You are trying to undermine me at every turn."

It's always been like this. Since we met. I thought it would be fun to have a sibling, even if we were a bit too old to enjoy the antics of childhood together. But from the very first time we met, Seth has been controlling, argumentative, and a downright pain in the ass.

Makes my attraction to him all the more complicated.

"Guess what, Seth. I'm a grown woman."

Something flashes in his clear blue eyes. "You don't have to remind me."

The quality of his voice renders me mute. It's not just

the deepness that's increased as he's gotten older. It's the acknowledgment that I'm a woman.

What gave that away? The age on my birth certificate? Or the way my body has –

Don't go there. You know you can't go there.

"Answer my question, Bridget. Were you watching?" His leaning in is hardly more than a hare's breath, but I almost feel it on my skin.

"You didn't answer my question. It's a double standard to expect answers from me when you're so cagey about everything."

Seth doesn't respond right away, sizing me up with those intense blues.

It's always a conflict with him. Always picking a fight, always pointing out something I'm doing wrong.

He nods. "Fair enough."

Talking to him is always an ordeal and my breathing has become labored, as if I've just been running. Or...doing something else. "Anyway, have fun, I guess."

I give the dungeon master another look.

I know she won't be his scene partner, but she's the closest thing I have for my imagination to punish me with a play by play of her on her hands and knees before him, accepting "funishments" like a good girl.

I step away from Seth, touching the spot on my arm he grabbed only moments ago. "Oh, will you be at family dinner tonight?" I smile, feigning innocence, blinking my eyelashes.

Seth sighs. "Yeah. I will. I'm always at family dinner."

"Just checking." I shrug and then leave, all too pleased with myself that I've reminded him of his mother and step-father before his scene.

And maybe I'm a little pleased to remind him of me too.

When I step out of the Underground, I'm back in the members club.

And though the door to the Underground is not too obvious, it's still obvious where you've come from.

And though no one is looking at me, I feel watched.

I'm not ashamed for liking what I like. I'm not.

I'm ashamed I can't have the real thing.

I get out of there as fast as possible and head right home.

I still live in the townhouse I grew up in with Dad and Amelia, my stepmother.

Over the years, though, Dad has had construction done to give me a private wing with my own entrance. I want nothing more than to go out on my own and take the world by storm, but I love home too much. It's safe and warm. A place that knows me as well as I know it.

I go in through my private entrance to avoid talking with Dad or Amelia and head straight to my bedroom.

The feeling between my legs was building during the scene and somehow, for some god-awful reason, got even more desperate feeling from talking with Seth.

I splay out on my bed, grab my little box of toys from my nightstand, and pick out my favorite vibrator. Without wasting a moment, I shove it under my dress and into my panties, letting it ride on the highest setting.

I attempt to imagine everyone. Anyone. The sexy, dark, and handsome Dom I watched today, my high school crush, Ryan fucking Reynolds, but no one does the trick like my stepbrother does.

Touching myself always results in thoughts of Seth. Of him taking all of his coldness to me, his brand of domination, and translating it into his own form of primal worship.

When I climax, I can only find one word to moan.

"Seth."

2

SETH

Family dinners are one of the most grueling tasks on my to-do list, having to endure sitting at the dinner table across from Bridget while my mother and Solomon, my stepfather, do everything they can to get us to talk to them about our lives.

Bridget and I have never spoken about family dinners. There's just this unspoken thing between us, an implicit knowledge that we have to do this for my mom and her dad. They've both been through too much for us to be difficult about a few dinners every month.

Not to mention, Bridget and I are well into adulthood and don't really have room to pull the whining "But *moooooommmm*" card.

"You two should see what your dad got up to today," Mom says, smiling ear to ear across the table at Solomon. "It's remarkable."

I glance at Solomon. I don't call him dad, and I know there's no expectation to. But the second he walked into my mother's life, all six something of him with his shiny balding eagle nest head and pointy nose, she was so excited to get her life back. The life she had before Dad, my real dad, died.

I've never had the heart to tell her it will never be the same. I think she knows that deep down. "What'd you get up to, Sol?"

Solomon smiles, then blots his mouth off with a napkin. "Well, I don't know if it's *remarkable*."

"It's remarkable!" my mom says, her blue eyes bugging out and curly, brown hair bouncing. She's stopped covering up the silver strands with dye. "Don't sell your accomplishment short."

Solomon blushes. Like actually blushes. I can only hope that one day I'll be able to have the woman of my dreams that makes me blush like that well into my fifties.

I look over at Bridget and immediately feel my stomach curdle. I'm suddenly not very hungry.

I'll never be able to have the woman of my dreams. That much has been clear for ten years.

"Well, I should just show you." Solomon pushes himself up from the table and scurries into the room off the kitchen, his office, which is more like a workshop. He's not yet retired, but in his free time, he certainly acts like a retiree. From the woodworking and the puzzles and the–

"Ta-da!" Solomon returns, holding a bottle with a model ship inside.

Bridget gasps. "You made that, Dad?"

"You bet your ass I did. And it was like hell getting it in, god almighty," Solomon says as he sits back in his seat with a heavy sigh. He turns the bottle back and forth. "A brigantine in a bottle. Who would have thought, huh?"

Bridget smiles, corners of her pink lips pitching as high

as they'll go. Makes me warm in the chest. She's never smiled at me that way. Never will, in all likelihood.

"That's amazing."

"See? Amazing, Sol." My mother points her fork at him.

"Anyway..." Solomon places the ship in a bottle in the middle of the table like a centerpiece. "Now that you've all heard about my very exciting day–"

I chuckle, "Can't say I've ever accomplished something like that."

"I'll show you!" my stepfather says with eagerness. "I mean, that is, if you want. You know. If you have time. You're busy. Which reminds me, what did you get up to today?"

I push at my side of mashed potatoes, wishing I could stomach eating another bite so I wouldn't have to respond. "Not much. Work. Work is work. You know how it is."

Bridget giggles. My eyes shoot to her. What the hell was *that?*

"Something you'd like to share with the class, Bridget?" My eyes are square on hers.

Her cerulean eyes dare to stay on mine, twinged with fear at the corners, and her smile falls. "Nothing. Nothing at all."

The table settles into another silence, one we're very good at.

I chew on my lip as I watch Bridget. I know she knows I'm watching her.

After all these years, I know she's come to disdain me for watching. Thinks I'm controlling, overbearing, maybe a freak. If only she knew how I fucking can't help it. Haven't been able to since she was sixteen years old, and I felt like a total creep lusting after her. Too young for me. My *stepfather's daughter*. I refuse to think of her as my stepsister.

"What about you, Bridget?" I take my glass of wine and swirling it in the crystal glass. "What'd you get up to?"

Her eyebrows rise, dark like her flowing locks. "Nothing. Just some sketching."

"At the club?" I offer.

Her eyes flash.

I bite back on a laugh.

She's so cute when she's annoyed with me. Perhaps that's why I can't help pushing her buttons all the time.

Solomon looks her way. "You were at the club today, pumpkin?"

"Yes, weren't you, pumpkin?" I say with a teasing lilt.

Under the table, Bridget's foot makes contact with my shin. Harder than I anticipated. I grip the bottom of my seat to keep from reacting to the pain.

Bridget lifts her chin, maintaining her good girl persona. "Yes, I was visiting Sonia."

"Oh, that's nice of you," my mom says.

"Yes, you know, I always like to visit my friends."

That's one way to put it. And sure, she was walking out of the viewing gallery with Sonia. But I've heard through the grapevine she enjoys herself in the viewing gallery far more than I ever anticipated from pretty, sweet Bridget Vance.

Of course, I've always been able to tell what she needs.

Every cell in my body screams for Bridget because she is as submissive as they come.

And for years, all I've wished was to be the one she submits to.

But that is forbidden fruit. And besides, just because I know what she needs, doesn't mean she knows it too.

Would she even let me? Would she want me to?

God, I need to get out of my head. Now.

"That's the only reason you were there?" I half-smile.

Bridget's nostrils flare. "Why do you care, Seth?"

I shrug. "Just curious."

I love watching her squirm. I could drop a bomb on family dinner in one fell swoop by telling the truth about where she was exactly. What would I get out of that, you may ask? A reaction. If I have to live a half-life and settle for subs that don't quite satisfy me, if I can't have the sub of my *dreams*, then I want to enjoy my time on this earth any other way I can.

But just because I like to see her reactions to me, imagine how she'd react to my hand as I spank her for being this fucking irresistible, I would never actually out her like that. It means crossing a line.

The sanctity of the Underground is worth everything to me, just as it's worth everything to Bridget. Not only because we've signed legally binding documents, but because it's a place where we can express our desires.

Our needs.

Our cravings.

I wouldn't jeopardize that.

"What about you, Seth?" Bridget offers. "Why were *you* at the club?"

My heart stutters in my chest. It's only fair.

Well played.

There are any number of reasons I could be at the club. I'm a member in my own right, not just by familial attachment. I could have been using the fitness facilities or indulging in a meal midday. Maybe taking a meeting with potential investors in my tech company.

However, every excuse eludes my tongue because the truth was I left my office in the middle of the day because I was desperate for a release. Desperate to be free of my ever-present thoughts of Bridget for an hour or two. Needed a sub to take my mind off of it.

And by the way Bridget is staring at me, she knows. Does she know that all the teasing and poking is a reaction to not being able to have her? If that's the case, she's got a better poker face than I thought.

"Business lunch."

"At three?" Is that a smirk on her lips?

"*Late* business lunch." My jaw tightens.

Mom tsks. "No wonder you're not eating much. You're not hungry."

"With whom?"

If Bridget were my sub, she'd be getting the spanking of her life tonight.

I lean toward the table, my eyes locked in hers.

Her smile grows. "Well? Is it a secret, Seth?"

Out of the corner of my eye, Solomon squirms in his seat. "You two, always with the arguing," he mutters.

Solomon knows about my... inclinations. Though he isn't in the lifestyle himself, he accepts that we all have needs, I am rather open about mine around everyone except my mother.

Thankfully, she's not all that invested in the club scene, much prefers to keep to her own hobbies and hiking trips.

Solomon wants me to like him. Always has. So, as he says, this stays "between us guys."

I'm an adult, a man with needs, and she doesn't need to know of my need to always stay in control because life seems to find a way to elude accountability.

I throw out the first name that comes to mind. "Cal Ferrano."

"Cal Ferrano." She nods. "Isn't he in Portugal, Dad?" Her eyes swing toward Solomon.

He shakes his head, looks into his lap. "Don't ask me. I didn't work today."

"What is going on with you all? You're acting funny," my mom says.

"Yeah, I had a meeting with Cal Ferrano." Who cares if he's in Portugal? "Sonia was working, though, she must have been busy, right, Bridget? So, what were you doing while she was busy?"

Bridget's mouth grows small, eyes darken. I withhold a laugh. How is it she manages to look adorable even when she's serious? If she knew what that does to me, she wouldn't pick a fight with me.

She looks back at the plate in front of her, pushing her food around like she is working on some kind of masterpiece. "Working on final details for the wedding."

"Oh, the wedding. What kind of details?"

Bridget jerks forward. "Why do you need to know?"

I match her. "Just curious."

We could go on like this all night if we had to. It's a stalemate. I have a secret of hers and she has a secret of mine. If one of us reveals the other's, it's mutually assured destruction. Could be fun...

Except it's not fun when our parents are the ones in the crossfire. I would do anything for my mother. And I know Bridget feels the same for her dad.

"Oh, my goodness, you two!" my mom cries out. "Can't we ever just have a nice dinner without you two going at each other's throats?" She shoves herself up from the table.

"Amelia –" Solomon calls to her.

She waves her hand. "I need some fresh air."

Mom walks across the kitchen to the sliding glass doors into the garden.

We all watch in silence.

Once she's outside and the door smacks closed behind her, Solomon sighs. "You guys…"

I shrug. "We're just having a conversation, Sol."

He looks at me. Defeated. "You know that's not true."

"Sorry, Dad," Bridget says in a small voice. Docile and wanting to please. Would she be that way for me too?

Not the time.

I look at Solomon and then toward where my mother left.

Fuck.

I hate apologizing, but this is not all on her. "Yeah, sorry."

Without another word, Solomon gets up from the table and follows the path of my mother outside.

Leaving Bridget and me alone. A rare occasion. Often, we're surrounded by our friends or our family, interacting at events, not left alone to deal with what is between us.

Or isn't, which makes my chest ache.

"Were you seriously going to tell my dad?" Bridget whispers in a way that pulls on my heart strings.

"Were you going to tell my mom?" I shoot back.

"As if that's nearly as a big of a deal." She shakes her head.

I scoff. "Of course it is!"

"You're a guy! It's not the same if people know you're into… the lifestyle."

I frown. "What's the difference? Between me and you, then?"

"Are you kidding?" She huffs. "My dad knows all about your…" she waves her hands wildly, "what you do and doesn't bat an eye. If he were to know *I* was doing that, then I wouldn't be his good girl anymore."

Not my cock growing hard at that.

Good girl.

What the fuck, that's so unfair.

"And that's what my dad expects."

"You seriously put on the good girl persona just for your dad?" I scoff.

She rolls her eyes. "It's not just for my dad."

"People see you walking out of the Underground. They see you in the gallery. It's not like people don't know that you–"

She shakes her head. "It's just different. You know it is. And if you don't get that..." Bridget stops.

"What is there to get? I've got my needs and you have yours." Fury flashes in my brain for all the men who have gotten to touch her and kiss her the ways I always have wanted to. "And neither of us want our biological parent to know. Although I really don't think you should waste your time in the Underground with any more than watching. Those guys...they won't know how to take care of you."

Bridget's brow pinches at the center. "And you would? No, don't answer that. I don't know why I continue to try and make you understand when you never will."

A knife to the gut would have been less painful than that. "The fuck does that mean, Bridget?"

"I'm so tired of you speaking to me like I'm some kid who doesn't get anything. You're only three years older than me, Seth."

"You're my..." No, I can't even think it, let alone say it. I don't care what society or law say. I'll never seen her that way. I swallow before adding, "We're family, I'm trying to look out for you."

Bridget shoots out of her chair. It tips back and smacks the ground. "You're trying to control me! You're always trying to *control* me and tell me what's best for me and threatening me with my secrets to keep me down and–"

"I've never threatened, Bridget." At least, I haven't intended to. Is that how she sees it?

She puts up her hand. "Look, I don't think we should talk anymore. Okay? Unless it's family dinner."

I shake my head. My heart is being ripped in two. "What?"

"I don't want your commentary on my life or my choices. I don't want you to interfere. And if you do–"

"You'll what?" On the outside I need to keep my poise. Calm and collected. I need to have control over this situation.

I. Have. Control.

Bridget's mouth twists. "I don't *know*. I just don't want you to talk to me anymore, alright?" Her voice pitches high, warbling with tears.

Double fuck. I don't want to be the cause of her tears if there's no pleasure involved. "Bridget–"

She turns, hands over her face, and runs out of her room, up the stairs to her wing of the house.

I remain seated at the table, staring at all the half-eaten plates of food, the empty seats. Empty because of me and my inability to get a handle on my emotions.

My inability to let Bridget go.

How can I after ten years of pining?

I grab my fork in my fist and close my eyes, trying to level my breath.

Now she doesn't want me to talk to her because, in her eyes, I'm some sort of monster.

But I'm not a monster.

Bridget just doesn't understand.

She'll never understand.

If I'm cursed to want my *stepsister* the rest of my life, I want to at least be able to talk to her.

But I've fucked everything up by being too much. As fucking always.

Maybe I *am* a monster.

3

BRIDGET

"Tʜᴇsᴇ sᴋᴇᴛᴄʜᴇs ᴀʀᴇ ғᴀɴᴛᴀsᴛɪᴄ, Bʀɪᴅɢᴇᴛ."

I smile, hoping it's not obvious how nervous I am. "Thank you."

Deborah looks out from under her dark-framed spectacles at me for a brief moment, then back at my sketchbook. "I really like how bravely you shift your dynamics between your pieces."

Deborah Angelise complimenting the dynamics of my drawings? I feel faint.

She continues to page through my sketchbook as I try to ignore the club around me.

I've been trying to get an audience with Deborah for months now. She's very busy, a tycoon of the fashion industry, famous in her own right, even if most of her money comes from her French billionaire husband.

And right now, she's looking at my sketchbook.

Is everyone watching us wondering if Angelise will give little Bridget Vance, daughter of the Lyons Club CFO, a chance?

I want to get things on my own merit, however the

connections made through the club are invaluable. Besides, even if I can get an audience with some of the most powerful people in the world doesn't mean they'll just give me what I want.

"Oh! Well, this is surprising…"

I snap my attention back to the design she's looking at, and my heart stops. "Oh, oh, that's not part of the collection I wanted to show you." I reach for the book.

Deborah smiles, lips full of mischief as she slides the book out of my reach and leans back in her seat to take a closer look at the page. "This is closing in on fetish wear, I'd say."

"Yes, that's why…it's more experimental." I half-laugh.

"Bridget, please. Let your work speak for itself. Don't do it the disservice of qualifying it."

I nod. "Very well."

"GOOD." DEBORAH FLIPS THE SKETCHBOOK AROUND and shows off the design.

One of my favorite pieces.

In the sketch, the model wears a pair of see-through black pants that look light and flowy, but on top, she's strapped in by a harness with metal rings. However, instead of being made of leather, it's lace.

"Tell me about your inspiration."

I clear my throat. "Well, my philosophy on lingerie first and foremost is to make the wearer feel beautiful. And I'm interested in the intersection of physical beauty and power. It's like a chicken and the egg almost. Does beauty make you feel powerful or does power make you feel beautiful?"

"And that's what you're playing with?"

I swallow. "Yes, with my last few sketches."

Deborah flips through the last few. "You see this as being marketed toward the average woman?"

"The average *sexually enlightened* woman."

I almost cringe at my own words. Because how dare I say that when I've never had sex myself?

But that is the goal. I want to be that woman. "Women who understand what they want and what they like from their encounters."

"Hmmm..." Deborah pinches her lips that are painted in a barely-there nude color. She's silent as she flips through my sketchbook. From the beginning to the end. "You're certainly versatile. That's important in a world where anyone can be anything."

I shrug. "I just have a lot of interests."

"Do you?" Deborah's eyebrows waggle.

"I —" My throat constricts. "When it comes to fashion and trends, yes."

The older woman readjusts her glasses and scratches the back of her close-cropped gray pixie cut. "I like it, Bridget. I like it. You've got a vision. But it's not overt. It's being cultivated. All you need now is the power to stand and say what you mean."

"Working on it." I half-laugh.

Deborah flips the book closed and places it back on the table between us. "You said you have samples?"

"Yes, I do." I touch the garment bag beside me. "They're made by my own hand which is to say if they were done by an actual garment house, they'd be much more well-crafted, but —"

"Bridget! Stop selling yourself short." Deborah's hands tap the air in front of her like bongo drums.

"Would you like to see them?" I take the zipper of the bag in my hand.

Deborah shoots up out of her seat. "Yes, I would."

But then she just begins to walk away from our table and cluster of chairs in the main hall of the club. What is happening? Did I miss something?

Deborah turns and jerks her head toward the stairs that lead down to the Underground, her chunky necklaces clacking. "Come along. We need models, don't you think?"

I blink a few times. "O-of course! Of course, we do!" I grab the bag and the book and follow her down to the Underground.

"Hazel!" Deborah calls out to the sub manning the front desk.

Hazel smiles. "How can I help you, Mistress Angelise?" Hazel leans to the side and smiles at me. "Hi, Ms. Vance."

I want to crawl out of my skin.

I know they have to refer to us that way in the Underground, but I've spent enough time with Hazel up in the Lyons Pride, the night club that's open to the public, to call her a friend. Feels weird to be treated as though there's some power dynamic between us. "Hi."

"Do you have some people available who might want to play dress up for a bit? I'll pay if I have to."

"No, if any payment is involved, it's on me." I step up to be even with Deborah.

"Nonsense. This is my idea. It will go on my bill. Or, more specifically, Michel's."

I can't argue with the bank account of Michel Angelise.

Hazel calls out two women who are just hanging around close by. One is Mistress Morgona, a Domme, and the other is a sub, Penny.

"I have a couple of pieces of art here that I think may be of interest to the both of you, and I'd love to see how they would fit a body. Would you be willing to try?"

Penny smiles, her head down as she nods. "Yes, Mistress."

"And you, Morgona?"

"Sure, I can play along. Let's see what you have there."

Deborah hands a piece over to each of them to put on. "We'll do a little fashion show out here when you're done." She gestures to the stage in the main room of the Underground where often times there are burlesque shows or public scenes.

When they return, they get up on the stage and show off the goods.

And I'm stunned. Truly.

I've actually never seen this side of my work on anyone but me. I do well on social media selling unique, reproduceable pieces. But I've never had room for the more "edgy" looks. Probably because my brand is billed as "sultry for sweet girls" even if I also get customers more interested in having little rosettes and bows on their pieces than leather and latex.

Penny wears one of my earlier designs, a matching green set with a garter belt and stockings. Morgona wears something closer in attitude to the black number Deborah pointed out in my book, except this one is a dark blue corseted piece with a pair of leather pants that snap up the sides so they can be torn off in an instant.

"How do you feel, ladies?" Deborah asks.

Morgona shifts in her hip, swinging her long box braids to the side. "Hot. And comfortable."

"It's so comfortable, oh my god," Penny agrees with an almost erotic eye roll. "I mean, I like a little pain and discomfort here and there, but not when it comes to clothes."

They both laugh.

"Comfortable and sexy, that's good." Deborah gets up on the stage and begins to circle the models. "You've sold your tailoring abilities short, Bridget."

I blush. "Well..."

"These leather pants, especially, I mean that is not easy to accomplish." She lifts a hand and makes eye contact with Morgona. "May I touch?"

Morgona grins. "Only if you want me to punish you later."

Deborah clutches her chest. "That shouldn't turn me on as much as it does."

We all laugh.

Risking a lost hand, or eager for the punishment since she is apparently a switch, both Domme and sub depending on her mood, Deborah runs her hand down the length of the leather pants. "Sleek. Intense. Yet delicate." She lifts her eyes to me. "Powerful, yet beautiful."

My heart flutters. "You think it works?"

"Absolutely. And these *stockings*–" Deborah moves on to Penny.

I grin. "I can't take credit for the embroidery. I had them done by an expert fiber artist. The filagree is placed so that–" I get up on the stage next to her and point to the way it swirls around the Penny's thigh, "—it accentuates the curves of the body. To heighten the beauty that's already there."

"And green is a powerful color. Even your softer designs encapsulate your artistic vision."

I've never thought of myself as having an artistic vision.

One of the Doms emerges from the back room. The one I was watching just the other day. He's wearing a harness today and pants so tight his junk is basically out.

"Heard there was a fashion show?"

"What do you think, Lex?" Morgona says. She grabs the front of the pants and rips them off, leaving her clad in a scandalous little thong.

Lex laughs. "Wow, those are amazing." He looks at me. "You made those?"

The glint in his eye tells me he knows. He remembers me watching. However, his smile is affable and real.

"I did."

"Damn, I want a pair..."

I shrug. "That can be arranged."

Lex's eyelids lower, and his smile goes from friendly to frustratingly charming.

Before I can reply, though, the girls start in on more conversation, questions I have to answer, details I need to point out. Deborah has me on my toes, but I can tell it comes from a place of confidence in me rather than trying to trip me up.

Amidst the conversations, I can't help but notice the door to the Underground open.

Seth.

God, I can't catch a break.

Since dinner went sour the other night, he has left me alone, thank god. Then again, I haven't been in the same place with him, so he hasn't had an opportunity to annoy me with his controlling antics.

Our eyes meet. I don't smile. I don't give him any indication I'm trying to be nice, which is *hard* for me as resident nice girl. As a sub with the need to please.

Seth looks away.

Though I'm glad he's respectful of my coolness, I can't lie. It hurts.

I wish it didn't. However, it's taken me ten years to push him away. It had to happen sooner than later.

He might blow my cover.

Or worse. I'll be unable to resist him.

Seth goes over to the desk to talk to Hazel. Another appointment today? God, he really has no shame, does he?

"Bridget–" Deborah calls my attention.

I flip back to the task at hand. "Yes?!" I say with more urgency than the situation needs.

Deborah points to Penny and Morgona. "I want them to try on a couple more pieces."

"Sounds great. Your call."

The older woman furrows her brow, but I can't manage control right now. Not when my nerves are starting to tremor, and my mouth is growing hot.

Jeez, just being in the same room with Seth is painful.

She doesn't question me, though, and moves on with Penny and Morgona to pick out the next round of looks.

As they go, Hazel laughs from her spot at the desk. I glance over at them.

Seth is making her laugh. How come he's so nice to everyone else but only gives me grief?

Hazel leans on the desk, her hands clasped under her chin as they discuss...whatever.

Seriously? Doesn't he have an appointment or something?

Hazel lifts her phone. "All available subs to the reception area, please."

So, Seth is going to look at a line of women and get his pick...I see how it is. No wonder he doesn't want his mom to know. He's a veritable manwhore.

Amelia doesn't need the horror of knowing that.

Fine. Two can play at this game.

I pull in a deep breath and turn back to Lex. "You really want a pair of those pants?"

He nods. "You kidding? The drama involved in that would be too good to bear."

My cheeks get hot. "I bet."

"You could make them, and then we could give them a trial run?" Lex winks.

My eyes widen.

Lex holds up his hands. "Only if you wanted."

He flirts with everyone. It's his personality. It's not about me. Still, I can't ignore the way my stomach drops. "That might be good. Durability test."

He laughs, loud like Hazel. I can't help but hope Seth is looking.

"Yes, exactly. We need to know just how sturdy your work is."

I bite my lower lip.

I'm not going to do anything with Lex, but the banter is fun. And pushing Seth's buttons is more enjoyable than it ought to be. "I have a measuring tape. We could get started on them now if you like."

"Bespoke tearaway pants? For me?"

"I've wanted to get into men's intimate wear. You can be my guinea pig."

Lex steps back and spreads his arms.

God, he's ripped. Muscles bulging out from the harness, thighs threatening to rip through the pants. A perfect specimen.

Perfect...but not Seth.

No matter. I reach into my purse and grab the rolled-up measuring tape. "Let's start with the inseam."

Lex raises an eyebrow. "You want to get familiar fast?"

"Alright with you?"

"Always, Ms. Vance."

I want to tell him to call me something more familiar.

Like Bridget. Or something even more...intimate. But he's not my master. Wouldn't be fair to cross boundaries. Unfurling the measuring tape, I give him a sweet smile. "Just doing my job."

"Sure you are."

I crouch down to the floor, level with his dick. My heart pounds as I place the measuring tape at the top of the inside of his thigh, mere centimeters away from his package.

"Don't make it too roomy in the crouch," Lex says. "I like the challenge."

Okay, Lex might kill me. He really might–

"What's going on?" Seth voice comes from close behind me.

I look up over my shoulder. He's abandoned the front desk in lieu of confrontation. "I'm measuring Lex for a pair of pants," I say with an innocent air. "Is there a problem?"

Seth's jaw tightens, and his usually bright blue eyes darken.

As he stares down at me, I feel smaller and smaller.

Overwhelmed by his power. His dominance.

Dear god. I'm panting. And it's not because I'm close to Lex's cock.

I'm at the mercy of Seth's gaze.

And that alone has made me wet.

This isn't good. Not at all.

"Get up off the ground, Bridget. You're making a fool of yourself."

Seth's words compel me to obey. As I stand, I try to tell him to leave me alone, not to talk to me. But I can't.

"You don't have to speak to her like that, Carlton," Lex says. "Alright? We're all just here to have a good time."

"Are we?" Seth asks.

I keep my eyes downcast. The annoying tickle of tears is beginning.

Why is he doing this to me?

But beyond the shame, there is something I...I crave. I crave being under his control. It's why I've had to push him away. When he checks on me, tries to rein me in, it makes me feel like he cares.

Like he might want me.

Like he is my master.

What a silly thought, though. The truth is he's just an asshole.

Before I can answer Seth's question, Penny and Morgona reemerge from the back in new outfits. I don't have the wherewithal to clock what they are. I'd just like to get out of here to deal with these swirling feelings of shame and want.

"I really like this one," Penny says with a bold grin.

Before I can respond, Seth abandons our conversation, goes to Penny, and grabs her by the wrist. She lets out a gasp of laughter. "I'm already booked, Master Carlton."

"Not anymore," he growls.

As they walk away, Penny looks over her shoulder at me with an apologetic smile.

I swallow back the jealousy, except it sits at the base of my throat, threatening to make me sick.

"What a jackass," Deborah says. "But I guess it does the job. I mean, he *pounced* on her."

I force a smile. "Yes. Yes, he did." I wish now with all my heart I wasn't a good designer. I wish I couldn't manage more than a paper bag.

I turn back to Lex. "Let's get you measured for these pants, huh?"

4

———

SETH

I slam the door harder than I mean too. My breath is heavy in my chest as I pant.

What the hell was that? How dare she cut me out of her life then make a spectacle out of herself? Doesn't she know that a Dom at the club only wants her body? Her temporary submission? It's selfish attention. Not the real kind.

Not the kind I could give her. Desperately *want* to give her.

I turn around and jump at the sight of Penny on her knees before me, her eyes on the ground in front of my feet.

I stare at her. Penny is called so for her hair, the silky copper coif she keeps in a desperately tight ponytail that can be used for pulling or can be released into cascading coils.

Penny is beautiful. A good sub.

But not the one I want. Not today. Not ever.

I gnaw the inside of my cheek as I look at her. "Are your limits as usual today?"

"Yes, Master."

"What is your safe word for today?"

"The color scheme works for me, Master. So, yellow to pause and red to stop."

I nod. I always check their limits and their safe words. Since we are both unattached, but don't scene together often, it is a good reminder for me, and a way to see if anything changed since last time.

If I had any say in it, I wouldn't be unattached.

Because the thing I long the most for is to be in a committed relationship. I crave to have *my* sub. Someone who only bends to *my* will, not to anyone else's.

And my body and soul crave only *her*. My sweet forbidden fruit. The bane of my existence.

So, I'll have to settle for Penny for now.

I look at the wall which is laden with a variety of toys and tools. I grab a flogger off the wall, the leather strands dripping just like Penny's ponytail.

My eyes scan the room.

What should I do with her?

Lay her down on the spanking horse?. Doesn't feel right. Or exciting. I turn back to the wall and put the flogger back, before reaching for a set of silky restraints. Could be fun to tie her up. Tie her down. Overstimulate with a toy. Make her beg so nicely.

Except, imagining her moans and her begging sounds nauseating.

I came here today because I can't focus. Again. My mind has been all Bridget all the time. From the second she told me I couldn't speak to her, all I've wanted is to speak to her, and now I've broken her rule.

The one rule she ever set. Her hard limit.

Fucking hell, what kind of Dom am I?

Ignoring the restraints, I blindly reach for the flogger

and stand before her. I place the tip of it under her chin, bidding her to look me in the eye.

Penny does so. Her brown eyes would be inviting to anyone.

To me, they just feel wrong.

"On the horse."

Penny nods, her head back down and goes to the spanking horse in the corner of the room.

As she stands, my eyes take in her attire today...delicate teddy that parts right below her breasts and scrapes the ground as she stands.

I dare not look any lower for fear of my stomach turning on me completely. It sickens me as it turns me on because it's Bridget. Not just because it's her design. It exudes who Bridget is and that only muddles my brain further.

But undressing her feels wrong. Her naked form might be perfect to another man. To me, it's just a hollow counterfeit of the one I really want.

Penny lays herself prone on the spanking horse, and it does absolutely nothing for me.

Maybe if I go through the motions, I will get into it.

I clip her wrists in, then her ankle.

"Good girl." The words burn my tongue on the way out as each action I take brings me further away from what is happening. From me.

Who is this person? Where am I?

I grip the flogger in my hand and pass it over her backside, clothed with a thin layer of mesh. I could say I'm teasing her. Making her yearn for my touch.

Truth is, I'm just buying time. Because I don't want to do this. Not with her.

I pull my arm back and swat her backside once. Twice.

I stare at her ass.

I feel nothing. Nothing at all.

Maybe if I keep trying...

Again, I wind my arm up, decided to do right by the sub. Just because I feel hollow, doesn't mean I won't try to make it worth it for her.

"Red," Penny announces.

I drop my arm, frowning but relieved, the flogger hitting the outside of my leg. "Are you alright?"

I hurry to release her restraints.

As soon as she is free, she sits up on the bench, looking at me before lowering her eyes again. "I'm sorry, Master Carlton."

"Is everything okay?"

Her eyes fleet to mine again before she nods. "It's just that... I'm not comfortable going on with you like this." She is twisting her hands. "You don't seem like you want to be here. It's like your head is miles away."

I raise my eyebrows. "Is it that obvious?"

Penny smiles and gets to her feet, her head down and her hands holding each other in front of her. Still the perfect submissive. "Please forgive me, Master Carlton, but perhaps we can do this another time."

"I'll compensate you for your time," I say.

Penny shakes her head. "That's not necessary, Master. But thank you."

It's a fruitless argument. I'll see to it that she gets something as an apology at least. "You are free to go, then. Thank you, Penny."

Penny gives a single nod, then disappears through the door back into the atrium of the Underground.

I lock the door behind her and take in the empty room.

Except it's not empty. Not when my imagination is running so wild.

It's the same as always.

Bridget, Bridget, Bridget.

Bridget in my arms, Bridget on her knees. Bridget on my cock.

I take the flogger, wind it back, and with all my might, hit the bare spanking horse.

"Fuck!" I yell. Thank god the rooms are soundproof.

The leather on leather lends the air a raw smack. It would sound so much better on skin. On *her* skin.

I try to even my breath as I stare at the table.

What if...

No, I couldn't think about that. It's bad enough I've had fantasies about Bridget since I met her. I can't imagine her *now*. In the one place I've always gone to get away from fantasies of her.

It's too late.

I can see it. Clear as day.

Her, bent over the spanking horse, wearing that damn outfit Penny was in. The thin fabric covering her alabaster ass. She's already pale enough in the face, lord knows her ass must be white as a canvas. Even better for spanking. I'd get to see every bit of redness. Every welt.

I'd paint the best work of art yet.

Fuck, I'm hard.

I resituate the flogger in my hand and give the bench another smack.

I imagine her under the leather, body balking and bracing. Arms locked in restraints. The sounds she'd make.

She wouldn't call me Seth. She'd call me Sir.

"You like that, pet?" I say softly as if she's in the room with me. It's foolish. But I have to let it out.

"Yes, Sir."

I blink. It's like she's right here in the room with me.

Her dark hair falling to the side over the table, her face turned to the side, her expression wanton.

Chest heaving. Breasts smushed against the leather, threatening to spill out of their cups.

No, fuck it. This is my fantasy. She'd be naked.

"Do you want me to do it again?"

"Yes, Sir."

I do.

The funishment I wasn't able to hand Penny comes effortlessly now.

I release a thrall of slaps with the flogger.

My cock grows harder with each one.

I don't care how pathetic it is, me alone, playing out my deepest, darkest fantasy. To dominate the one woman I can never have.

The woman the world deems forbidden to me just because our parents decided to marry each other.

It doesn't matter that we were already in our teens. It doesn't matter that we never even knew ourselves before then. It doesn't matter that we never considered the other a sibling. Everyone insists on seeing her as my sister. My *step*sister.

It doesn't help that we've been taking family pictures for years, having family dinners, talking about family plans.

This fixation I have for her, this yearning, this craving, it's sick and disgusting in the eyes of society.

And with every day that passes, with every look her way, I just want her all the more.

Why do I always end up wanting what I can't have? It used to be for my dad to come back to life. Then I met Bridget, and my impossible desire became all *her*.

I want to hear her begging.

So, the Bridget of my imagination begins to beg.

"Please, Sir. More, Sir. I want all of it, Sir."

I exchange the flogger for a crop.

I'd take it slow with her. I doubt she's ever been disciplined like this. And with her fair skin, I'd never use a whip or a cane.

I trace the empty table with the crop.

Oh, how I'd tease her...slide it between the cheeks of her ass, down to her pussy, shove it up against her clit.

I wonder what she sounds like when she comes. When she's desperate to come.

The crop takes less work to flick. I could pepper her ass with red welts in thirty seconds, cover the area with my marks. Brand her mine.

And how I imagine she'd buck. And plead. And moan.

That fuck Dom couldn't give that to her.

No Dom other than me can give it to her. Not like she deserves it.

Why doesn't she understand all my efforts of control have only ever been because I want to please her? I want to be the only one to–

My imagination conjures the possibility she'll forget herself. Won't call me Sir. Will sing out my name with rough and curdled desperation.

The crop falls from my hand.

I am weak all over.

And my cock is aching for release.

I drop my hands onto the table, press my cock up against the edge through my pants and I rut hard, as if it was Bridget. If she was right there to take every inch of me, to accept that I am the one. The true master of her mind and her body.

"Fuck, Bridget. *Fuck.*" I drop my head.

Don't care how ridiculous or how crazy I seem. I need her. Even the imagined version.

I'd make her come first. I'd last.

I'm thankful in my fantasy, I can make her come first regardless of how long I'm fucking her because I'm about to burst.

I'm about to–

"Haaaa*ohmygod*." The sound I release is unearthly, something I never knew I had in me.

I release a deluge of come straight into my boxer shorts, the wetness reminding me of just how alone I am.

I can't enjoy the high.

I just pretended to fuck my stepsister. *Pretended.*

I'm so fucking pathetic.

Bridget might have been right to stop talking to me.

5

BRIDGET

"Let's put Abigail with Theo." The wedding planner, Cara, looks down at her clipboard, scanning the list of wedding party members with her pen.

Abigail flicks her red hair and goes to stand next to the tall, dark, and handsome Englishman who seems to almost lean away from her with his body, though his smile is inviting her to come closer.

I stand with my arms crossed. Nerves are at an all-time high since the wedding is tomorrow and we only have a half hour to get the rehearsal right before we're to head off to the rehearsal dinner.

Not even the beautiful garden scenery or the temperate evening can make up for my mood.

I'm waiting to be paired with one of the groomsmen for my walk down the aisle.

It's customary for the maid of honor to walk down the aisle with the best man, but Edwin's best man is my dad. In theory, this would be fine, but Dad is actually going to walk Sonia down the aisle since her father passed away several years ago.

So, now I have to be saddled with someone else.

"Bridget and…"

I glance over at the groomsmen. There's Nate and Jack, Edwin's sons. Jack's walking down the aisle with one of Sonia's friends from California. Nate's already spoken for in the form of Laney, and so is Mason. The three of them are in a throuple situation that has been both strange and beautiful to watch come to life.

I can't imagine *one* guy falling in love with me, let alone two.

Anyway, they've already insisted on going down the aisle together in a trio, throwing off the numbers even more.

Then there's Theodore Wallington, Theo to his friends, apparently an old buddy of Edwin's from his salad days. He's already been paired with Abigail, Edwin's daughter.

"Okay, let's have Bridget and Seth," Cara says, lifting her head and giving a bright smile.

As if she hasn't just said something absurd.

My gaze shoots to Seth who stands among the boys with a petrified stare in my direction.

Great, he knows just as well as I do how horrendous this situation is.

"Oh, my god…" Nate says, covering his mouth with his hand to cover up a snort of laughter.

Mason boxes him on the shoulder. "Bro."

Nate isn't the only one reacting this way.

Abigail is doing her best not to look shocked, but her big green eyes betray her. Edwin's mouth opens and closes like a fish. And Jack is rubbing his face like he's an old man, already exhausted by the events of today.

"Bridget and Seth?" Cara repeats, confusion starting to register on her face. "Is something wrong?"

I purse my lips. "N-no, nothing's wrong." Because it's true. Nothing's wrong.

Seth and I won't be walking down the aisle to get married ourselves. We're just part of the wedding party. There's no reason everyone has to be making a big deal about this. In fact, it's making it worse.

"We can't," Seth says, jaw set.

I know I'm the one that put the embargo on our communication, but I can't help being hurt by his response.

Cara's forehead puckers with so many wrinkles I'd swear she was a pug in a past life. "W-why?"

My father steps forward from his place behind the action, waiting with Sonia to do the final part of the walk-through. He gets Cara's attention with a delicate touch to her shoulder. "Bridget and Seth are siblings."

I feel sick with myself.

"Step siblings, but still," Dad adds with a forced chuckle. "I think everyone's just responding to the weirdness of that? Maybe?" His eyes skitter to the group for approval.

Nate shakes out his beachy blond hair. "Yeah, I'm sorry. Sometimes, I'm surprised these two didn't grow up together the way they go at it."

"Cats and dogs," Mason adds.

"Guys..." Laney admonishes in a soft tone that always gets them both in line. To have that kind of power...I want to be her.

Sonia steps forward as well. "Bridget, would you be more comfortable walking with someone else?"

Leave it to Sonia to put the power back in my hands. I wish I could claim it myself, but I've never felt powerful enough for that. I don't feel comfortable with having control in situations like this. Which is just another reason I crave my own Dom. I want someone to save me from embarrassing myself. From the agony that is to be required to speak up for myself when I flounder with what to do.

But Seth's already made it clear he won't walk with me. No need to add insult to injury.

I hope it's not obvious from my expression how strange this all is, so I just smile. "Yes, it's just a little weird. Could we figure out something else?"

Cara pages through her clipboard. What could she possibly have to look at on the clipboard when it comes to making an order of a bridal party walking down the aisle?! "Oh, um, of course, I'm so sorry. I thought I had gone through all the relationships and details and–"

I want to crawl inside a hole and die. "It's alright." Last thing I want to do is make someone as uncomfortable as I am with the situation.

"How about, Theo, you walk with Bridget and Abigail walks with Seth and then I think–then I think–"

"That will be fine, love." Theo takes a step away from Abigail in my direction. His smile is so easy, like cream being added to coffee. "Alright with you, Bridget?"

"Y-yes." I don't mean to stutter. It just happens.

And I know Seth notices. I see it out of the corner of my eye. His whole posture tenses.

"And Seth and Abigail, is that–"

Abigail rolls her eyes, but wears an effervescent smile. "What do you think, Sethy? Can you put up with me for a bit?"

Seth closes his eyes. "Fine."

"Better than me," I say under my breath as Theo navigates into position beside me.

"Say something, dear?" the tall Englishman asks.

I glance up at him.

His hair is a wonderful mess of curls that seem to fall in perfect choreography over his forehead. And that smile is contagious.

I find myself smiling with ease, no force about it. "Nothing. It's nice to finally meet you." I hold out my hand.

Theo takes my hand in his. He's taller than Seth by several inches, would be a gangly beanpole if not for the clear density of his muscles beneath his tailored khaki suit.

He doesn't shake my hand. Just squeezes it, thumb sliding over my skin. "Pleasure's all mine." He lifts my hand to his mouth and kisses it with gentleness before his eyes rise to meet mine. "Bridget."

I know Theo knows what he's doing, but I can't help but swoon. My name in his British accent is like heaven.

My face burns. Not from blushing. But from Seth's eyes boring into my skin.

What the hell is his problem. He is the one who didn't want to walk with me.

I hate that he doesn't see the capable woman I am. Why won't he just let me be? It shouldn't bother him so much that I've grown up and am more than ready to interact with other men. I'm not some little fragile thing that needs to be protected.

I'm twenty-fucking-six years old. When will I be mature enough in his eyes to handle myself?

And if he was any other guy, I might be tempted to think he was jealous, but this is Seth. And hell is far from freezing over.

Whatever. Let him be an asshole. I don't care.

I'm going to have fun with the older British man.

How old is he? In his forties? Not really my cup of tea, but hey, maybe I need to change tack, try something new.

As Cara rounds everyone up in the order we'll go down

the aisle, Theo leans down toward my ear and speaks in a low voice as to not be overheard, "Sonia's very lucky to have such a beautiful maid of honor."

"Is she?" My heart is flittering like a thousand butterfly wings.

I'm not *good* at this kind of thing. I'm good at being a good girl who trips over her words and is shy and polite. Not the flirting thing. But I'm going to try my level best to push past that.

Who knows what worlds might open up to me if I do?

"I'd say so. She should also be grateful she's already taken. I'm sure when the two of you go out, you're the one who gets all the attention."

I can't keep from flushing.

And I can't ignore the fact that Seth keeps turning his head the slightest degree from his spot in front of us in line. Is he trying to eavesdrop?

"I think you're flattering me, Mr. Wallington."

"Oof, remind me of my age, why don't you?" He clutches his chest.

I laugh. "I'm just trying to be polite."

"Well, Bridget, you needn't ever be *polite* with me." He grins, and *oh, god*. It's devilish and delicious.

My eyes catch Seth in front of me. His jaw his ticking so hard it could be seen from space.

Abigail pulls on Seth's arm. "It's our turn! Pay attention!"

The two of them begin their walk down the aisle.

"You should take my arm, probably," Theo says. "Customary, I've heard."

I slowly slide my hand around his bicep.

Holy crap. His muscles are firm even through his jacket.

Theo's hand shoots out and grabs mine, pressing it harder to him.

I can't hide my shock, eyes wide as I look up at him.

"Like I said, don't be polite."

It's our turn to walk down the aisle, and so we do. It is rather uneventful because the least I can do as a maid of honor is be easy to work with.

However, the one thing that nearly throws me off balance is Seth. As per fucking usual.

He watches from the top of the aisle. Eyes glued to me. Unapologetic. Not trying to hide. The tension remains in his body, in his hands folded in front of him, wringing.

Why? Because I'm of me on the arm of a man?

I know he thinks Theo will chew me up and spit me out, but why can't he just relax? Just because another man is touching me doesn't mean he's going to–

For one fleeting second, as my mind gets away from me, I concede maybe Seth is right to worry about me. But before memory lane takes me down hurtful paths, I shut it down.

As Theo and I arrive at the top of the aisle, he relaxes his arm, lets me step away. "Until we meet again, Bridget."

He's too charming for his own good.

I try to reply, but I'm distracted by Seth behind him.

Yes, his body language makes him look angry. But his expression is...is that hurt?

I would call Seth many things. Temperamental, domineering, *exhausting*.

The number of times I've seen a grief-filled look in his eye have been few. Very few.

I go to my spot as maid of honor and try to focus on what is happening, but it's no use.

I'm fixated on Seth. That final look he gave me.

If he's in pain over not walking down the aisle with me, which is a long shot, then he only has himself to blame.

Of course, that is just wishful thinking because Seth would never even consider touching me with a pole, let alone let me walk with him arm-in-arm.

AFTER THE REHEARSAL, THE WEDDING PARTY FLOCKS out of the garden and into the big estate house where dinner is being held and other welcomed guests are already congregating.

I walk next to Theo who hasn't left my side since we walked back down the aisle together. He's been chatting with me, or at me I should say, considering I'm not very good at keeping up conversation with my head is full of so many thoughts.

"Anyway, enough of me talking, what about you, Bridget? What do you do?"

I smile to myself. My answer always excites people, men and women alike. And it most certainly keeps conversation going since they have questions for me, and I don't have to keep the ball of conversation in the air. Unless I have a couple drinks in me...that helps immensely.

My smile grows as I remember that's how Sonia and I became friends in the first place, when I cornered her in the bathroom at Lyons Club her first day here.

That feels so long ago now.

"I design lingerie."

Theo's head jerks back with a laugh. "What?"

"Did I surprise you?" I grin.

"Yes. Very...surprised."

We begin to walk up the steps to the archway entrance of the mansion. "Why does that surprise you?"

"Because you're..."

I raise my eyebrows.

Theo catches his next laugh in his hand, runs his hand down his clean-shaven chin. "So *polite*. I'm shocked, truly. How did you get into that?"

I am careful as I climb the steps, scared my heels will have me tumbling down at any moment. "I've always loved fashion."

"Well, I can tell. You're very well dressed."

"Thank you," I reply. "And I know it's not really cool anymore, but I always loved watching the Victoria's Secret Fashion show. Something about how every garment was like a puzzle and yet was made with so little fabric."

"A puzzle. That's one way to describe lingerie," he says with a suggestive tone.

I laugh. "Well, I'm sure you have other reasons for enjoying it. But I really fell in love with the craftsmanship and...now here I am."

We make it to the top of the steps.

Theo slides his hands into his pockets. "Well, I'd love to see your work."

"I'm on Instagram." I smile.

Theo's eyes narrow, and he smiles. "That's not how I meant, love."

My stomach plummets in the best way. It's clear this man is after one thing and one thing only. And I know myself. I know what I need. And I know that isn't Theo.

But a little flirting doesn't have to end in bed, does it?

"I'm sorry, perhaps that was too forward," Theo says.

"You're not sorry at all." I smirk.

His tongue slides across his lower lip. "I'm happy to give

an apology when it's very necessary. Is it?"

I am about to tell him no when a hand grips my bicep. A hand and a grip I know too well. Looking at Seth over my shoulder, I glower. "Seth!"

"We need to talk." With a simple nod to Theo, he says, "Sorry to interrupt."

"No apology ne–"

We don't remain long enough to hear the rest of Theo's sentence.

Seth yanks me over to one of the tall columns making up the façade of the mansion.

"You're hurting me!" I hiss.

"Sorry," he grumbles, lightening his grip but not letting go. "Need you away from the stairs."

I scoff. "What?"

He glowers at me. "Don't act like you don't remember."

Shit.

The memories that tried to creep up before threaten to resurface again, and I can't let them. Because I know exactly what he is talking about. Too bad *he* doesn't know what he is talking about.

No one knows. And no one will ever know if I have any say in it. Not even my family. *Especially* my family.

I shake off the past.

"I can handle steps, Seth." We stop at the base of the column, out of sight of most everyone. "What do you want?"

"What the hell are you doing with Theo?" His chest rises and falls with clear pent-up frustration.

I shake my head. "Talking?"

"No. That's *not* just talking. He's flirting with you. And you're flirting back."

"So?!"

Seth's eyes widen. "*So?!* He's a total womanizer."

"It's just flirting, Seth."

"Not with him it's not."

My shoulders slump forward.

I'm exhausted by this game, this back and forth. "I'm a grown fucking woman, Seth. I can make my own choices."

"I'm protecting you!" I can tell he is holding back, because if he could yell it, he would.

"You're *manipulating me!*"

His brow furrows. "Manipulating?! I'm–"

"I told you to stop talking to me. And twice you've crossed that boundary. I don't want you involved in any part of my life."

Seth face slackens. "You don't mean that."

Of course, I don't fucking mean that.

Seth has preoccupied every other one of my thoughts for years now.

I *want* him.

"I've never given you any shit for the way you fuck around at the club or any of the girls you've ever–"

"It's different!"

Is he kidding right now? "How is it different?"

"Because someone needs to protect you! I'm not worth protecting like you need to be."

I frown. "You really think that?"

Seth finally drops his hand from my arm and steps back. "Just stay the fuck away from him, alright?"

I blink.

"I'm done with this, Seth." I take a couple steps away, trying to keep my composure. "Just stop."

He doesn't reply.

So, I walk away, setting an intention in myself. I'll make the best of this wedding weekend. And I don't care how mad Seth gets in the process.

6

———

SETH

I don't know where Bridget is.

She disappeared right after the photos of the wedding party were taken and hasn't returned to the gardens since.

I'm doing everything in my power not to ask if anyone knows where she went or to go after her but every nerve in my body screams at me, begging to go after her.

It's not even just a bad habit from all these years of adoring her. It's something necessary to my lifeforce. I feel like I'm dying not knowing where she is.

It was like this when she went away to college too. Didn't matter how busy I was with my work, didn't matter the pictures I saw she posted on social media. I was desperate to know that she was safe at all times.

That's when the texts really began. My check-ins. My begging to know where she was. Of course, she didn't see it as begging. She saw it as *manipulation*.

I wasn't able to enjoy the rehearsal dinner whatsoever last night after our confrontation under the column. I had to watch as Theo flirted with her, ogled at her, sat next to her, the place I have wanted to take for *ten years*.

And then I had to watch her walk down the aisle with him. Arm and arm. The way he leaned down and whispered something teasing in her ear. How it made her laugh.

Drove me fucking crazy.

But what really pushed me off the deep end was Bridget. How beautiful she looked in the olive-colored dress that brought out the green in her eyes. The elegant line of her bare collarbone. Her head held high, dark hair in luscious tumbling curls.

God, what am I supposed to do?

Keep it together, Seth.

That doesn't stop me from scanning the garden for any sign of her just one more time.

Instead, I lock eyes with Mason.

He's standing with Nate, talking low and close. He jerks his head to draw me closer.

I head over. That will hopefully be a good distraction. "What's up?"

"You still good to help us tonight?" Mason asks.

I smile. "Of course, I am."

Nate sighs. "We're nervous, man."

"Most guys have to propose on their own," I say. "They don't have backup."

Mason scoffs. "You know it's not like that."

I roll my eyes. "I'm joking, joking." I grab both my friends' shoulders and give them a squeeze. "It's going to be great."

They both smile.

When I found out that they'd gotten permission from Sonia and Edwin to propose to Laney at the reception, I offered my services right away. After all, I was one of the first ones in on the relationship, when Mason called me almost in panic when they were in the cabin where their throuple's story began.

Now they've been official for about eight months and, while I think it's a little fast for a proposal, when you know, you know, I guess.

"So, you'll go out and make sure the lights are set up, right? Abigail's on musician duty and–"

Laney appears at Mason's shoulder. "What are you guys talking about?"

All three of us jump at the sound of her voice.

Mason gasps. "God, you scared me!"

Laney frowns, smiling at us like we're dummies. "Sorry, didn't realize you weren't ready for a jump scare."

Nate tries to laugh.

Laney puts her hands on her hips. In her heels today, she's almost as tall as me. "Seriously, why are you being all secretive?"

Mason and Nate look at me for an excuse because "planning our proposal to you" isn't going to cut it if they want to keep the element of surprise.

"Just checking if they've seen Bridget." God, I'm obsessed with her.

Laney looks around as I've done twenty times already. "Oh, weird. She was in the photos, right?"

"Yeah, pretty sure..." I trail off when I spot Theo stroll by. On his own. Tip tapping away on his phone. The business type. Doesn't have time even for personal events like a wedding. Works hard, plays hard.

Yeah, don't want him anywhere near Bridget.

"Sorry, I gotta go do something." I duck away from the conversation, leaving Mason and Nate to stew in their nervous energy in front of their soon-to-be fiancée.

My focus is lasered in on Theo.

He must feel me coming because he lifts his head and locks eyes with me. Offering me one of those smug I'm-god's-gift-to-women smiles.

I'd love to punch that smile off his face.

"What's up, mate?" he asks as I close in.

Shit. I can't just come up and start talking about Bridget, can I? Would that be weird? Do I need to make small talk? "Enjoying yourself?"

Smooth, Seth.

Theo holds up his phone and grimaces. "Work never stops, does it?"

"Know the feeling," I say. "I'm in tech."

"Edwin mentioned. Baby prodigy or something, eh?" Theo pushes his elbow toward me, not daring to touch me.

I nod, attempt to smile.

I made my fortune at fifteen by working on a crypto algorithm that took off like gangbusters, especially when the market blew up. Now I'm proprietor of my own financial software company. Been working since before I could drive.

No wonder I'm tense.

"Yeah, hey, listen–" Fuck small talk. "I want to talk to you about Bridget."

Theo's eyebrows pop up. "Oh?"

"Yeah, just...I'm her... brother." God, I feel sick. "So, you know, I'm just looking out for her."

He nods. "That's good of you."

You probably wouldn't say that if you knew the way I think about her most the time. "I can tell that the two of you are getting kind of close."

Theo's eyelashes flutter, eyes rolling back. "I mean, you know, it's all in good fun."

The exact reason I was wary of him. He's just biding time. Having *fun.*

Bridget isn't deserving of some guy's attempt at fun at a wedding.

"I totally get it. But Bridget, she's sensitive."

The Englishman cocks his head to the side. "Oh?"

"She's..." *Now or never, Seth. What kind of guy are you going to be?* "Just gotten out of a relationship."

A liar, apparently.

"*Oh*," Theo repeats, this time with a knowingness I wish I could celebrate with a happy dance.

"Right. So, she's very vulnerable, and I wouldn't want her getting confused that your flirtations are anything more than–"

Theo puts his hand to his chest. "Oh, of course, mate," he says in a dower, low voice. Quintessential British person. "You needn't worry. I'll be very careful. In fact, I'll keep it strictly friendly from now."

"Yeah, thanks. I appreciate that."

He holds out his hand to me. We shake on it.

I'm such a slime ball for lying like that, making up a relationship Bridget hasn't been in. But it was the right thing to do. That way, I protect her.

And protecting her means protecting me.

Shit, maybe I *am* a manipulator.

Before I can make other false claims, Solomon approaches. A relief for pulling me from this conversation. A shame for the way I just lied about his daughter.

"Am I interrupting some sort of business deal?" he says with a *daddish* lilt on the phrase "business deal."

"Always," Theo says, then gives us both a nod. "Gentlemen."

The guy might be a Casanova, but he knows how to read a situation.

"What's up, Sol?" I ask.

Solomon grabs my shoulder. "Your mother wants a picture of the four of us while the photographer is doing portraits, but I can't find Bridget. You mind taking a look inside?"

I look back at the manor house and gulp. "Sure." I try to play it cool.

Solomon smiles. "Thank you, Seth."

I head out of the garden and up the stairs to enter the mansion. Past the column where I feel the ghost of Bridget and me sniping at each other in low tones.

All I can hear in my ears is my heartbeat.

Where could she be? Camped out in the bride's quarters? Trying to calm her nerves with a glass of champagne?

I walk the halls calling out her name. Event staff are scurrying past me carrying trays and linens, trying to set up the reception room while cocktails take place out in front of the manor.

If I know Bridget, which I think I do in some respects, she wouldn't be camped out around the chaos. She'd be taking a breath somewhere quiet.

I head up the grand staircase to the second floor and head to the west wing. Us guys got ready at the opposite end of the hall in the west wing from the girls' room.

Once I get to the bride's quarters, I rap on the door. There's no response.

With care, I open the door and peer inside.

"Bridget?"

The empty room doesn't answer.

I begin to close the door but stop when I hear the sound of a woman's voice. Distant and muffled. In pain?

"Bridget?" I say again.

Still nothing. But another...moan?

I go into the room and stand there for a moment, waiting for the next sound.

Sure enough, with my ears tuned to the sound, I am able to identify the direction. And it's coming from a door I didn't see before. Must be a bathroom or...

"*Oh god...*" the voice whimpers.

Okay, that's not pain. That's *arousal*.

And it's not just any woman's voice.

It's Bridget's.

"Bridget?" I ask once more, except my voice is nothing more than a whisper. I'm not sure how to keep my nerves steady. If she's in there fucking some guy, I'm going to lose it. But if she's alone...

I can feel blood rushing to my cock already.

"*Fuck, fuck, fuck,*" I hear from behind the door.

I stop in front of it, stare at the wooden panel. I can't very well interrupt, can I?

Then she'll know I heard her, and she'll be embarrassed, most likely angrier at me than she already is. But if I stand here and listen–

"*Get out of my head...*"

Yeah, there's no way I'm walking away.

"*No, no. Shit.*" She huffs out a long breath.

I smile to myself. She sounds frustrated.

Is she touching herself? I don't hear the breath or sounds of someone else...

I'm growing harder by the second. I wish I wasn't...

"*Come on, I'm– I'm going to–*"

I grab the doorframe and close my eyes. All I want for her is this release.

She sounds so desperate, so needy.

I've been there. So many times.

"*Fuck, Seth, please.*"

My eyes shoot open.

Did she just say my name?

"*I hate that you do this to me...*" her voice pitches higher at the end of her sentence.

God grant me the strength not to tear open this door right this fucking second and show her what I *am* capable of doing to her.

"*Seth, Seth, Se–*" The last mention of my name is interrupted by a shrieking sigh.

My cock jumps in my pants. All I'd have to do is touch it and I'd come, Jesus Christ. I try and steady my breath, think nasty gross thoughts that will reduce my horniness.

That's better...mildly so, but better.

There is silence for a few moments.

Then, I hear the door handle jostle.

Shit.

I stumble back, hurry out of the bride's quarters, and stand in the hall and wait for her to emerge. A few seconds pass. Then a minute.

Finally, the door flies open, and Bridget appears, cheeks flushed from her release.

"Hey," I say, my smile not able to hide my nerves.

Bridget leaps into the air. "Oh, my god!"

"Sorry, sorry, I didn't mean to scare you. I–"

"What the hell are you doing just standing here like a creep? What the fuck is..." She tries to catch her breath. "What is that about?"

Poor thing doesn't know I just heard her coming with my name in her mouth. But *she* knows she was repeating my name. Begging a version of me in her imagination to release her from the shackles of her arousal.

She wants me. Bridget fucking wants me.

I clear my throat. "Sorry, our parents–" *Ugh, I hate*

saying that. "—they want a family picture before the photographer moves onto the cocktail hour. Your dad sent me to look for you, and I–"

"Okay, well, let's get it over with I guess," Bridget says, blowing past me toward the staircase.

I withhold a laugh.

She's so flustered. Because I was just on her mind. More than that. I was in her body. In her blood coursing through her, the pounding of her heart, the wetness of her pussy.

As I follow her, I swear I can smell her, the remnants of her arousal between her legs. Not the first time I've felt able to smell her. I've been attuned to her since I first met her.

Fucking pheromones. They're stronger than ever now that I know...she wants me.

My insides are like a circus over that. Backflips and acrobatics.

Elation.

Once we get downstairs, I catch up to walk beside her. "Bridget."

"What?" she replies, clearly short with me.

"You look...really nice today." God, how old am I? Thirteen? Telling a girl at her bat mitzvah her polka dot strapless dress looks *nice?* "I mean, you look amazing."

The tension in her face melts, but she doesn't look at me. "Thank you."

We are silent the rest of the way to meet our parents out in the garden.

My mom grins. "There she is!" She gives Bridget a loving hug.

I try to ignore the guilt building in the back of my throat.

Mom has always treated Bridget with love and closeness. Unlike me, Bridget lost her mother when she was too young to have many memories of her. That allowed for my mom to give her more than Solomon has been able to give me.

We are a weird little family.

But all of that is eclipsed by the memory of my name in Bridget's mouth.

We allow our parents to jigger us around since my mom wants to show her good side. Finally, we settle in a row, Bridget and I next to our respective parents.

"Alright, big smiles." The photographer ducks behind his mammoth lens.

And boy, if I don't follow that direction. I beam, lifting my chin, puffing my chest. Proud.

Not for my family. Not for how we look like the perfect American Dream from the outside.

No. For the way I feel. That after ten years, I can be proud of the way I want Bridget. There's no reason to be ashamed.

Not when my name is in her mouth. Not when she wants me in her most primal, private moments.

I'm right. Right to want her.

And now...I have to have her.

7

BRIDGET

Couples are flocking to the stage as the band begins to play a cover of some eighties ballad I've heard on the radio while in the car with my dad and have never known the name of.

I watch Edwin and Sonia at the center of the dance floor swaying together, whispering in each other's ears.

It's clear their big day has been everything and more to them. They look more in love than ever. First comes love, then comes marriage, and I wouldn't be surprised if they fulfill the third part of that saying on their honeymoon.

Laney, Mason, and Nate all also head out on the floor, doing their usual sharing dance which would be awkward if it were anyone else. The three of them make it look seamless, the way Mason and Nate share Laney without any competition, without any strangeness.

Then I spy Amelia and my Dad bobbing back and forth.

I laugh into my hand.

Dad has two left feet, but Amelia doesn't care at all. I couldn't have chosen anyone better to love my dad. And me.

I scan the rest of the room, feeling myself wilt. Most of

the people who aren't on the floor are families with kids, people in deep conversations, older folks who are blissed just to watch.

No singles. They've all paired up and gone onto the floor, happy for just a night together. And certainly no one walking my way.

However, out of the corner of my eye, I spot Theo. He's leaning against one of the walls, typing on his phone as he's been doing from time to time throughout the reception.

I take a deep breath and down the rest of my lemon drop martini.

Fuck it. I don't want to be someone on the sidelines. I want to dance. And I shouldn't hold back just because Theo is a womanizer.

Stupid Seth got into my head, just like he always does.

So much so I had to get him out *some* way.

I try to push the thought of Seth away for fear that thinking of him too much will put me on edge again, force me to flee to the bathroom and touch myself until I come *again*.

Nope. No more of that. Tonight, I'm having fun despite all the crap he's put me through.

Holding my head high, I stride over to Theo.

He senses me coming, lifting his eyes to meet mine. And he smiles.

The smile makes me uneasy. It's not rude but it's not necessarily inviting. It's almost...pitying.

That doesn't stop me. I've had a couple drinks, maybe I'm not reading it right. I smile back and throw a look to the dance floor. "Too busy to dance?"

"Ah, no. I hadn't even realized..." he trails off and holds up his phone. "Distracted."

I tilt my head to the side, hoping it's flirtatious enough

he gets the idea and asks me to dance. "Isn't it the middle of the night in England?"

Theo chuckles. "Oh, yes. But some things require immediate attention, don't you think?"

I'm not sure how many emails are more important than a friend's wedding, but that's not why I'm standing in front of him. "Well, if you have just three minutes, there's a power ballad I'd like to dance to, and I don't have a partner."

Theo nods his head toward me with politeness. "If that's your way of asking, I'd be happy to accompany you."

As we walk toward the dance floor, arm in arm, I can't help but dissect every word he's chosen.

Happy? That's not good enough. He should be doing cartwheels to dance with me.

Accompany? That sounds clinical.

I think I might be reading into it until we position ourselves for a spin around the dance floor.

His hand doesn't touch my waist but just above it. And the grip he has on my hand is cool and professional.

Something is different compared to how we were walking down the aisle earlier. His charming chat in my ear, obvious flirtations, thinly veiled double entendre.

Now, he's avoiding eye contact and touching me in a platonic way.

What changed?

"I'm surprised nobody else has snatched you up to dance, Bridget," he says.

Our eyes meet. There's no glow in his. No spark.

"Yes, well, I think they might have thought I already had a partner." I try to close the space between us an inch more.

Theo doesn't allow that, pulls back just as much as I stepped forward, like we are magnets repelling each other.

"Yes, I'm sure if it's new for you, people haven't gotten used to you being unattached."

I furrow my brow. "What?"

Theo smiles at me. And it *is* pity. I can tell because his eyes are sad. "I heard you're newly out of a relationship."

Have I stepped into the Twilight Zone? "Where did you hear *that*?"

"Doesn't matter, I just, you know, I know what it can be like to want to–" Theo clears his throat, shakes out his curls. "Get over by getting under, you know?"

My eyes widen.

"And while I don't want to assume, based on our rapport...well, I'm flattered to say the least if you were looking for something like that with me, but I find that situations like that always end up complicated, so I'd rather not. For your sake."

Thank god he's still dancing because if he wasn't, I wouldn't be able to move my feet. I'm too dumbstruck to make sense of what's happening. "Someone told you I went through a breakup?"

"Yes. It's nothing to be ashamed of, of course."

Any possibility of an attraction I could've had to Theo the past two days releases like the popping of a balloon.

First off, how dare he assume I wanted to sleep with him? And second of all, how dare he assume I'm ashamed of a breakup? And third of all, what fucking breakup is he even talking about?

"But take it from me, I've been around the block. Don't know if you can tell from the gray in my hair," he says on a soft laugh. "Sometimes what's best is to take some time away rather than to rush into..."

As we circle around to the beat of the song, I get a new view of the room, and over Theo's shoulder I spot him.

Seth.

He's just reentered through the doors to the garden, shoving his hands in the pockets of his trousers, scanning the room like he's just been up to no good.

The bastard. It was him. I know it!

He scared Theo away. Pulled him aside and told him some fib about my love life to scare him off. Under the guise of trying to protect me. All he's doing is isolating me.

This is textbook Seth.

And I'm fucking fed up.

Theo's voice comes back into focus. "You understand what I'm saying?"

I don't take my eyes away from Seth as he crosses back to his table.

I won't let him walk away like that.

"Yes, of course," I say, pulling away from Theo. "You're right. Thanks for the talk."

Theo tries to hold onto me, say something more, but I elude his grasp and head in the direction of Seth.

I bunch my skirt in my hands so I can walk as fast as possible over to Seth.

We lock eyes as I charge in his direction. And I can tell that for *once* he's scared of me.

"Bridget–" he begins when I'm in earshot.

I grab him by the arm and yank him toward the doors out of the ballroom and into the long hallway. "You've got a lot of fucking explaining to do," I growl.

"I thought you weren't talking to me," he says with a smug tone.

I glare back at him before grabbing the knob of the first door I see and yanking it open. I pull him inside, slam the door behind us, and then flip around to face him.

Seth is closer than I expect, making me gasp, not

because he's scared me, but because he's much closer than… than he should be.

"What the fuck is wrong with you?" I move around him into the room.

Moonlight streams in through the drapes. I can make out the lines of beautiful leather couches and bookcases lining the walls. We've tripped into the estate's library.

"Care to enlighten me on what you're referring to?" Seth crosses his arms over his chest.

I stare at him, unable to speak.

My anger roils in my belly and yet…I can't help but think he's beautiful as the silvery light cuts across his face. Across his tight, closed-lipped smile and the dimple that appears in his left cheek. The one that shows me he thinks I'm some silly kid that doesn't need to be taken seriously.

I'm done with that. I'm *done*.

I'm a fucking woman. And he has to let go of me.

So I can let go of him. And find someone. The one truly meant for me.

Between measured breaths, I answer, "Theo."

Seth raises his eyebrows like he doesn't know what I'm talking about. He's a good actor. Knows how to be stoic and stone-faced. A Dom.

I won't believe him.

"What about him?"

I start to laugh. Wry and dark. "You're kidding, right?"

He shrugs a shoulder.

"Someone told him I just got out of a relationship."

"That's weird."

I stare at him.

He doesn't back down.

Wait. Could someone else have lied to Theo?

But why? No one else has any reason to.

Seth has always vied for power over me. Vied for control.

Doesn't he know how that screws with my head? How confusing it is when for ten years I've wanted him?

Fuck.

"Yeah, I thought so to. I asked him to dance and though he agreed, he let me down easy. Which was really embarrassing considering whatever he's been told is a lie."

For a split second, there's something like an apology in Seth's blue eyes. A softness that betrays his dishonesty.

"And I know you did it."

Seth shakes his head. "I didn't."

"Seth–"

"What would I get out of that?" He takes a step further into the room. Closer to me.

I hold my ground, remain steadfast. "You want to control me."

"That's not true."

"Admit it."

"That's not true, the way you say it. *That's not true.*"

I step closer to him. "What the hell does that mean?"

His jaw tightens.

Fuck, I can smell him. Smell a fresh scent of cologne mixed with the tingly saltiness of sweat, a smell I have known as *his* all this time.

God, I want him. Being in this little room alone with him is suffocating me with desire.

If I'm not careful, I might...I don't know what I'll do. Because I've never felt anything like this.

"Answer my question, Seth."

"I already did."

I shake my head. "Answer it *honestly.*"

"*Bridget...*" It's a warning. Of what, I don't know.

But we are too close. A foot apart.

I can't be here any longer if I don't want to do something I'll regret. "Fuck you," I say in a soft voice before walking past him to the door.

"Wait."

I stop, my hand on the doorknob. I don't turn, though. Not yet.

"I'll answer honestly if you agree to answer a question in return."

I look over my shoulder at him.

Seth's fists are balled at his sides. Is he nervous?

"Honestly, of course," he adds with another smirk.

I narrow my eyes. "You have to answer me first."

He nods. "Of course." Then, with his chin lowered, his blue eyes flip up to mine, darker in the shadowy room. "Do we have an agreement?"

Huffing, I drop my hand from the door. "Yes. Fine."

"Then, as we agreed, you go ahead and ask."

"Seth, did you lie to Theo and tell him I just got out of a relationship?"

Seth holds up his hands. A reveal. "Yes. I did."

My eyes pinch with tears. "Why?"

"You've already asked your question, Bridget."

I cover my eyes in frustration. "That's not fair, I deserve to know why, I deserve–"

"It's my turn."

He's closer.

I remove my hands from my eyes and tuck them against my sides, under my arms. I want to disappear. "Fine. *What.*"

Seth doesn't speak right away. He tilts his head to the side, watching me as if timing is just as important as the question.

"Seth, *what?!*" I cry out.

Seth's eyes drop from mine. His tongue slides across his lower lip.

I hold my breath.

"How often do you say my name when you touch yourself, Bridget?"

Time freezes. I stare at him. Unsure if the question he asked was a real one or if maybe it was actually a different language and I just misunderstood. "What?"

His eyes lift and when they meet mine, I know. The same way I knew that *he* was the one who ruined my chances with Theo for the night.

He heard me when I was touching myself earlier.

I knew it was suspicious the way he was standing outside the bride's quarters, but I pushed it away because... because...

Without considering the repercussions, I turn on my heel and rush for the door again, grabbing the knob, twisting, and–

The door only opens an inch before Seth comes up behind me and slams it shut, his palm pressed against the wood. "Answer the question, Bridget."

I try to pull harder, but his strength is too much for me. "Let me go."

"You promised. A question for a question."

I pull again. "This isn't *fair*, Seth. This–"

"*Answer me.*"

He grabs my shoulder and pulls me around to face him, pressing me up against the door, his hands on both my biceps. It doesn't hurt. And if it does, I don't feel the pain.

I am flooded with pleasure at his touch. At his control.

Our faces are mere inches apart. His breaths land across my skin.

"Look at me."

I close my eyes and duck my head.

"Be a good girl and *look* at me."

Electric pulses warm my core.

What the fuck is he doing calling me a good girl? Trying to make me a mess?

Of course, he is. If he knows I moaned his name with my fingers delved between the lips of my pussy, he knows what one 'good girl' will do to me.

It will destroy me.

But all I've ever wanted to be is a good girl.

If this is my only opportunity to have that with Seth, I will take it.

I lift my chin, my mouth sealed closed. I will wait for his instruction. Be obedient. Listen.

I'll be so good. For him.

Like I've always wanted.

"Let me ask again." His voice is so calm and steady it's hard to imagine how much power he's exerting keeping me up against the door. "How often do you say my name when you touch yourself?"

"Very often," I say, my voice ragged and quiet.

"Louder, Bridget."

I swallow, get my strength. "Very often."

"Were you saying my name earlier today?"

It's not fair for him to ask another question. But this isn't about fairness. It's about finally serving him. His purpose. His desire. I want nothing more. "Yes."

"Yes, *what?*"

I blink. I have heard what he is called at the Underground. Master Carlton.

Master.

I have never used the word for anyone. I have wanted to.

But with him, it doesn't feel right. It's what everyone else calls him. And I don't want to be like everyone else. I want to be his good girl, yes, but not just another one. I want to be his best girl.

There is no question, though. I have dreamed about this too many times not to take my chance.

"Yes, Sir."

Seth's eyes darken, almost all pupil, no iris. His eyes fall to my lips, then dart back to meet my gaze.

His hands slide down my arms to my wrists and in a fluid motion, he pins my hands roughly above my head.

I gasp as he presses himself against me, his face to my temple, his chest to my chest, his...

Oh god. I can feel his cock through his pants.

I've looked at it before. Couldn't help it.

I've always known it was big.

But no.

It's huge.

I can't help bending my body toward him, rubbing myself against him.

Seth's cock. I'm rubbing myself against *Seth's cock.*

"What the fuck am I supposed to do about this, Bridget?" he growls in my ear.

I don't have an answer for him.

"What the fuck am I supposed to do when I know what you want, and I know I can give it to you, but I..." Seth trails off.

But I can't.

And I know why he can't. Why *I* can't.

What if he could, though? What if we threw away convention and did? Just once. He could teach me. Break me in. Make me good for the Dom of my dreams.

Except I know the truth. If he gave me one inch of his

power, I would try and take all of it. I would want to bask in it the rest of my life.

Which is why, as much as it breaks my heart, I have to stop. Now.

"It was a mistake," I say in a soft voice.

I don't mean it. None of it has been a mistake. *None* of it.

Seth's grip loosens on me. We droop together, his hands still on my wrists as I draw them back to my sides.

"It's just a mistake. I meant someone else. Or I..." It hurts to swallow. The tension in my jaw.

There's no going back. There's no going forward either.

Seth releases me and takes a step back. Without his touch, I feel naked, stripped of anything meaningful or true.

He rubs his chin, can't look me in the eye.

I grab the doorknob and move so fast I'm close to flying, I can't bear to hear him apologize. Can't bear to know his regret when mine is so heavy.

I return to the ballroom as if I was never gone and fold myself into the throng of dancers doing the electric slide, bumping up against Sonia who grins at me in a champagne haze. "Having a good time?"

"Great!" I say without missing a beat.

We dance.

But all that's on my mind is Seth.

Now that I've had one little taste, I know I will crave him every moment of every day.

For that, I regret everything.

8

———

SETH

I haven't paid attention during this meeting for one single second. In fact, haven't paid attention at work all week.

I sit back in my rolling chair at the head of the conference table, my feet propped up on the table edge, squeezing a stress ball in my hand. Being the owner of a tech company, I've always kept things rather relaxed. Casual dress, comfortable furniture, etiquette be damned. I save all the strait-laced behaviors for the Underground.

Today, though, I could use some of that discipline here at work to at least look like I'm engaged. No one wants a CEO off in la la land.

I can't help it, though. Can't control my own thoughts, can't whip them into submission.

My brain has been all Bridget all the time since our encounter at the wedding.

I almost kissed her. I almost *fucked* her.

She felt me.

And now that I know she wants me, every part of my body wants to be near her.

I'm dying inside. Betraying myself by keeping my distance.

Not a second goes by I'm not thinking of her.

I barely sleep. I can't eat. I'm in full body mourning for what I shouldn't have. Because no longer is there a wrought iron gate of "can't" in front of Bridget.

She moaned my name. She obeyed me.

I *can* have her. If I'm ready to break everything.

Someone's voice cuts through my aching thoughts. "What do you think, Seth?"

I raise my gaze to the presenter at the front of the room, one of the new recruits fresh out of MIT. Rodney.

He's helming the development of one of our new algorithmic products, trying to make it both marketable and user friendly.

I stare at him.

God, he's so young. Still splotchy with acne and hasn't quite nailed down his hygiene routine. The glare of the grease in his dark hair is nearly blinding.

"It's good."

Rodney smiles, eyes bright. "Really?"

Is he really asking me to double down? Fine. "Really."

Yeah, I haven't been listening, but I'm not about to admit that. And I'm also not going to dash his hopes in front of all these people. I'll take a look at the proposals later and make sure everything is above board.

I push myself up out of my seat before anyone can comment. "Let's table the rest of this to tomorrow's stand up. There's some things I have to get done before end of day."

"You got it," my assistant, Camilla, says. She's quick to type a memo to herself in the calendar, her wild curls falling over her face.

I can't manage a thank you, though my team deserves it, before I hurry out of the room to my corner office, shutting the door behind me and triple checking it's locked.

I lumber over to my lounge chair in the corner and sit with the heaviest sigh, as if I'm Atlas deciding to no longer hold up the sky.

Through the floor to ceiling windows, I get a fantastic view of Manhattan across the East River. As high up as we are, it's impossible to have any peeping tom neighbors.

Which is great for me. That way, no one can see the CEO of Firmament Industries unzip his pants and release himself into his hand to jack off for the umpteenth time this week. It's unceremonious and unfulfilling every time, but since the night of Sonia and Edwin's wedding, my cock has been half-hard. All the time.

Each time I jerk off to thoughts of Bridget, I think and pray it will be the last time. That I just have to get it out of my system.

And each time I'm disappointed when my cock deflates only to harden not half an hour later because I can't turn my thoughts away from her.

I shut my eyes tight. It doesn't feel good anymore. It's painful to touch myself to thoughts of her when I know I could have the real thing if our circumstances weren't so fucked.

I stroke myself to completion, coming sadly onto myself as usual. What a fucking waste of my virility.

Leaning back, I catch my breath which isn't nearly as labored as it would be if I was able to release the way I wanted to. Fucking Bridget. Dominating Bridget. Making Bridget come and using her for my purposes.

I shut my eyes, and I'm greeted with the image of her under me. The memory of her up against the door, pinned by my hips and my hands. Her heart pounding against my chest, want so clear I could *smell* it.

She was such a good girl for me. Just that minute against the door.

Tears sting at the back of my eyes. I don't cry and know I won't. It's been years.

Not since the day I lost my dad.

But to be *threatened* with tears is enough to show me that my want for Bridget might break me if I'm not careful.

Unless I completely abandoned my life...which I don't want to do.

I like my life. My work, my family, my friends.

Bridget.

I make a fist and smash it against my forehead. Breath growls in and out of me.

If something doesn't change, I'm going to break.

Which means I either break my world or it breaks me.

And for Bridget, I'm willing to burn it all down.

Jack holds out the controller in my direction. "You want a turn?"

I shake my head. "I'm good, man."

He snorts. "Suit yourself."

It's guys night. A usual great distraction from any racing thoughts. But no dice. Bridget is still first and foremost on the brain.

But I'm okay with that now.

Because I have a plan. I just need to get Nate alone.

"Okay, another round?" Mason navigates the Call of Duty menu with his own controller.

"I'm down," Jack says.

Nate shakes his head. "I need a break."

My heart lurches in my chest.

Perfect.

Maybe I can lure him out of Jack's living room and into the kitchen for a chat.

Jack looks to Mason. "Tag team?"

Covering his mouth with his hand, Mason starts to laugh. "That doesn't mean what you think it does?"

Nate laughs too, causing Jack to roll his eyes.

"Oh, my god," Jack says. "You guys only have one thing on your mind, don't you?"

Nate shrugs. "Kind of."

Mason lifts his hand for a high five, which Nate reciprocates.

With an annoyed look in my direction, Jack sighs. "Do they annoy you like they annoy me?"

"No comment," I say. I'm not going to rain on Nate and Mason's parade. Their proposal went exactly to plan. Laney said yes and now they're engaged, date of the commitment ceremony to be determined.

Anyway, I don't care about whatever innuendos Nate and Mason make or really anything about anyone at all. I've got a one-track mind.

I get onto my feet. "Anyone want anything? I'm gonna grab another beer." I shake my empty bottle.

"Yes, please. Beer." Jack gets into a ready position as Mason starts the game.

"I second that," Mason adds.

I give Nate a look. You wouldn't know from the way he is snuggled up in the couch under a blanket that he's actually a buff surfer dude who most of the time can't be made to sit down. This is going to be harder than I thought. "Nate?" I prod.

"I'm good, man." His eyes stay glued to the screen.

I stand there and gnaw on my lip.

Fuck.

"Could you..."

Nate looks at me, obvious confusion on his face.

I groan to myself. "Could you come help me?"

Mason smirks, eyes on the game, fingers clicking on the controller. "You can't carry three beer bottles?"

I grunt. "Yes, I can carry three beer bottles."

"Okay, good. Because I'm super cozy." Nate buries himself under the big blanket.

I continue to stand there. I've never been good at asking for help.

Nate blinks. "You good?"

"Can you..." I gesture over my shoulder, at a loss. There's no getting around just asking the question. "Can you just come with me? I want to talk to you. In private."

Jack laughs. "You gonna talk shit about us?"

"Yeah, that's what I need to do," I say in a dry tone.

Nate groans and pushes the blanket off of himself. "*Fiii-iiinnnne.*"

"Thank you." I jet out of the living room and into the hall. Thank god the kitchen is at the other end of Jack's Financial District apartment, so we won't be overheard.

Not that Mason and Jack seem to care since they're pinned on their tag team round of Call of Duty.

Nate's padding feet follow me, and I can't resist a small smile. Just a year ago, he was still learning to walk after his surfing accident. Now, he's the same old Nate.

Once I enter the darkened kitchen, I head right to the fridge for the beers.

"What's going on, man?" Nate prompts.

I throw him a fleeting glance, unable to hold eye

contact. "Um. Well." I grab three beers, place them on the counter beside the fridge. "I have a question for you."

His eyebrows twist. "Okay."

I grab a bottle opener off the counter and pop the caps of the beers off.

Nate juts his head forward. "And your question is…?"

"Give me a second, I'm trying to get the nerve to ask." I huff.

"You're scaring me, Seth."

Yeah, I'm scaring myself too.

I take a swig from one of the open beer bottles. Wish it was something like whisky or tequila, the real liquid courage. "I need a favor."

Nate shakes his head, still confused. "I mean, anything. If I can. Anything."

I press my lips together, attempt to smile. I've got great friends. Great family. I'm not sure I deserve them when I'm willing to go so far to push the boundaries of my relationship with Bridget. "I need to rent out the Underground."

Nate's confusion breaks, and he smiles. "Oh! That's nothing. Of course. I mean, it'd be better to talk to Sonia about that, but–"

"She's on her honeymoon," I interrupt.

And she's Bridget's best friend. Don't want to cross the streams.

"Right, right…well, I'm sure we can make that happen for you. You want to throw a party or something?"

"No! Nothing–nothing like that," I say with more urgency than I mean to.

Nate's eyes widen. "Oh, okay."

Shit, this isn't going well. "I just…need it for myself."

"Kinky, but respect."

"And..." *This* is the big ask. "I need it in the next couple days."

Nate's eyebrows leap up. "You want to rent out the whole Underground in the next couple days?"

"Yep."

He shakes his head, searching for words. "That's not possible."

"That's why I'm asking *you*."

"But that would require disappointing a lot of the members and I mean, a turn around like that–"

I walk closer to my friend. "I'll pay double. Triple."

Nate backs away. "You're scaring me, Seth."

Am I? Is it the crazed look in my eye? The way I'm stalking toward him like an animal who hasn't eaten in days? Weeks?

"I'm desperate, Nate," I say, my voice higher-pitched than usual.

"What–why do you need it?"

I shake my head. "I can't tell you."

My friend runs a hand through his blond waves and squeezes his eyes shut. "Um..."

I need to make the deal as sweet as possible. "I don't need any of the subs. I don't need a mistress at the desk. I just need the Underground. All to myself. No distractions."

Nate scrubs a hand over his face. "That's a huge ask, Seth."

"I know it is. And I'll owe you. I promise, I'll–"

"Fine. I'll get it done."

I blink at him. "You will?"

He slides his hands into the pockets of his joggers, glancing over his shoulder down the hall. "If it wasn't for you, we probably wouldn't have worked things out with Laney."

I smile. I remember the phone call Mason made to me all those months ago when the three of them were vacationing together at the cabin upstate. How confused he was over his feelings for Laney and the lack of jealousy he had over her relationship with Nate. "I didn't do anything, Nate. Not really."

"Don't sell yourself short."

If it gets me what I want, fine, I won't. "You're right. I am the reason you three are together."

He laughs, head thrown back.

"And I helped with that amazing proposal."

"True, true."

"At this point, you should name your first-born son after me," I egg him on with humor.

Nate lifts a finger. "Now you're pushing it."

I laugh, then lock eyes with my friend. "So, we have a deal?"

Nate holds out his hand.

I take it and we shake.

"Deal," Nate replies.

Step one of my plan to burn down the world, complete.

9

BRIDGET

I run my hand down the bolt of burgundy fabric.

The velvet caresses my hand, soft and whispering. This might be perfect. I slide the bolt off the shelf.

Abigail groans. "Another one?"

I smile at her over my shoulder and drop the bolt onto the stack she's already balancing in her arms. They're all moody and dark, a far cry from my original pastels and florals. I have a whole new collection in mind. "This is what you get for being my assistant."

"Begrudging assistant," Abigail mutters.

Laughing, I continue down the rows of bolts, squeezed onto the shelf, a library of fabrics. The fabric store is like my church. The place I can go to worship, to expand, to create.

My mind has been racing with new ideas since the wedding.

All it took was two minutes. Two minutes of playing in the world I've coveted for years. And everything clicked into place. Made sense. Broke open.

I'm a different woman now.

I can't help but wonder how long that will last before I start craving more.

For now, I'm riding the wave of creativity. Picking out fabrics to test with my new design of luxurious sub wear. Edgy designs that will be delicious to tantalize Doms... that may or may not all look like Seth in my head.

"You're really going all out today," Abigail says.

"Yep. I'm inspired, what can I say?" I pull out a bolt of black, wide knit lace.

"Any particular reason?"

I glance at her. Abigail blinks her green eyes almost hidden under her feral red bangs. "That question sounds pointed."

I slide the black lace out and plop it on her stack.

She yelps.

"I'm just saying." She tucks her chin on top of the bolts to look at me. "You and Theo were kind of cozy."

Laughter falls out of me. "You're kidding, right?"

"Well, he was flirting with you, you were dancing–"

I leave the aisle, Abigail at my heels, and head to the front counter. "We were literally paired together, and I had no one to dance with. That's all it was."

"Well, good," she says, the good punctuated as she drops the bolts on the counter in front of the seamstress who runs the shop.

The bolts slide across the counter, creating a mess. The seamstress raises her eyebrow over the thick glasses.

Abigail grits her teeth, trying to smile. She's in her early twenties, still clinging onto that childlike, oops!-Did-I-do-that? mentality. "Sorry," she says.

"Three yards of each please," I ask the seamstress, who gets to measuring and cutting quickly.

I turn my attention back to Abigail, crossing my arms

over my chest. "Why are you so concerned with me and Theo anyway?"

Big laugh from Abigail. "Because I'd be concerned about anyone with Theo."

I narrow my eyes. "Why?"

"Because he's such a fraud," she whispers.

"A *fraud*?" That could mean any number of things.

Abigail blows out an annoyed breath. "He has the whole charming Brit thing going on, but he's got baggage. So, I don't want anyone I love getting involved with him."

"Well, we're not involved," I say. But I can't leave it there. I'm nosy. "But what's his baggage?"

The seamstress continues cutting, but I can see she's interested too, turning an ear toward us.

"Well..." Abigail puts on her gossip columnist face, her lips pursed together, eyes widened. "My dad met him when he was traveling Europe after my brothers were born. And Dad always says that if there was one guy wilder than himself, it was Theo. You know, drugs, partying, the works."

My lips tip down in a frown. I guess I could see it.

"When they're together, my dad is just a different person. Like, I see the guy who has three baby mamas and has never been married. Until now I guess."

"I didn't see that at the wedding," I say, not sure I buy it.

"Of course you didn't, Dad was busy," Abigail says. "Anyway, Theo runs his family's investment firm, which, ew boring, right? But he and his brother are both total assholes. They've done so much shit no random person would get away with. Public indecency, assault, money laundering..." Abigail sneaks a smile. "Of course, that all changed when Theo's wife left him for his brother."

I gape and smack my hand over my mouth.

"Yeah. I know. So, after years of covering up for that

piece of shit, he ran off with Theo's wife. Well, ex-wife now. Left him with a little girl too."

"Aww..." I say.

Abigail slaps my arm. "Don't aw that!"

"He's a single dad. That's cute."

"No. He got what was coming to him."

I frown.

"Besides, he leaves his little girl with his parents all the time while he travels and goes to weddings and–"

"I think you're too hard on him."

Abigail's face grows red. "He's a jerk, okay? And no one needs to get involved in his mess. That's all. I'm protecting you."

Saved by the buzz in my pocket. "Alright, alright..." I pull out my phone and open the message.

It's from the automated BDSM Underground concierge. I frown.

Your appointment at two-thirty has been confirmed.

"Huh..."

"What? What is it?" Abigail sticks her nose over my arm to look at the message. She gasps. "Bridget! You're going to finally rip off the band aid?"

I swipe my phone out of her line of sight. "No! I didn't make an appointment. This must be a mistake. Or..." A light bulb goes off in my head. "You're *kidding* me."

"What? *What?*" Abigail gabs my arm.

I shake my head with a chuckle. "Sonia."

Abigail frowns. "Sonia?"

It's as clear as day to me. An unexpected appointment in the Underground? "She's trying to push me to...you know."

"Do a scene?" Abigail looks down her freckled nose at me.

I sigh. "Yeah."

Of course, Sonia would arrange this when she's impossible to contact on her honeymoon island retreat and I can't call her to yell at her.

"I'm sorry, Abs, I have to go deal with this."

Abigail smiles. "No big. I've got to get back to some grad school work anyway. And...maybe you should consider going and enjoying yourself."

I open my mouth to protest but am interrupted when the seamstress drops the bag of my fabric yards in front of me. "On your tab?"

"Please." I swipe the bag. "Thanks."

I give Abigail one last look.

She's smirking.

"Stop thinking about it."

"I'm not," she lies.

WHEN I ARRIVE AT THE CLUB, IT IS PRETTY QUIET. Afternoons have a usual lull after the lunch rush and before the it's-almost-five-o'clock-somewhere drinks. The quiet makes it easy to duck into the Underground.

The desk is unmanned at the moment. No big deal. I can wait.

I go over to it and lean on the desk, waiting for someone to show up so I can clear this up.

Only a few seconds pass before I realize how quiet it is.

I look over my shoulder. No subs or Doms are out on the floor. No one is preparing for a scene in the main room. And from the looks of it, most of the lights are off in the private rooms.

All except one.

Strange.

I turn back to the desk and notice the ledger is splayed open. Every page is usually filled to the brim with names scribbled into the time slots in ink, the old-fashioned way.

Sonia has told me they put it all into a computer for posterity, but for aesthetics, masters and mistresses use the ledger.

Today's date, though, is empty past noon.

I furrow my brow and try to look closer.

Not empty. There's an arrow drawn down from the name written beside the twelve o'clock time slot all the way down.

Whoever that is has booked the Underground for the rest of the day.

I guess it should be my name except, if my theory is correct, Sonia can't be so unhinged as to think I would be able to make use of the Underground for an entire half of a day.

I bite my lower lip and look up to the door to backstage. Someone could walk out at any moment, and they'll accuse me of thumbing through private information. But I can't read upside down, especially not when the name is written in cursive.

As quick and as careful as possible, I take the cover of the ledger and spin it toward me until it's at an angle I can read the name.

My heart drops.

It's not my name.

It's Seth's.

No mistaking the swooping curve of the 'S' or the loop of the lowercase 'L' in his last name.

"You made it."

Seth's voice sends my blood coursing through my body.

I am terrified to turn around and face him. "Seth," I say, the simplest thing, the only thing I can will myself to say.

The heels of his dress shoes clack against the floor. "I wasn't sure you'd come."

"I almost didn't." I tuck my chin against my shoulder, preparing myself to face him.

Seth chuckles. "Are you afraid of me, Bridget?"

"Of course, I am," I say without thinking. I've been afraid of him for ten years. Since the moment I met him. Not because of his coldness or his control, but because there is something about him that makes me want him, want him with such a desperation I can't control myself.

Seth sighs, continues walking. "You don't need to be scared of me. That's not what I want."

Before the wedding, I would have told him he could have fooled me. Now I know he is telling the truth.

There is a clicking sound.

I turn toward it.

Seth is standing at the door to the Underground. He's just locked the door, made it impossible for anyone outside to disturb us.

Whatever this is.

Seth looks at me, blue eyes penetrating to my most secret depths. My most coveted wants.

"You brought me here," I say.

"I'm glad you've caught on."

"Why?" I have a guess, but I wouldn't want to make a fool of myself.

Seth pauses, leaves enough of a gap in the conversation for me to fall into. "Why did I bring you here?"

"Why did you trick me? That text, how did you–"

"I had Hazel send that off before dismissing her," he says. "In fact, everyone has been dismissed."

I stare at him and *lord,* he looks nice. Suit and tie, the kind of Dom that will be a perfect gentleman in the light of day and behind closed doors, tie me up and whip me into submission.

Where did that *thought come from?*

I've had thoughts like that before, but they've all been paired with mental apologies. This thought drove a stake into my middle, pinning me to my want, making sure I don't back away.

And hell, I'm not backing away.

Not now.

Maybe not ever again.

"We're alone, Bridget."

"Yes, I realize that…" I tighten the bag of fabric to my shoulder.

Seth's brow tenses for a moment.

"Why do you want me alone, Seth?" I'll make him spell it out. I want to know what happened in the library wasn't a fluke of love drunkenness or real drunkenness.

His Adam's apple bobs, the strong defined lump creeping up and back down.

"I'll be brief." Seth walks toward me. "I can't stop thinking about you. Not just since the wedding. I've *never* been able to stop thinking about you. Since the moment we met."

The gears in my brain gridlock.

What did he just say?

Seth stares at me. "Say something, Bridget."

This can't be real. I've either stepped into an alternate universe or Seth is screwing with me.

I don't mean to laugh, but I do. A weak one. A defense mechanism. "You're playing a joke on me."

His dark brows scrape down his forehead and his gaze intensifies. "Do I look like I'm joking?"

My muscles all want to turn to jelly but I remain resolute.

I spin around, trying to spy hidden cameras or anyone watching from the sidelines holding in laughter. "This...if you're trying to make a fool of me–" My eyes well with tears. "This will be the worst thing you've ever done to me. This will–"

Seth stops a foot away from me. That foot is a dangerous space for us. It is far enough to maintain a distance and close enough to destroy it. "What happened the other day, that wasn't a mistake."

He doesn't ask. He states it as a fact.

I open my mouth to rebut, a squeak coming out of the back of my throat. But no words. None.

Because...he's right. It *is* a fact. And I don't regret it.

I've been replaying it in my head over and over, refining the moment to use for the next time I touch myself.

Am I so easy to see through?

"You want me too."

That's a fact too, one I don't have the wherewithal to attempt to argue.

My cheeks burn with shame that it's been so obvious. "Seth–"

"And now that I know that, I'm not going to be able to survive until I have you as my sub, Bridget."

My body is made of one thousand matches, and Seth has just set me alight.

What does a person say to a request like that? A *demand* like that?

"How did you..." I trail off.

Seriously, Bridget? Can't manage anything but questions

about the hows and the whys when the man you've wanted to be your Dom all this time has decided he wants you?

"I pulled some strings with Nate."

My eyes widen. "He–"

"*Doesn't* know why," Seth finishes, reading my mind. Of course, he can. He's a Dom. Wants to be *my* Dom. He should know what's best for me.

It hasn't been even a full minute of Seth asking me to be his sub, and I've already given into the role. Into the dynamic.

However, that's not shocking. I've been waiting for this. Craving this.

For ten years. Since I was sixteen, when a relationship between us would have been even more perverse than it is now.

"We have the Underground to ourselves until midnight."

"Then my carriage will turn into a pumpkin, I guess," I mutter to myself.

Seth smirks.

And though that was a stupid thing to say, a childish thing to say, I don't feel childish in his eyes. Not anymore.

"You don't want me," I say in a small voice.

"You don't think I know what I want?" he asks, not with unkindness, but a firmness that reminds me his want should always go unquestioned if I am going to be a good sub for him.

"I just mean..." I dip my head down, avoiding eye contact. I know from the reading I've done and the scenes I've watched that I must be invited to do something like that. "You have experience. And I don't. You will grow tired of me."

Seth's hand envelops my chin. His fingers are softer

than I've ever noticed. He tilts my head upward, so our eyes meet. His are glowing. "On the contrary, I would love to have the honor of training you, Bridget."

I am not sure I exist anymore. I have floated out of my own body. This must be a dream.

"I've watched you go through life trying to be brave," he says. "Trying to match yourself with the person you know you are, always falling short. And I know why."

My lips part.

"You need direction. You need someone who can protect you. Who can control you."

"I need a Dom."

Shit, I should never speak without prompting.

The scene hasn't begun, yet. We haven't set a contract in place, limits, anything of what I heard happens between subs and Doms. But I wanted to be his perfect sub from the start.

I don't want to give Seth any reason to change his mind.

Seth chuckles, a dark and luscious roll in his mouth. "Yes, Bridget. You need a Dom. And I want it to be me."

God. Letting the thought that I might get a Dom, and he might be the one, wash over me releases tensions I didn't know existed in my body.

I have been holding, bracing, trying to be a good girl and a professional young woman, attempting to navigate life.

I have been forced to live in a world where I need to be assertive, decisive, confident. In control.

I'm not in control. Ever. I hate it.

And to know I might not have had to for so many years if Seth had only said something.

But maybe I was not good enough before. Maybe I'm not now. But I will try my best to show him what a good girl I am.

"Will you accept my offer?" he asks. "If only for the night?"

The last thing I want is for him to mistake my eagerness for immaturity. But to be his. To submit to him *every* night. This is a need. Not a want.

"I will. I mean, yes, I'll be your sub."

A smile spreads across his face, a bold one. A proud one. I've given him what he's wanted.

And to know that I have pleased him pleases me. Pleases me so much I already feel blood rushing to my core and swelling my lower lips. I know once I take a step, I'll notice how wet he's made me.

I don't know if I'll be able to handle how good it will feel to submit to Seth.

"Good." He drops his hand from my chin. "Follow me."

Seth strides toward the open chamber at the other side of the hall.

I watch as he goes, his tight ass in black slacks looking so fucking good. And with no one around, I don't have to worry about being caught looking.

I drop my bags and rush after him.

10
———

SETH

Bridget enters the chamber like a child entering her classroom on the first day of school. It isn't too far off, anyway. I will be training her tonight.

I was at a loss for words when she told me she had no experience.

The hours I spent agonizing over her with other Doms.

And now, I get to show her what a real Dom is. How she deserves to be worshipped.

Me! As it should be.

"Let me take your coat." I come up behind her.

Bridget undoes the belt and allows me to remove the long, cream-colored coat from her arms. Just because I will be dominating her soon does not exempt me from being a gentleman. Besides, we haven't begun. Not yet. Not for a little while yet. There are details to be discussed first.

She says nothing.

I think she is trying to mimic what she's seen which is both a blessing and a curse in the eyes of an experienced Dom. On one hand, it shows me she is as eager for this as I am. On the other, she now has misconceptions and maybe even a few behaviors that need to be corrected, I'm sure. She needs to learn how things work in real life and how different they are from reading them in a book or watching others participate in a scene.

Being inside of a dynamic like ours will become is a different beast.

"We aren't in scene yet, Bridget. You may talk to me."

"Thank you...Seth." She hesitates when she says my name. I know her mind is going to the same place as mine. Her calling me Sir at the wedding. I've been dreaming about it ever since.

"Take a seat, Bridget." I gesture toward the luxurious chaise in the middle of the room.

The Underground chambers are all a little bit different, but this one is my favorite. It is the most like a home with the Persian rugs, the chaise, the coffee table, a four-poster bed against the hall and decadent mirrors hanging in various places for watching. Even the toys are out of sight, stowed in a wardrobe.

She follows my direction with ease, sinking down onto the settee and smoothing out her skirt as she does so.

Didn't even know today would be the day that changes everything, and yet she's wearing an absolutely life-altering outfit. Of course, everything she wears is, in my eyes, stunning. But today, it's like she felt what was about to happen to her.

Skin-tight, navy dress stopping mid-calf. Buttons all down the front. Heaven for a Dom who likes to unwrap his reward. To watch each inch unveil.

And oh, how I want to watch Bridget.

"Do you know what this is?" I step toward the table before the chaise and point at the papers on top of it.

Bridget nods. "It's a contract."

"Good." I hold back on the 'girl.' Just barely. Because that's going to push us both over the edge. "This is a standard contract for tonight only. If we decide we want to continue after that, we will go over everything, and you will need to catalog all your hard and soft limits and we will talk about each of them at length. Since we won't go too deep tonight, I stated my limits in the contract as well as a few I think you will agree with."

I push the contract toward her. "Take a look and see if there's anything you would like to add or remove."

This contract is standard here in the club for new subs and new Doms that just want to scene for the night before really committing to the Underground side of the club.

The last thing I want to do is cross any of Bridget's limits tonight. Especially since I'm not even sure she knows her true limits yet.

After the well of silence, Bridget takes the pen from beside the paper to sign.

I hold up my hand. "Read it again."

She nods, places the pen back down, and does as I ask. It sends a shockwave of delight into my groin. That wasn't meant to be a test, but she's already so good at obeying directions.

I just...need this to go right. I need it to be perfect.

Because while we've agreed to the night, I know I'm not going to be satiated unless I have her much longer than that.

Probably forever.

I pack that thought away. No use thinking about forever when we haven't even started.

Bridget clears her throat. "I've read it again. May I sign?"

I withhold a smile.

She's so dear, trying to be all good and proper. How could that not make me smile? "You may."

She picks up the pen, signs, and places it back down with utmost care.

"Good."

The corners of her lips tick up.

"If at any point you find yourself feeling unsafe, you will tell me with a safe word. Going forward, if that is what we decide to do, you may choose one. For tonight, let's keep it simple and use the colors of a traffic light. Green means you are enjoying what I'm doing, and we can keep going, red stops everything and the scene is over. We will talk about why and what happened, but we are done scening for tonight. Yellow is almost like a pause button. The scene doesn't stop, but is put on hold, and we talk about what you are unsure of or what's making you uncomfortable. Does that make sense?"

Bridget nods. "Yes."

"The first thing you need to learn, Bridget, is that communication is the most important thing between a Dom and a sub. And in this dynamic, though it might not look like it, you have all the power."

"Wh-what do you mean? I thought you were in control."

I smile. "Oh, I am. Always."

Her flushing face has me fighting against myself with the need to touch her, to caress her soft skin, to feel her heat.

"But a word from you has the power to stop everything. That is why I said you have the *power*. And that is why we use safe words. Your consent is key here."

"So is yours." As her mouth gapes for a second before she bites her bottom lip, her eyes widen, and she lowers them to the table, almost as if she is afraid she just did something wrong.

But I am taken aback.

Because with her words, I am reminded of what we are risking by being here together. The reason I rented out the entirety of the Underground, have worked to keep it a complete secret, including ensuring Hazel's confidentiality with an extra tip.

We aren't just consenting to the dynamics between a Dom and a sub.

We are consenting to never being able to go back to what we were.

"I'm sorry," Bridget says in a soft tone. "I shouldn't have–"

I clear my throat to cut her off.

She's done nothing wrong.

"Let's begin, shall we?"

She nods and keeps silent.

I stand before her with my hands behind her back. "First, I'd like you to put your hair up in a ponytail."

"I...don't have–"

I pull a scrunchie out of my pocket and hold it out to her. "You should never question that I'm prepared, Bridget."

She nods before taking it from me, a cautious raise of her green eyes to meet mine. "Thank you."

"Look at me while you do it. In the eyes."

Bridget sits up straighter and collects the dark tresses of her hair into a ponytail. Eyes not leaving mine.

My heartbeat quickens.

I knew she'd be a good girl. But for me? Is it possible?

She snaps the elastic into place, the ponytail waterfalling from the back of her head.

"A ponytail..." I circle to the back of the chaise. "Is a tool of your own making that I can use." I run my hand through her hair, rolling it around my fist until I have a firm grasp on it. "You understand?"

"Yes, I understand"

I release the ponytail, though my instinct is to yank her head back and kiss her on the lips. "Good."

Looking at her bare neck, I can't wait to see my collar there, branding her as mine for all to see. I've never trained a sub, never had the opportunity to bestow a collar. It all hinges on tonight.

Regardless of what happens, though, I still want the full fantasy. I want to know what she will look like with my collar on. So, I remove a thin, blue ribbon from my pocket, a chocker that clasps at the back. It is simple and it is fragile. Like tonight. Like our budding sub and Dom dynamic.

However, I intend for this night to be a courtship like no other.

I raise the choker between my fingers. "Will you wear this for me, Bridget? We'll call it a consideration collar of sorts. Just for tonight. If you accept."

She smiles, this time with teeth. Her cheeks glow. "Yes, I accept."

Relief floods through me.

"Let me put it on you..." I try to keep myself steady. "That way we can practice the ritual to the fullest extent."

Hopefully one day, I'll get to do this for real. A real collar. My collar. And Bridget...

She'll be *mine.*

I take ribbon in both of my hands. Feels as light as a feather, something that might blow away in the wind.

"Stand," I command her.

She does so. I guide her out from behind the table to stand with her back to me.

I loop the small band around her neck.

Bridget's skin breaks out in goosebumps.

I clip the choker closed, then turn her back around to observe how it looks against her skin. Pale white and deep blue.

How I want to add red to the mix by marking her skin with my teeth.

In due time...

"There. Beautiful." I drop my hands to my sides. "During your training, you will address me as Sir. Is that clear?"

"Yes, Sir."

I inhale as deep as I can to keep from coming straight away. I haven't waited all these years only to waste the night. "You will keep your eyes down unless I say otherwise. Is that clear?"

A smile appears on her lips, her eyes veiled by her long ink lashes. "Yes, Sir."

I run my teeth over my lower lip. "Good girl."

Though she can't speak, the minute movement of her lips tells me how good that felt.

I cross to the armoire of toys and grab a pair of soft cuffs for her wrists, ignoring the gleaming spreader bar hanging on a hook.

The image of her splayed before me sends another shock to my pelvis.

Soon.

If I don't take it one thing at a time, I risk making a mistake. Risk ruining her trust and faith in me as a Dom. As a man.

Domination is a high wire act, a constant negotiation of exercising my authority and reading my sub. She is the center of my world while we are scening, and all I do is for her pleasure, even over my own.

"You like to be called a good girl, don't you?"

"Yes, Sir." Her eyes are on the floor.

I chuckle to myself. "Kneel, pet."

Bridget hurries to obey. So eager.

"If you like to be called good girl, you will continue to act like one. So, from this moment forward you will not speak unless I address you first."

"Yes, Sir," she says in such a simple, reflexive way, it takes her a second to realize she's spoken out of turn.

Bridget smacks her hand across her mouth and looks at me. When our eyes meet, she realizes another rule has been broken and she claps her eyes closed.

"Now, now, Bridget." I shake my head. "I know you know better than that. I guess you're just too excited for your own good."

I go over to her.

From her tense posture, I can tell she is bracing for punishment.

Running my hand through her ponytail again, I let the moment linger and tremble.

She will not know it's coming, nor does she deserve it. But this is too good an opportunity to waste.

I wind her hair around my hand and pull back.

Bridget lets out a gasp that she tries to muffle by shutting her lips.

"I told you that you couldn't speak. Not that you shouldn't make a sound," I say through clenched teeth.

Bridget breathes heavily. Cheeks flooding with color.

"Are you enjoying this?" I smile.

She nods.

"I asked you a direct question, pet. I need your words when that happens."

"Yes, Sir. I am, Sir." She keeps her eyes averted. Good girl.

But not what I need.

I pull her hair more, bending her back further. This time, she lets her sounds free, a loud cry. But it's not pain. Shock and… arousal?

"Look me in the eye and say it again."

Her green eyes blink open and meet mine.

I almost falter. Almost end the scene.

She is sixteen again, the pretty teenager who sat across from me at dinner as we met for the first time, the pretty, shy girl who couldn't look me in the eye more than a second at a time.

My pretty little sub. From the beginning.

"Yes, Sir," she says, throat straining.

I want to kiss her, want to bite her neck, want to plunge my hand into the bodice of her dress and feel her breasts. "Say you're sorry," I say, stone-faced.

"I'm sorry, Sir."

"Good." I push her back onto her feet and release her hair.

I'm having to breathe quicker to keep up with my heart rate. "A good sub should be naked."

Bridget's hand flies up to her collar.

"Everything but the collar." As soon as I say the words, I have half a mind to tell her she doesn't have to. That this is all a mistake. I know she's agreed to my demands, but I can't help but feel–

Her hand drops to the top button on her dress.

She undoes it.

I try to stay composed, but holy fuck, it's impossible.

Bridget undoes each and every button, one by one, fabric parting more and more to reveal the pale skin of her sternum, her belly, her thighs.

In one go, she lets the dress drop from her arms, leaving her in just a matching black underwear set and a pair of black pumps.

Of course she's wearing matching underwear. For one, she's Bridget. And for another, she's Bridget Vance, *lingerie* designer.

Fuck, how did anyone ever expect me to stay away with *that* job description?

Bridget goes for her bra first, not the shoes, which is a darling example of her fluster.

I've never had a sub so flustered, only experienced ones. And the ones who I've asked to act naïve no longer quite grasp the true newness of it all.

She unsnaps the bra and it slides down, exposing her breasts.

Her nipples tighten, the bud poking out.

She drops it to the side, still following instructions and not looking at me.

It's all happened so fast, I'm not sure how to process it.

Her nearly naked pale form is exquisite. The bones of her hips protruding against her underwear, a tiny softness at her middle, breasts fuller than they look when they're trapped in her clothes.

I want to kiss every inch, want to worship every piece, want to claim her. A collar won't be enough, nothing ever will.

"You're fucking gorgeous," I say in a voice lighter than I anticipate. I'm marveling and I can't be stopped. "Like a sculpture."

Bridget twitches and looks away, but with her hair in a ponytail, she can't veil herself away from me.

Her hands ball up at her sides. She doesn't know what to do with herself.

How long has it been since someone has seen her like this? Could I be the first?

Bridget hooks her thumbs into her underwear, but I step forward and grab one of her wrists to stop her. "No. That's mine. Is that clear?"

"Yes, Sir."

I want to be the one to slide her panties off. Like a present that I can't wait to unwrap.

I am so close. For a kiss. One kiss.

What kind of Dom am I to melt at the thought of one kiss?

But her glossy cherry lips look like they'd be sweet, and her pink tongue would feel perfect rolling against mine.

Not yet.

"On the bed. Now."

I release her, and she is quick in her high heels, close to tripping up the two stairs to the platform the bed sits on.

She crawls onto the bed, her ass in the air, and then lays in the center of it.

Unlike her hurriedness, I take my time striding over, twirling the cuffs in my hands. "Restraint is a form of control. Not everyone likes it. Not everyone can handle it." I approach the side of the bed. "I'd like to try these on you. I'm only asking this time, because you didn't set it as a limit, but I want to make sure just the same."

Bridget looks even better lying down. Christ almighty.

"So, pet, if you agree, arms up."

She rests her arms over her head on the bed.

"Good girl," I coo.

Bridget bites her lip. I wonder if it is to keep from moaning or smiling.

"You don't have to hold back." I sit at the edge of the bed. "Unless you're being a brat. Then I'll punish you for that. Clear?"

"Clear, Sir," she says.

I run a hand up the length of her arm, then wrap a cuff around her wrist, connecting it to the bed frame that has been crafted for the exact purposes of BDSM.

There are hooks and loops for whatever one might need for restraining, swinging, straddling. The list goes on.

"Comfortable?" I test how tight they are by fitting my pinky finger between the cuff and her wrist. I want her restrained, not hurt.

Bridget rolls her wrist around. "Yes, Sir."

I nod and move to the other side of the bed and cuff her other wrist, repeating the process.

"Color, pet?"

"Green, Sir."

With both her arms over her head, her body is stretched and long, a masterpiece waiting to be birthed. A canvas to paint as I please. Clay to mold to my will.

However, this scene is not about me. It's about her.

"I realize you might have expectations about what should be happening or what should have happened by now, especially since you've watched so many scenes, but think of it like I'm taking your temperature," I say. "I want to know where your strengths and weaknesses are so we can both enjoy as much as possible. We have all the time in the world, so I want to take my time and make this right."

Bridget's chest rises and falls, her breasts begging to be touched.

"Does that make sense, pet?"

"Yes, Sir."

I climb onto the bed and straddle her, then press my palms into the mattress by her head. "So, before we really begin, we have two punishable offenses to deal with... if I remember correctly."

Bridget seals her lips together, eyes wide. Pupils dilated. Body open.

She is enjoying this.

What I would like to do is kiss her senseless. However, punishments must be doled out.

I dismount her. "Roll your legs to the side, sub."

Bridget follows directions, exposing her barely clothed rear.

That fucking ass is swallowing her thong completely.

I slide my hand across her bare ass cheek for a few seconds. Caressing and enjoying the feel of her on my skin. How long have I craved this?

Ten years.

Now I'm finally able to live my fantasies.

"This is for speaking out of turn." I draw my hand back and smack her. With less than half the power I know I have. Way less than she should be able to take.

Bridget lets out a quick, "Hm!"

I'm preparing her as well as myself as the light tingle dissipates through my hand.

I twist her legs back so she's flat on the bed. "This–" I mount her again, eyeing her breast. "Is for not calling me 'Sir'."

I descend upon the swell of her breast, above the nipple and bite down. Enough to mark. Enough for her to feel it. Not enough to break the skin.

I want her to hurt, but I also want her to enjoy it, even if this is supposed to be a punishment.

Bridget yelps and squirms under me. The links on her cuffs rattle. Her pelvis rises to meet mine, causing me to buck.

Fuck.

I bite harder.

She moans but settles down.

When I'm happy, I pull away, favoring the slick image of my teeth marks on the skin of her breast.

That will leave a mark tomorrow. So she can remember.

"Look me in the eye," I growl.

When our eyes meet, my strength eludes me. Because her eyes are begging. For release. For more.

Now. I have to do it now.

Each of her breaths creates gravity, pulling me closer and closer, inch by inch until we are centimeters away.

"I need to do this," I say.

Though it breaks protocol, I don't care when Bridget responds with a desperate and whimpering, "Please."

I need this just as badly as she does.

Our lips collide with a harsh neediness, starting at a level ten of passion. Lips pressing, tongues winding.

I am a lost cause for Bridget. For her mouth. For her touch.

I don't know if I can do this.

I break the kiss, pulling away, though Bridget's mouth hungers for more. "Stop," I say, a mere croak.

"I'm sorry, Sir. Did I hurt you?" Her eyebrows raise with concern.

"No, no, I just..." I run my hand down over my mouth. "I'm afraid I might lose myself. Because I...want you *so* bad."

Bridget is quiet for a moment. She's about to tell me to release her from her restraints and disappear from the

Underground never to be seen again until the inevitable family dinner we have to sit across from each other and pretend like we were never here.

I brace myself. This is it. I screwed up everything.

Instead, she smiles. "So, lose yourself. Sir."

I want to. So bad. "I can't."

"Seth."

My name is a shock to my system. As much as I love hearing her call me "Sir," the sound of my name brings me back to myself.

"I want you, too," she says. "Please. I'm begging."

I screw my eyes shut. "Fuck, Bridget."

"What, what's wrong?"

Through my haze of arousal, I take her in.

Hair splayed on the pillow, breasts aching to be touched, her beautiful, wanting expression.

I swallow, a lump of desire dropping into my belly. "I can't resist begging."

11

BRIDGET

THIS IS HAPPENING.

I'm tossing out my v-card tonight.

Seth sits back on his knees, the heat between his legs pressed to the heat between mine. His coiffed hair is now a bit off-kilter and, once I get my hands on it, will be a complete mess.

If I can get my hands on it.

I never thought it would be him, as much as I wanted it to be. As much as I've desired him over all these years, I never thought that he would be the Dom I would trust enough to take me there.

Now, with my hands cuffed to the headboard and my body nearly naked before him, I am about to give him the one thing I've kept a secret.

As long as Seth doesn't change his mind.

He knew it would lead here, didn't he? Maybe not so soon?

"You want me to beg?" I ask.

He shakes his head once. "I didn't say that."

"I'll beg for you," I say. "Fuck, I let you bite me, begging is the least I can do."

His eyes flick up to the mark now forming on my breast.

"I like it," I say. "I promise, I liked it. But I want–" I grind myself against him, feeling a rolling wave of pleasure of my body.

My clit is perked, and my insides are dying for more.

"*Bridget*." Seth lunges forward and presses his hands to my shoulders, sealing me to the mattress.

I gasp as he hovers over me, rendered silent by the intensity of his gaze.

Seth scans my face.

I can feel the way his eyes travel over my skin. Creeping over me and sizing me up.

"You're a virgin," he says.

I open my mouth to respond but say nothing.

"If you want to go there, we can, but you can't get that back after it's gone."

"How did you know that?" I whisper.

Seth hesitates. "I just...had a feeling."

"How did you *know*?"

"I know everything I can about you. You haven't had a boyfriend since college, and I know he didn't touch you like that."

I screw my face together. "How could you possibly know that?"

"I don't *know*. Not in the factual sense but in the feeling sense. This is all this is, Bridget. I can feel that you're–"

"Fuck you," I say. "You can't know anything by feeling it. And now you've just made me tell you that I'm–that–" I pull at my restraints. "Let me go. Red. *Red*."

Seth puts a hand against my sternum. "Easy. Take it easy."

My pulse skyrockets. A claustrophobia I've never known is taking over. "I want to get out, I want–"

Seth rubs my bare breastbone with one hand while trying to reach the key with the other. "Shhh...I'll let you out, but you have to calm down. Breathe, honey."

His touch is warm and comforting. I follow his instruction without thinking.

He releases one wrist from its binding. "I didn't mean to trick you. I'm sorry."

I roll my free wrist, then watch as he undoes the other. But he keeps my hand in his, cupping it like a wounded bird.

"I wish I could make you understand how much I've thought about you since the moment I met you. Not only have I wanted you like this..." Seth rakes his blue eyes across my body. "But protecting you, keeping you safe. It's a compulsion I can't quit."

I don't say anything. Because it all makes sense. All the texts and phone calls. The insistence at having my location at all times while I was away at college. Warding other men off. "Why didn't you just say something?"

"How could I? When we're..." He closes his eyes and shakes his head.

Silence falls between us. Seth pulls the inside of my wrist to his mouth, kissing it softly, then presses it to his forehead. He releases a deep sigh, the weight of the past decade melting out of him.

I open my palm, letting my fingers tickle through his hair.

"If you want this, you have to tell me in no uncertain terms, Bridget," Seth says. "I do not take the job lightly to be your first."

I can't help smiling, though his expression is distraught. "Seth, I have been saving myself for my Dom."

His brow is pinched at the middle.

"And if you'll continue to have me after today, that's you."

His jaw steels. The way the persona fits him is as visible as a superhero putting on their cape. A total transformation.

It's so fucking sexy.

"So, yes, I want you to be my first," I say. "Under one condition."

"You have a contract?" he asks with a half-smile that is at the same time smug and tentative.

I shake my head. "You'll just have to be a man of your word."

Seth nods. "Always."

One shaky inhale.

Say it.

A steadier deep breathe. "I don't want you to be gentle with me."

Seth's breathing stills.

"I want you to fuck me like I'm your sub. Because I am," I say. "Aren't I?"

"Damn right you are." Seth nods before rolling off me and getting to his feet. Our eyes lock. "Are you ready to begin again?"

I divert my eyes from his. "Yes, Sir."

"Fuck, I love it when you call me that."

Seth grabs my ankle and yanks me across the bed.

I yelp as he positions me across the bed, then flips me onto my belly.

He grabs my ponytail and presses my face into the mattress. "Face down." Then, his hands slide into the pockets of my hips, and he yanks them back. "Ass up. Got it?"

"Yes, Sir," I pant into the mattress.

"Repeat it."

My chest warms at that. "Face down, ass up, Sir."

"Good girl."

With my face down, I do not have a view of what Seth is doing, which means *feeling* him is everything I have.

Seth presses his clothed erection into my backside and hums. "Goddamn it..."

Same.

He drapes himself over me and begins to press kisses down my spine.

I melt further into the bed with each touch of his lips.

It is such a small and gentle gesture, yet knowing he has complete control of the situation sends my head spinning.

Then, his fingers tuck into the band of my underwear.

He begins to work them down, a sharp inhale when they're halfway down my thighs. "Christ, you're *glistening*."

For you.

"Straighten your legs for me, pet."

Oh, I love when he calls me that.

With my legs straightened, Seth guides the panties all the way off, then taps my heels off the backs of my feet so they fall to the ground.

Now, I'm naked in front of the man who is going to take my virginity. The man I've tried to stay away from for so fucking long it's caused physical ache in the pit of my belly and the apex of my thighs. The man I've touched myself thinking about. The man who has owned every single one of my climaxes because I want him that fucking badly.

Seth pushes my knees back into position. Face down, ass up.

"I'm going to taste you. Get you ready for my cock."

I turn my face to the side, eyes shooting open. I've never had that done to me either.

"Be a good girl for me and let it all out," Seth says in a ragged voice before pressing his face into my groin and enveloping my clit with his lips.

I cry out.

My clit perks with a sensation of pain that is quick to turn into pleasure.

My moans can't be contained as Seth works my pussy with his mouth. Tongue flicking, mouth humming.

I garble all my words with groans and sighs, masking "oh gods" and "fucks" left and right to avoid breaking his rules.

I am still a beginner after all and want to be the goodest girl I can be for him. My Dom.

I squeal inside each time I remember.

And while pleasure builds between my legs, Seth's grip on my thighs reminds me of the thin line between pleasure and pain.

His fingers dig into my skin, pinching with abandon.

I don't mind, though. Not only because I relish the pain, but because it reminds me of how bad he wants me. Of that erection he was sporting, harder than I thought was possible.

The pleasure zips through me like crests of building waves.

I shift forward and back on his face, Seth's grip never faltering.

"Oh, oh, oh–" I offer because I can't tell him I'm so close he might push me right over the edge.

However, Seth is well practiced and pulls away right at that moment, accompanied by a staggering growl. "You want to come?"

"Yes, Sir. No, Sir. I... I don't know."

He laughs. Big and vibrant, filling the room and shaking the walls. "Shall I edge you?"

That sounds like a delicious torture. "Yes, Sir."

"Hmmm." Seths hand forces it's way between my legs, two fingers pinching my clit. "Next time. Now be a good girl and give me what I want."

With one twist of the bundle of nerves, he sends a powerful and sharp orgasm through me. The noise that comes out of me is one of jerking surprise and tremendous pleasure.

"If you think I'm ever going to resist the urge to give you an orgasm, think again," Seth says.

I expect him to remove his hand from between my legs, but he doesn't. Instead, he circles my clit and then prods it again.

A painful shock cracks my body, and I shoot forward, trying to get away from his fingers.

Seth grabs ahold of my ponytail and pulls it back. "*Stay still.*"

To further emphasize his point, he smacks my ass a little harder than he did earlier.

That's something I want more of.

Two fingers work my clit again, sending pangs of euphoria-edged pain through my body, while two more of his fingers plunge into my pussy, working me from the inside.

Soon enough, my clit is no longer screaming for a break but begging for release.

I push my hips back on his hand until the tremendous release mounts into a somehow even stronger orgasm.

Again, I scream out, slicking his fingers with more of my essence.

"Holy shit, your sounds," he says through a disbelieving

laugh. "I always knew you'd be perfect for me, but your sounds are better than I could've imagined."

Seth releases my ponytail, and I drop back into position.

"I can't wait any longer."

Me either.

Seth grunts as he steps away. The clinking of his belt sliding off and hitting the ground with a clank, then the zipper of his pants running let me know what is coming. And god, I'm so ready!

"I need to be inside you."

I moan.

"Use your words, pet."

"I want you, Sir." The words come out of me like a song that needs to be sung. I can't keep them in. "I need you inside me so bad."

We didn't discuss contraception, but if Seth knows everything about me, he knows that I've been on birth control since I was eighteen because his mother went with me to my first gyno appointment and thought it would be best. It's only come in handy for less painful periods.

Until now.

"I'm big, Bridget."

"I know, Sir."

Seth grabs my hips and pulls them back until I bump into his bare cock. Hot, hard, and huge. He drags himself across the seam of my pussy and my backside, coating himself in my juices. "Tell me how much you want me."

"I want you so bad, Sir," I whine. "I've wanted you for years."

"Fuck yes, you have."

"I have been a good girl for years so that one day you would finally fuck me, Sir."

As soon as I say the words out loud, I know I mean them

with all my heart. And though it was never a conscious thought of mine, the truth is I have been craving this attention from him for years.

He laughs low. "You've been a good girl for me?"

"Yes, Sir."

"Well, good girls deserve rewards."

It is painful at first, the way he sticks his cock inside me. My whole body bracing. I fist the sheets, hoping that will help.

"Tensing won't make it feel better," Seth says in a soft manner.

Still my Dom, the one who knows everything I don't. But not set on inflicting pain.

Further proof it was right to wait for him.

"Relax around me, pet."

I let out my held breath, let the term of endearment wash over me.

Seth is being...gentle. One of his hands slides across my backside, not prepping me for another lashing, but encouraging me to give in.

After several breaths, my muscles unfurl and it's starting to feel good. To be filled by him.

Seth inches a bit further inside me.

The stinging pain threatens to return, but I remind myself to just relax and let him take me away.

"God fucking dammit, you're tight," he says through clenched teeth.

That helps me to relax further, knowing just how good I'm making him feel.

We both need this. Have both craved it.

On one hand, that's a lot of pressure, to make it feel as good as possible. And on the other, there's so much inside we've been waiting to release.

The latter will win out.

Seth starts to move his hips forward and back with careful slowness, dragging his cock through me. He can read my body, can sense when I am ready to be pushed just a little farther. He is such a great Dom.

Such a great man.

Seth's hands move to the pockets of my hips.

He begins to use my body as leverage, pulling himself inside, pushing me away.

I lock into the rhythm too, begin to push my hips back as he thrusts inside, hips kissing.

"Tell me how you feel," he grunts, voice growing ragged.

As I stretch, I burn. Not a bad burn, not at all. It is as if *I* am the fire, the way my insides are starting to swelter and flare with pleasure.

It's different than the orgasms he gave me already. Those were hot and sharp. Immediate. This one, as it builds, threatens to be bigger, brighter, longer.

"So fucking good, Sir," I moan.

"That's not good enough."

Seth cups the base of my neck, presses me tight to the mattress and begins to thrust harder, faster.

As pleasure overwhelms me and envelops me in a beautiful cocoon, I can no longer keep up with him. I am at the mercy of his rhythm and his cock.

Each press of himself inside me elicits sounds from the back of my throat, sounds I've never heard myself make. They are unfettered and sometimes choking and ugly, but Seth matches me.

His groans and curses rip and roll out of him as if he can't hold them back.

"You like it when I fuck you?" he calls out.

How is he holding so tight to his control? I feel like I

might burst into flames or shatter into a thousand pieces any moment now.

"Yes, Sir," I squeal.

His hand attaches to my ponytail again, and he yanks on it, pulling me back so far I'm sitting on his lap with my back against his front.

I yelp, all my weight poured down onto his cock, skewered with pleasure.

Seth twists my face toward his, kisses me fiercely.

I have forgotten how wonderful his kiss is. I haven't had nearly enough of his kisses. I want more, more, more.

But one is enough to sate him. He pulls me again by my ponytail, away from his mouth.

The look in his eye is dark and primal, pupils overwhelming his irises.

His nostrils flare with heavy breaths.

"Tell me..." he says with dark softness. "Tell me how bad you want to come on my cock."

"I..." I struggle to find my voice, buried deep under heavy moans and sighs. "I want to come on your cock so badly, Sir. Please let me. Please."

Seth says nothing, mouth a thin line. He ghosts his hands down my arms, takes my wrists, and pulls them back so my arms are looped around his neck.

He tucks his chin on my shoulder and runs his fingers down the front of my body.

I watch his fingers trace the bite mark he left on me, then my pebbled nipples, all the way down my navel, and to the glistening spot where our bodies meet.

"You're perfect," he whispers.

My eyes flutter shut.

I don't think that was Seth the Dom coming through. I

think that was Seth who has watched me for the past ten years, desperate to have me when he knew he couldn't.

Tonight, I am his dream come true.

And he is mine.

When his hands reach my thighs, he grabs them tight, wrenches them back so I am straddled over his knees.

"Let me hear you," he growls.

Then, he lets me have it. Driving harder and faster up into me if that were possible.

My head drops back onto his shoulder, and I moan, scream out for him. "Sir, please, Sir…"

The pause in stoking the fire has only made it burn brighter.

I feel it climbing up my body, engulfing each one of my nerves, snaring and snapping until, until–

"You need to come," he grunts in my ear. "Don't you?"

I try to speak, but I can't get out more than, "I–I–"

"*Don't you?!*"

My voice pitches to new heights as the orgasm rattles the bars of its cage. "I need to come, Sir. Please, I need to–"

Seth's hand snakes down to the spot we meet, fingers locating the button of my clit. And just a press of his fingers shoots me into the heart of the fire.

I combust, every part of me hot and thrumming with pleasure.

My pussy contracts around him, pulses, making the space smaller, tighter for him.

Seth's arms wrap around my chest. He thrusts just a few more times before a strangled sound jabs out of him and lands against my neck.

I feel him inside as he throbs and releases, painting my insides.

I cannot ignore the feeling of accomplishment inside me.

I made him come. He wanted me so badly...

Seth's tight embrace relaxes around me. His head drops forward and he drags his lips across my shoulder, back and forth, before dropping a single kiss to my skin.

His heaving chest presses against my back.

I can feel his heart racing, racing, racing...slowing.

Seth swallows, thick and loud, and he lifts his mouth to my ear. "Are you okay?"

"Yes, Sir." That's all I can manage when my mind is still swimming with the wonderful flush of sex.

He rubs my arms up and down. "Lay down with me, Bridget."

I nod. It is heavy and unwieldy on my neck. I'm here, but I'm not. I'm out flying somewhere. Could this be the subspace I heard about?

I'm in heaven and I don't know if I should come back down to earth.

Seth takes control. He slides out of me, leaving me empty and sated, and guides me to lie on the bed. Then he rolls me onto my side to face him, covering us and holds me tight. Like he is keeping me tethered here, to him.

"I'm going to get you some water and some chocolate, okay? It will help you."

I nod.

He snugs the covers all around me, like my own little snuggle cave, before he heads to his bag.

After rummaging inside, he comes back, and helps me drink a few sips and feeds me two squares of chocolate. Lying next to me, he pulls me close, and his free hand moves to my ponytail.

With utmost care, he begins to undo it.

Slowly, I came back into my body.

Wow. I had no idea it would be like this.

When I watched scenes, the aftercare has always confused me. The switch in energy never made complete sense.

Now I get it. I understand. After all the intensity, it is necessary to slow down, remind us both who we are beyond the dynamic of sub and Dom.

We are Bridget and Seth.

There is so much baggage that comes with that, baggage I was able to push away in the throes of pleasure and self-discovery.

Baggage that now threatens to scare me away.

"Bridget, could you open your eyes, please?"

I do.

All the fear of baggage melts away when Seth's blue gaze meets mine while his lips linger on my hands.

I find myself smiling. A stupid smile, most likely.

"Here, have some more water," he says.

I realize just how parched I still am.

He wraps his hand around the back of my neck. So tender... "Tilt your head back."

"I can..." I reach for the bottle. "You don't have to."

"I want to," Seth says.

My eyes widen, but I follow his instruction, tilting my head back.

Seth brings the bottle to my lips again and tilts it so the water runs gingerly into my mouth.

A sip of water has never tasted so good.

I suckle at the bottle until it's half empty, then draw my lips away, panting.

"Had enough?"

I nod. "Yes, thank you."

"Do you need more chocolate?"

"I don't think so."

Seth watches me for a moment. His watchfulness is now so clear to me.

The way he was taking me in while we were in scene isn't that different from what he's doing now.

Except now, rather than dominating me, he's...taking care of me.

"It's important," Seth says, his voice deep and firm, "for both of us, that after a scene I take care you."

He guides his fingers across my temple, pushing some hair away from my face.

My eyes flutter shut.

God, his touch is so nice after all these years.

"So you don't go into sub drop," he says. "And we can... reconnect."

My heart swells.

In truth, Seth and I have always been connected. There have been moments of distance, frustration, annoyance, yes.

But we both admitted it. We've been dying for this.

Seth leans in, kisses my cheek. "Are you cold?"

I snuggle closer to him for his body heat. "I'm okay."

Seth chuckles. "Let me tuck you in better."

God, this is so different from the Seth I knew before. A million miles away.

I never thought I'd let myself feel this, but I need him. Need his surety. Need his control.

This can't be only tonight. It can't be.

After making sure no inch of me is uncovered, he looks into my eyes, frowning. "Better?"

I let out a long sigh. "Feels nice."

He relaxes beside me, pulls me close again so I'm nuzzled into his chest.

He clears his throat. "So...what did you think?"

"About?"

Seth hums, a warm resonance in his chest. "All that happened here, I guess."

My mind is swimming with thoughts.

There are so many ways I want to express how *much* I enjoyed it. How grateful I am. How amazing it all felt. How much I'd like to do it again.

Desperate. I'm desperate to do it again.

"It was all..." I sigh. "Better than I could have imagined."

Seth tips my head back so he can look into my eyes.

His thumb traces my lip. "Would you like to do that again some time?"

I nod, smiling. "Again and again and..."

Seth's lips tip up into a boyish smile. Rare for him. "Then tonight, Bridget, was the first night of your training."

His eyes fall to my neck and his fingers follow the thin, blue ribbon to the back of my neck, pulling at the clasp.

"Don't!" I cry out and press the ribbon to my throat.

Seth's brow furrows.

"Let me...let me leave it on. I feel safe with it. Is... is that ok?"

His brow softens, surprise shining on his face. "Are you sure? People will see."

"Yes. It doesn't have to mean anything if you don't want it to, but please. I'll wear turtlenecks or... maybe it can be a fashion statement." I lower my eyes.

Seth smiles at me like I am dear and small and worth being protected. "You have no idea how much I like that idea. How much it means to me that you want to wear my collar. Even if it is just a placeholder."

I can't restrain myself. I push myself upward and kiss

him. We are out of scene, anyway. I am in need of training. I'm still wily. Need to be taught.

But this I must do.

After I kiss him, I draw back only an inch and whisper, "Thank you."

Seth cups my cheek.

And in the place of the, "You're welcome," I expect to hear, are echoes of my own words.

"Thank *you*, Bridget."

There's no going back now.

We remain in bed together for as long as we dare. Sometimes, our mouths gravitate toward one another in soft, angelic kisses. So opposite what we just experienced together.

I am sore between my legs, otherwise I would invite him in again. They say the first time hurts, and while it did upon his initial entrance, all the pleasure made it so worth it. Still, though, I don't want to bite off more than I can chew.

Besides, it's not just sex.

It's submission too. And I still have a long way to go before I'm good enough for him.

12

———

SETH

I walk down the street, bottle of wine in my grip, a hand shoved in my coat pocket.

I have never felt so tall as I have the past week.

Since my first scene with Bridget, I have felt unstoppable.

Now, instead of haunted by thoughts of Bridget, I am invigorated by them.

I have been more productive this past week at work than I've been in the past *year,* and certainly the last couple of months, what with mounting tensions between Bridget and me.

After our first encounter, we laid in bed for a long time, discussing her training plan and what the next couple of months will look like as we try her limits and get her to a place where she feels she has reached her zone.

I want her to see me as the perfect Dom for her because she is *my* perfect sub.

And because she has agreed to be mine with such whole heart, I feel like this must be a dream.

If it is, I never want to wake up.

Since then, though, there's been no contact, other than a few run ins and the club. I told her that my schedule might be uncomfortable at first. I also laid a few ground rules because that's my role as her Dom.

She agreed to it all. Said she trusts me.

My chest puffs with the reminder.

I reach the family townhouse and take it in.

First family dinner since everything has changed.

I shake myself off and sigh.

It's going to be interesting, to say the least. Could be a make or break it moment.

The danger in putting distance between myself and Bridget so early on her training is the possibility she changes her mind. Of course, she can change her mind whenever, but this period is the most fragile. Early enough that the investment is low. Early enough to get cold feet.

If Bridget got cold feet and backed out of our arrangement now, it might kill me. But I'm not going to think about that right now.

Besides, I'm the man who took her virginity. The one she was *waiting* for. Surely, she wouldn't change her mind now, right?

I take a deep breath, straighten out my coat, and head inside.

The townhouse is old-fashioned compared to my penthouse in Manhattan. Been in the Vance family for generations, apparently, and it looks it. But it's quaint and charming and worth way more than you'd think despite the narrow hallways and low ceilings. Not to mention the grandma-style furniture.

Mom's Siamese cat, Darla, slinks in from the sunroom to get a look at me.

"Hey, Darla."

She winds through my feet but eludes my attempt at petting her. Typical.

"Seth? Is that you?" Mom calls out from the sunroom.

I poke my head in.

Mom and Solomon are sitting across from one another on the floor, working on a puzzle with too many pieces splayed out on the coffee table.

"Wild Friday night, huh?" I smirk.

Solomon lifts his head and beams at me. "You know it!"

I get a pit in my stomach, unable to think any thought but, "I fucked your daughter," over and over again.

"I was going to make chicken piccata." Mom pushes herself up to standing and waltzing over to me. "But we got caught up in the puzzle and we ordered Chinese instead. Is that all right with you?"

I shrug. "Don't know if chianti goes as well with orange chicken, but–"

"Goes best with liver and fava beans, actually," Solomon says.

Mom rolls her eyes. "Ugh, enough with *The Silence of the Lambs*," she says, then wiggles under my arm and gives me a fond hug.

"*Enough?* Has there been more than one Hannibal Lecter joke today?" I ask.

"I don't want to talk about it."

Solomon gets a shit-eating grin, then gets up too, groaning with a hand on his back. "I can't sit on the floor like that anymore, Mimi."

I gnaw on my lower lip and look around the room one more time as if Bridget will somehow appear out of nowhere. I don't want to ask where she is for fear of rousing suspicion.

The doorbell rings, and Mom jumps. "Oh, that must be

the food!"

"I got it." I disentangle myself from my mom's embrace and turn back into the hallway.

I run right into Bridget, my chest colliding with her shoulder, throwing both of us off balance.

Bridget screeches, grabs onto me, dragging us both down.

Darla hisses and scrambles out of the way before the two of us fall right up against the wall of the thin hallway.

Effectively, I have Bridget pinned up against the wall, my body pressed to hers.

My *entire* body.

Her chest heaves against mine, her green eyes wide.

One of her hands clings to my bicep, tight and needy.

She's clearly put on makeup, her lips slick and glossy, lashes long and fluttery. And her long, dark hair waves down her shoulders.

I've missed having her face so close.

And the blue ribbon around her neck...

Fuck, I'm getting hard.

"Hi, Seth," she squeaks.

"H-hi."

"You two okay?" Solomon asks from over my shoulder.

I straighten up as quick as I can.

We lingered way too long in a precarious position.

"Great, I just pressed this," I say in a dry voice to add a tinge of realism to the interaction. After all, the way my mom and Solomon know us is tension-filled and constantly bickering.

"Sorry about that," Bridget says, avoiding my eyes.

I have to bite back a smile.

That's the way a docile sub should be. And from what I gather, Bridget wants the *full* experience. Which means she will always be at the mercy of my domination, even when we're around others.

"Bridget, you don't have to apologize for something like that, my goodness," my mom huffs, patting Bridget on the shoulder. "He's just a grump. I don't know where he gets it from."

Neither my mom nor my dad were the prickly type. I guess Mom should take it up with my trauma.

The doorbell rings again, and it's Solomon who goes to the door to collect the Chinese food from the hapless delivery person who has been waiting for the Vance-Carlton family to get their shit together and come to the door already.

"Sorry about the wait," my mom says, shuffling up to join Solomon in the doorway. "Tip him really well, Sol."

With their backs turn, Bridget and I have a moment to ourselves.

My mouth feels hot and my hands itchy. I want to grab her and pull her into my arms, kiss her with all my might. However, this is a moment where restraint is a must, especially since I'm supposed to be in control. Not to mention the whole parent and stepparent thing right in front of us.

I settle for a subtle glance at the collar of her shirt which dips down just enough to give a peek at the swells of her breasts. I lick my lower lip.

"Can I take this and open it for you?" Bridget gestures toward the bottle of wine in my hand.

She's so *eager* to please. To serve. "Sure. Pour yourself a glass too."

It is hard to explain, but Bridget's body exudes submission as she takes the bottle from me, clutches it to her chest, and almost bows her head before rushing off.

She has been waiting for me to return to her. I can tell

now I've been away too long. She needs my affection, my attention. She wants to do a good job, of course, but everything she knows other than what I taught her a week ago is guesswork.

I grin. Training her is going to be so fun.

Bridget disappears into the kitchen in the back, and we all follow shortly after, bags of Chinese in tow.

Dinner is enjoyable for once. Outward tensions are low, but inside they are set to snap.

Bridget avoids eye contact with me unless I call her attention toward me. Her jerking look reminds me of how things used to be. How scared she used to be of me.

I'm worried she's still scared, but only for a moment. Because when she rises to take her plate to the sink, she comes around and takes all the dirty dishes, including mine.

She hesitates before grabbing it. "Are you done, Seth? Or would you like more?"

"I'm done. Thank you, Bridget."

I swear her cheeks flush at that.

Such a good fucking sub.

Once dinner is cleared, Solomon claps. "Okay. Puzzle time!"

"You are *not* going to work on that puzzle before dinner is cleaned up," Mom snaps in a playful tone.

"I'll clean up," Bridget says, retrieving the last of the dishes. "You go enjoy."

I stare at her for a moment as she places the dishes in a stack at the side of the sink, then turns on the hot water and squirts some soap into the basin.

"Bridget, no, we'll help," Mom says and starts to get up to join Bridget at the sink.

I seize my moment. "I'll help."

My mom looks at me like I'm mad. "*You'll* help?"

"Yeah, is that so shocking?"

"Well, I just–" Mom cuts herself off with a nervous laugh, then glances at Solomon. "Leaving you two alone makes me worry only one will come out alive."

Solomon scoffs. "They're adults, Mimi."

"I know, but they fight like cats and dogs," she says under her breath, but not at all quiet enough for Bridget and me not to hear.

I touch my mom's shoulder. "We'll be good."

Bridget's shoulder tense. So microscopic of a movement only I would notice. Because my body, even after one night, is attuned to her like instruments in the same orchestra.

"Promise," I add with a smile.

"See, he promises." Solomon gets out of his chair and flocking to my mom's side. "And if I know one thing, Seth would never break a promise to you, my love."

He's right. My mom and I have been through too much for me to fuck with her. And she knows it by now. After my father died, we only had each other. I would never do anything to cross my mother.

Except maybe...with Bridget...

I cast the thought out of my mind and usher my mom and stepfather out of the room. "Now, go on. Puzzle isn't going to solve itself."

"You heard the boy! Puzzle time!" Solomon calls out.

Mom can't resist a laugh at that. She smiles over her shoulder at me as she goes as if to say, "Be good."

Well, I'll be good in the way she wants me to be good. My mom doesn't even know what kind of behavior she needs to anticipate now. Nor will she.

Not if I can help it.

Bridget has already started scrubbing the dishes, the sink full to the brim with suds and water.

I wait a moment to see if she'll look back at me. She doesn't.

So, I sneak in beside her. "I'll dry." I take a dish rag off the counter.

"You don't have to do that." She finishes scrubbing the most recent dish.

I swoop in and grab the plate before she can keep me from helping, then run the rag around the dish until it is warm and dry to the touch.

We go through the process of washing and drying. Over and over. Neither of us speaking.

Each moment that passes, I grow harder. Watching her pale hands growing red with the heat of the water, eyeing her neck covered by her dark hair where I want to lay a thousand marks with my teeth, wishing I could kiss her plump, pink lips.

When Bridget holds out the last dish to me, she smiles, a gentle and shy smile.

Fuck it.

I ignore the plate and grab her wrist instead, causing her to drop the plate back into the soapy water. Then, with my other hand on her slim waist, I press her up against the counter, kissing her fiercely.

Bridget squeaks into my mouth.

I pour my weight into her, make her feel my hardness, and relish the exhale from her nose as she kisses me back and wraps her hand around the back of my head, begging for more.

God, I adore her.

I rip my lips from her mouth, my forehead remaining pressed to hers thanks to her tight grip on the back of my head. "Fuck, you're such a good girl."

Bridget trembles beneath me.

I put my hands on the sink, framing her hips. "I would take you right fucking here if I–"

"You can't." Her eyes grow wide.

I chuckle low. "Don't be scared. I'm not going to. Not here." I lean into her, snag her ear lobe between my teeth and pull.

Bridget clings to my back, nails digging into my shoulders, repressing a moan in her throat.

I cup the front of her throat, running my thumb across the thin blue choker.

Bridget's face flushes, her mouth parts in awe. Remembering.

"Come to the club," I say. "Tonight."

Bridget blinks. "Tonight?"

"Is there an echo in here?" I tease, quirking my eyebrow and looking away.

"*Seth…*"

I laugh at my own stupid joke, then cock my head to the side. "You're a good girl, right?"

"I…am."

"Then you'll come see me tonight. In the Underground. I'll have our room ready."

Bridget's eyes alight at the mention of "our room."

I place a finger into the ridge of her clavicle where both bones meet. "I love that you are wearing your collar tonight, pet."

Her eyes shut.

I take her head in both my hands, kiss her forehead with finality. "I'll be waiting for you."

I leave her in the kitchen, say my goodbyes to my mom and Solomon under the guise of having an emergency at work, and head out to get ready for Bridget's next training session.

13

BRIDGET

Leaving the house is harder than it should be. I spend a little time helping Dad and Amelia with the puzzle, then say goodnight to them under the guise I will be returning to my apartment for the rest of the night.

"Sleep tight, pumpkin," Dad says before planting a kiss on my cheek.

I can't help but feel they can see the guilt on my face. The fact I've lied to him. Not only am I lying about staying in for the night, but I'm also lying about staying in for the night to go to the *Underground*.

And furthermore, the person I'm going to visit at the Underground...

No. Stop. I won't let my mind go there.

Not when I know what's on the other side of giving into temptation.

I get changed, opting for a black dress.

Once I'm dressed, I stand and stare in the mirror for far too long.

My heart has been punching itself out of my ribcage since I woke up this morning, knowing I would see Seth after what feels like so long. Then, of course, the second I come downstairs, we run into each other in the most literal sense.

I felt him get hard against me. Only took a single touch.

I was thankful he was able to pry himself off of me because I'm not sure I would have been able to handle my carnal impulses.

Every night, I touch myself to the memory of him fucking me. The fullness. The tender domination. The unrelenting pleasure.

I hope he will recognize how good I've been trying to be. I have not texted him or tried to reach out despite my anxiety flaring with each passing day. There's a niggling question in the back of my mind that enjoys taunting me in quiet moments.

What if he's changed his mind?

I draw my hand to my neck, stroke the choker. My placeholder collar. I touch it every time I start to get overwhelmed by fear.

It reminds me of our hours together in the Underground. All the times he whispered "good girl" in my ear.

The punishment...

Deserved punishment that made the pleasure *so much* *better*.

Should I follow his instructions tonight, we will move on to the next phase of our Dom and sub relationship.

That's all I want.

However, my bones ache knowing we are stepping beyond that into something else too.

Intimacy. One we will never be able to recover from. Whether it ends with broken hearts or...

I pause the roll of thoughts.

Enough thinking.

I need the one thing that gets me out of my head, the one thing that lets me relinquish control of my life.

I need Seth.

Now.

THE SAME AS LAST TIME, WHEN I ARRIVE, SETH removes my coat, except this time, he presses a kiss to my cheek as he does so.

I've always seen cheek kisses as something chaste and innocent. Not when he does it.

Something to remember him by before the scene takes over.

Also different from last time is Seth's immediate demand: "Strip, pet."

I try to steady my breath.

Seth smirks.

I obey. Shoes, stockings, dress, bra, underwear.

He watches the entire time, stone-faced, not betraying any enjoyment or feeling in the action.

In a strange way, it makes me feel giddy. Not knowing all that makes Seth excited means that everything is a free for all.

I only need to be focused on his demands. His orders. I don't have to worry about a thing because I know he'll take care of all my needs. He'll teach me all I need to learn.

And as he does, he learns me. My body. My reactions. He'll be able to read me like a book.

Those blue eyes, which have always felt cold to me, now feel like warm beams of light despite their lack of expression.

If only behind closed doors, while we are in this room, I am the center of his universe.

And he is the center of mine.

I fold all my clothing nicely into a pile and place it in the chest at the end of the bed.

Seth stares at my naked form, then tilts his chin toward the chaise. "Before we begin, I've drawn up our new contract."

I sit on the edge of the chaise, naked and proper, as if I'm at a formal dinner, my ankles crossed, back straight.

The new contract sits on the coffee table. We discussed my hard limits and the rules of our training before we left our first session, right here in this room, as if he hadn't just taken me to heights I'd never experienced before.

Seth had me fill out an exhaustive checklist of all kinds of kinks and experiences, some of which I'd never even heard of before.

Now, they are all listed in alphabetical order. All the dos and don'ts and maybes.

I have so much to learn. So much to experience. I'm like a kid in a candy store.

And best of all, his limits and mine are a match almost to a T, so if we continue doing this, we won't be settling, we are a perfect match.

I bite my lower lip. I can't help but be a little nervous to be pushed to my limit. I know Seth won't force me beyond what I can take. He suggested we take things slower since I am new at this.

And I can see his point, but I'm not sure. I've been watching from afar for years now. I've read all the books I can. I don't want to do anything halfway just because I'm "new" to this.

However, Seth is an experienced Dom. I need to trust

him to take care of me. To know what is best for me. Because he knows best. And he is my Dom, after all.

This time, I read through the contract twice, making sure everything is as we agreed upon, before picking up the pen.

Seth chuckles. "You're learning, Bridget."

I say nothing and sign on the dotted line.

"Very good. Now..."

Remembering last time, and before he asks, I pull my hair into a ponytail.

It is a strange sensation to have all my hair up off my shoulders. I rarely keep my hair in any kind of style but down. It makes sense that Seth would use this as a way to discern reality from the scene.

Not to mention, I know he loves grabbing it, using it as a way to control me.

As do I.

Seth retrieves a wooden box and sets it in front of me.

"We discussed that ribbon on your neck was a mere placeholder. So, since we now have a long-term contract in place, and I'm taking you as my sub, we need to let others in the community know you are not to be touched. Ever. So..." He opens the box. Inside are three beautiful chokers. Training collar options. "Pick."

I've been dreaming of this moment all week, and my eyes immediately fall to a chain closed with a lock.

Without looking at the others or hesitating, I point to the one that hypnotized me.

"Use your words, pet," Seth says.

"I would like this one, Sir."

"Are you sure, pet? You won't ever be able to take it off. Only I will."

Knowing I'm giving him a measure of full control over me makes me shiver.

I want to give Seth that control. That trust.

If he'd have me, I'd give up all control to him.

And I never want him to question that I trust him.

"Very well. Good girl."

Seth rounds the chaise, undoes the thin, blue ribbon, then places the training chain around my neck.

The metal causes goosebumps to break out on my skin. But it's also the pleasure at being claimed.

He snaps the lock right at the front of my neck, the click sending a pang of pleasure straight to my clit. Then he wraps his hand around my chin, guiding me to look up at him.

"Are you ready to start your training?"

I smile. "Yes, Sir."

"Good. Today, we will learn about some of the implements used in the lifestyle. Some of them, we will never use, but you should learn them just the same."

My insides flame with excitement and fear, for a moment painfully aware of how clothed he is and how naked I am. Not that I mind. Seth looks amazing in whatever he wears. All of his clothes are tailored for his perfect proportions. Strong, broad back, the vee of his waist, apple cheeks of his ass.

I swallow. I would love to see him naked one day. But that is not a demand I can make of him.

And as his sub...there is something so exciting about waiting for the privilege to see him naked. Not knowing if one day he will change the rules and allow me to see all of him the way I bare myself to him.

"Come."

I follow him to the wardrobe in the room and when he opens it, a world opens before me.

I recognize a few of the things in there, but others I've never seen before, and a few others downright scare me just looking at them.

"Let's start with the art of restraint, shall we?" Seth's voice is a low growl, sending shivers down my spine.

"Yes, Sir." A breath is all I can muster as I remember being cuffed to the bed last time we were here.

My heart hammers in my chest as his hand trails over a collection of restraints, and he explains how each is used.

His hand eventually stops at some colorful silky ropes.

He takes one out of the place where it is hanging.

"Ropes like this one offer both security and vulnerability. Same as neckties and scarves, they wrap around you like a lover's embrace. The difference is in the texture as it kisses your skin when you fight against them. Like all the others, they should add to the experience, not take away from it, so though they should leave you powerless to move, they should never be used in a way that will lead to unnecessary hurt or discomfort for you."

As he talks, the rope dances between his fingers with practiced ease.

My eyes can't pull away as I find myself captive of the intricate patterns he weaves, imagining how those soft strands would feel as they encircled my wrists and ankles.

He takes one end of the rope and skims it up my arm, over by breasts, and letting it caress my skin as he weaves it around me for a few seconds before taking it back and putting it away, leaving me panting.

Next, Seth takes out a set of leather cuffs, their metal buckles gleaming as he turns them this way and that. "These are similar to what we used last time, but a different material. As you could attest, they offer a more secure form of restraint. Unlike the ropes that can be used for full-body bondage, cuffs are mainly used for wrists and ankles, whether to tie them to each other or to secure points specifically designed for that."

He fastens one of the cuffs around my wrist, the leather tight against my skin.

I swallow hard, feeling a surge of heat pooling low in my belly.

"It feels different than the others last time. Sir."

"It does. The leather gives it a different texture. But just as nice to keep you still." He smiles.

He takes the cuff away from my wrist, and I feel its absence.

"Moving on." Seth selects a length of chain, its links looking cold and unforgiving. "This is a symbol of strength and submission, an unbreakable bond."

The chain trails along the curve of my spine, the metal cool against my skin.

I shudder as its weight presses down on me, anchoring me in ways I never thought possible.

After putting the chain back, he turns to me and skims a finger over my collarbone. "But the ultimate form of bondage is the collar," he says softly. "A symbol of ownership and devotion, this marks you as mine."

He traces the collar around my neck, his touch gentle yet possessive.

I inhale sharply at both his touch and the reminder of the utter control he has over me.

He turns back to the wardrobe. "Now let's see some of the instruments that can be used for both punishments and *funishments.*"

He goes through them all, one by one, and I have to

admit some terrify me, and a couple are added to my list of hard limits and a few others to my list of soft limits.

"I saved the best for last." His hand brushes over a simple handle with a circular, leather flat top.

It is smooth and unassuming.

He picks it up. "This, pet, is a paddle. It delivers a firm, satisfying smack, leaving a delicious sting upon your skin."

I swallow hard, my pulse quickening with anticipation.

He sets it to the side, on the table instead of putting it back like the others.

He takes a dark instrument this time, one that I've watched being used many times and have wondered about how it would feel on my skin. "This is a flogger."

He examines it, and when he talks next, his tone is filled with reverence. "It can be used for both pleasure and pain, its tendrils caressing or striking with equal intensity."

He twirls it in his hand, the strands whispering through the air with a tantalizing swish.

I bite my lip, imagining the sensation of the leather dancing across my skin.

Setting it next to the paddle, he reaches inside the land of treasure and torture once more to pull out something I am familiar with.

"The riding crop is perfect for precision strikes. It delivers a sharp, stinging sensation that will leave you trembling with pleasure."

He runs the tip of the crop along the curve of my spine, making goosebumps erupt all over. I gasp, as a delicious ache builds inside me.

Setting it up next to the other two on the table, he closes the wardrobe and turns to me.

"There's one more we haven't talked about yet, and it might be the most used of all."

Seth holds out his own hand, offering it to me with a tender smile. "This is the most intimate of implements, capable of delivering both pain and pleasure with a single touch."

I take his hand in mine and caress it, remembering last time, and how it had delivered it all.

He holds my hand in his, picks up the things he laid on the table, and guides me toward the bed.

"It's all nice and fine talking about it, but you need to *know* the difference between them. For that, you need to feel them. So... Are you ready, pet?"

I shiver. I am so ready. But at the same time, I don't want to disappoint him. What if I suck at this?

I nod. Once. Tentatively.

"We don't have to do this today, Bridget, but we do have to do it, so we might as well get it over with so we can move on to the more pleasurable part of the training. So, what do you say?"

14

BRIDGET

Now is the time to really show him that I'm his perfect sub. "I'm ready, Sir."

His smile is blinding. "On your knees." He points down at the floor beside the bed.

I obey.

Seth sits on the edge of the bed and holds out a hand to me. "Take my hand."

I do so.

He guides my hand to his thigh. "As we go, you'll learn some of my cues without me having to tell you."

I say nothing.

"Lie across my lap."

I resist scrambling, resist the eagerness inside me. Instead, with all the grace I can muster, I fold my body over his legs so my ass is up, and my torso is draping toward the ground.

"Good girl..." His hand starts to caress my ass. Almost like he's worshipping it. "You are less embarrassed today about being naked in front of me?"

"Yes, Sir," I say toward the floor.

"Good. Because your nakedness pleases me."

I smile to myself.

"That means you are being a good sub for me." Seth squeezes one of my ass cheeks. "Now, I'm sure you understand what this position is. We can use it for both punishment and *funishment*, and today, it's the second, and not a proper session. This is more about you learning how each implement bites your skin. Learning how you respond to pain. How sensitive your skin is. Are you ready for that?"

"Yes, Sir."

"Of course, you are. Because you're a good girl."

I hold back a giggle.

"Alright, let's get started."

His hand caresses my skin all over. The heat of his hand is warming me up inside and out.

Then is hand is gone, only to crack against my skin a second later. Not hard. Not painful. A preview and warmup for what's to come.

It is a strange sensation. The pain, the increasing tingling across my skin, the wonderful feeling of closeness by being across Seth's lap. It all comes together to make something more enjoyable than it ought to be.

Seth spanks me a couple of times more, increasing the intensity each time, then stops for a moment, rubbing my ass.

It is hot from his touch, and maybe a bit uncomfortable, but it feels good, and I moan.

"You're all pink for me. Just like when you blush. So beautiful." His fingers drop to my pussy and the tips slip easily inside. "So wet, pet. Good. Let's try something else, shall we?"

He reaches out to grab something out of my sight.

"Look, pet."

I lift my head and find the paddle from before held before me.

"You're doing amazing. You should be so proud."

My mouth is...salivating for more. And I find I *am* proud. I'm pleasing him.

"Perfect ass. So red. So beautiful." Once again, he touches me, this time teasing my clit, and I whimper, nuzzling my nose into his calf.

Seth chuckles. He puts the paddle against my skin, caressing me with it. My ass and the back of my thighs. "You feel it?"

"Yes, Sir."

He slides it across my skin. "Color, pet?"

"Green, Sir."

"Good. Are you ready to continue?"

I inhale. "Yes, Sir."

The whisper of the paddle moving is the only warning I get before it lands against my skin.

I cry out, my body jerking. The surprising sensation is entirely different. Not soft on soft, but hard on soft. The surface area is more and the pain it delivers is different too. More spread out. More bite to it.

It's official, I'm not a fan of the paddle.

Seth doesn't pepper my ass with more spanks. He lets that one linger in the air. Let's the silence come to suffocate me.

I want him to tell me the paddle is done, and at the same time, as the pain fades I want to beg for it. But I can't because I am *not* a brat and I don't need a punishment for talking out of turn.

This is the start of my training, and I will show him I deserve to continue being his sub. I am a good, good girl, and I will not ruin this for either of us.

The next slap comes without me expecting it, and I gasp. The place where he hit burns and stings, and I don't know how to feel a pleasure and pain mix together to create a confusing cocktail of sensations.

The pain starts to prick, starting to crawl down my thighs. My muscles react and I start to move, dragging across his lap, alleviating some of the pain in my backside, trying to get some pressure on my clit.

And my breath…god, I'm panting. I haven't even done anything, but I'm panting like I've run a marathon.

"Color?"

"G-green, Sir."

He caresses my burning ass with his hand for a while.

"How was the paddle, pet? Did you enjoy it?"

His fingers tease my clit as one slips inside my wet folds.

Did I? My head is swimming with thoughts, but none that I can grasp.

"It's okay if you didn't, Bridget."

"It hurts more than your hand, Sir. It bites and stings, and I'm not sure how I like it."

"Very good girl for expressing your opinion. We need to be open and honest at all times if this has any chance of going anywhere, okay?"

"Okay, Sir. Thank you."

He keeps his touch consistent, as one hand caresses my ass cheeks, and the other is in my pussy. It is not enough to make me come, just enough to keep me wanting more.

Once my breath has leveled out some, Seth takes his hand from my pussy. "Do you want to continue?"

"I do, Sir." I want to be his good girl, and this is part of the process.

And though it hurts, I am enjoying this so much. His

firm hand, his care. The fact that he is intent on teaching me. Training me.

The sting of the flogger spreads heat around the area where it strikes and tethers me to this world, but as he shows me how the remaining implements feel, my mind flies away from the here and now.

I am on a cloud, floating.

The only thoughts on my mind are about him.

I want to be so good.

I want to be the best.

For him.

I don't want Seth to even look at another sub ever again.

I want to be his sub forever.

I want him forever.

Tears slide down my face. Another strangled sound comes from the back of my throat.

His hand threads through my ponytail. He adjusts my chin onto my shoulder to look at him.

Seth's intense expression has disappeared. He's appraising me, calm and collected. "Can you give me a color, pet?"

I smile, though tears slide down my cheeks. "Green, Sir. A whole forest of it."

He smiles. I get more of his smiles now that he is my Dom. I cherish each one of them.

"Such a good girl." With a finger, he swipes away my tears. "So beautiful," he whispers.

He sits me on his lap and holds me to him for a few moments, feeding me a square of chocolate and having me sip water.

I sigh and let my head rest on his shoulder. He's got me, and I don't have a care in the world right now.

A couple of minutes later, when my mind is fully back

down to earth, he kisses my head. "Let me show you something."

I let him get me up, take my hand, and guide me toward a full-length mirror on wheels in the corner of the room.

He stands behind my naked form, glides his hands down my arms. "Look."

Seth turns me to one side, allowing me to catch sight of my ass in the reflection.

It is red with a couple of welts, but no torn skin and not a bruise in sight.

It's beautiful.

I smile.

"Do you see how good you were?" He caresses his masterpiece.

I drop my head down.

"You have something to say, pet?"

"I wanted to be the best for you, Sir."

Seth laughs, wraps an arm around me, and tucks his face next to mine.

I stare at our reflection in the mirror. How his tall, lean body fits around mine in such a beautiful way, like we were made for each other.

Is it possible Seth and I were fated from the start? Is that why neither of us have been able to give up on the idea of each other? Why we're here now, hiding from plain sight, trying to give each other *everything*?

"Look at me," Seth encourages.

My eyes meet his in the mirror.

"You are so good to me, Bridget," he says in a calm, steady voice. "The point of training isn't because you are not good enough. You are perfect as you are. Never doubt that." He caresses my cheek. "The training is a way to be sure that you know how to place yourself correctly and how to act so that this is both the most pleasurable and the most safe for us at all times."

I swallow. I know he feels that now. But this is all new. What if one day he wakes up and realizes I don't live up to his expectations? What if Seth invests all his energy, all his time into me and I fail him? What if he regrets ever wanting me?

I'm not sure I could handle that. Because he is such a perfect Dom for me.

I wouldn't survive if I lost him.

"And besides..." His hand trails up to my collar, framing the lock in his fingers. "There are so many ways for me to enjoy you. You will find so many other things that bring you to subspace. You trust your Dom, don't you, pet?"

Seth holds the key to my lock. That's not a euphemism. It's reality. And I would never have given that power to someone I did not trust. "Yes, Sir."

He lifts a finger and strokes my cheek.

I feel his hardness at my back. And I want it. Want it in my hand. In my pussy.

God, I even want it in my mouth, though blowjobs never appealed to me.

Unless I was imagining Seth's cock.

I reach back and try to stroke him through his pants without thinking.

Seth jerks away. "Ah-ah-ah, no. That's not for you to touch without my saying so."

I flip around to face him, grabbing at his waist. "I want to please you. Please let me please you."

Darkness clouds Seth's eyes. "You are being a brat, Bridget."

I suck in a breath. I don't want to be a brat.

"And I'll only say this once..." His hand slides between

my legs and then he holds my pussy again in his palm "Brats are not allowed here."

My fingers dig into him as his grip intensifies.

"Your submission pleases me," Seth says. "That is all."

Seth hooks his fingers inside me, this thumb working on my clit. Takes less than ten seconds for him to make me come.

I collapse into his arms.

"All your orgasms are mine from now on. Is that clear?"

"Yes, Sir," I whimper into his arm.

Seth sucks in a tight breath. "You may not touch yourself. May not make yourself come unless I demand it of you. Say you understand."

I clutch his arms tighter, fingers turning into claws. "I understand, Sir.

He hums in laughter. "So needy. So desperate. So *mine*."

Seth facilitates my sliding down his body until I am on my knees and my face is pressed up against his thigh. He fists my ponytail and jerks my head to his crotch, pushing his hardness against my face.

A moan escapes me.

"You want my cock, pet?"

"Yes, Sir."

Seth rubs himself against my face.

I can smell him through his clothes. It is an addictive smell, the salty pheromones of his groin.

"You will wait for my cock. Say it."

"I will wait for your cock, Sir," I say against the hard ridge, dragging my lips along the bulge.

"*Fuck*," he growls.

He wants me. I know he does.

But he is so strong. Because he can withhold his pleasure to train me. To make me a perfect sub.

I adore him.

Seth lets out a shaky breath, then releases his grip on me before stepping away. "Good girl."

Without anything to hold onto, I drop to my hands and knees. I am a shell of my former self, hollowed out by his domination and his power.

My body tremors from the soft echoes of orgasm, the pricking memory of pain, and anticipation. For the next time. The next lesson. The next touch.

I don't realize Seth has returned to me until his hand is guiding my chin up. He's crouching in front of me, a serene smile on his face. He releases the lock around my neck.

If we were in a relationship, we could be open about, I'd leave it on always like I had with the placeholder. However, a little blue choker is inconspicuous compared to a literal chain and lock.

Seth and I have agreed that it will remain in his keeping. That way, it will become part of our ritual. Putting my hair up and my collar on after taking my clothes off.

I steady my breathing, remember that there is a world beyond this room. One that would not welcome us together like this.

Seth's arms wrap around me, and he pulls me into his lap, burying his face in my neck.

"You're so beautiful," he murmurs.

My breath catches.

"So perfect."

I need to be good. Need to follow the rules, but I... "Will you kiss me, Sir? Please?"

Seth lifts his eyes to mine, a serene smile painting his

lips. Without a word, he presses his mouth to mine. Long and drawn out.

His fingers thread through my hair, cupping the back of my head as the kiss lingers and winds.

Together, we return. To Bridget. To Seth.

Seth carries me back to the bed, lays me down prone, and breaks out a tub of cream. With care, he rubs the cream onto my ass, reminding me of the searing pain I experienced.

"This will help with the redness. It will also help with any bruises."

The coolness of the lotion relieves the tension in my muscles.

Once he is done, Seth places a line of kisses across my shoulders. "Let me get you another glass of water...maybe some more chocolate..."

His voice fades into the background as I realize something.

I love being his sub so much I'm not sure the line between Bridget and sub exists anymore.

15

———

SETH

When Bridget arrives, she is dressed just as I specified. In a dark blue dress.

Low cut to show off her cleavage and skintight to display her tiny waist and round hips.

As the maître d' escorts Bridget to the table I've reserved for our *business lunch*, I rise from my seat to welcome her.

She is docile, eyes lowered, lips sealed.

Those lips...painted with a dark red lipstick I've never seen on her.

I can't shake the idea of her lip prints left around my cock.

Keep it together, Seth. Lunch hasn't even started.

I greet her with an open hand. "Hello, Bridget."

She takes my hand, lets me pull her close so I can kiss her cheek.

All outward appearances are friendly. Casual. If people we knew saw us together, they would think nothing of it.

Well, they'd probably be confused that we're even deigning to dine together since we have a decade's history of fighting like cats and dogs. But I am fine relying on their confusion to keep our entanglement hidden.

As I pull away, I am captivated by her scent. Sweet and floral, as always, her perfume and shampoo interacting to create a landscape for my senses I'd love to live in the rest of my life.

The maître d' pulls out Bridget's chair for her.

My temper spikes, but I have to keep it in check. Of course, he doesn't know that it's *my* job to care for her in that way. She is my sub, yes, but there are things I will do for her regardless of that dynamic. Because I am a gentleman.

And because a tiny part of me would love for Bridget to think of me beyond the dynamic.

It was easy to fall into intimacy when we have promised each other a release we have been craving. But once she's trained, I want to make sure she wants to stay in my life as my sub.

And I won't be sharing her with anyone.

Which means I have to be good enough to be seen with her in the light of day as well as dominate her behind closed doors.

I'm getting ahead of myself, of course. There will be lots of...barriers.

But for now, Bridget is in front of me, and we are having a very important training lunch.

"Thank you for joining me today." I settle back into my chair.

"Thank you for having me." Her eyes are still downcast, a small smile on her lips.

My chest warms. "You may look at me when we are out in the world, Bridget."

Bridget's eyes rise to meet mine. Stunning green, complemented by her blue dress.

"And you may speak more freely," I add.

Her lips curl in a nervous way. She tucks a lock of her long dark hair over her ear. "Sorry."

"There is no need to apologize."

"I just want to show you that I am committed to this."

I bite my lower lip and give her a tiny nod. "I haven't doubted that for a moment."

She smiles again, shoulders rising with what seems like an inhale of pride. Such a sweet sub for me.

"Of course, there are rules for when we are out in the world, and I'd like to teach them to you."

"Yes, Si–" Her eyes widen. "Seth."

I can't conceal my smile.

Bridget giggles and covers her mouth. "Sorry. Force of habit, I think."

"Well, in public, Seth works just fine."

"Yes, Seth."

My cock jumps. When she is submitting to me, Sir sounds amazing, but so does my name. In all the years we've known each other, my name has come from her mouth either in trepidation or in frustration. Now it's said with respect, even enjoyment.

How can something make me so horny and so content at once?

To me, sex and domination have been a way to fill a void inside me. Not make me content.

Dominating Bridget does more than fill that hole. It adds a cherry on top of this fucked up sundae.

A server appears beside our table dressed in a tailored suit. "Good afternoon, can I get you something to drink to start with?" The server gives us both genial glances.

Bridget hops to attention, opening the skinny, leather clad drink menu in front of her. "Oh, I'm sorry, I haven't had a chance to–"

I grab the menu, snapping it closed and snaking it out of her hand. "We'll have a bottle of Dom Perignon. 1975, please."

The server glances at Bridget for a brief moment before assuring me, "Very good choice, sir."

He scuttles off quick to retrieve our champagne.

Bridget's eyes widen. "Do I want to know how expensive that bottle is?"

I chuckle. "Probably not." Close to fifteen thousand. But that's a drop in the bucket for me. Not to mention, she is worth every penny. "You will never order around me, Bridget."

She cocks her head to the side. So adorable. So pure.

"It is my duty to feed you. Is that clear?"

She gnaws on her lower lip.

"Don't be scared." I hold out my hand to her across the table.

Bridget places her palm in mine.

The small gesture makes my insides sing with something separate from deep, carnal desire. It's...sweet.

I don't crave sweetness.

I might now, though, as long as it's Bridget's.

"This is something I need as your Dom. You understand, right?"

"Yes, I understand, Si-Seth."

I stroke the back of her hand with my thumb, then remember we are in a restaurant in the middle of the day.

Sure, a hand hold and a kiss on the cheek are innocent enough. But anything more might be misconstrued.

I squeeze her hand, then retreat, pressing my hands to the tops of my thighs to avoid doing anything more stupid.

Her eyes skitter across the restaurant. Everyone here is engaged in their own business dealings, from the literal to the figurative. I doubt they're concerned with Bridget and me in the corner.

"If we go out to dinner with friends, that will make for some weird conversations with our friends," she says with a gentle giggle. "Especially if you do it in front of Sonia."

Fuck our friends. Fuck Sonia.

I lean my elbows on my table and clasp my hands, looking over at her in a dark and appraising way.

Bridget's body shifts with my gaze. Her muscles go rigid, and she sits a little taller.

"When we are alone, I don't want to talk about anyone but us, Bridget. Is that clear?"

Her cheeks flush. "Yes. I'm sorry."

I swallow. As her Dom, I don't owe her explanations on my rules. But I don't want to hide things from her. In a strange way, I want her to understand me. "All the mentions of our life beyond our dynamic remind me of...perversion."

Bridget's eyes grow sad.

"I've already had to do the mental gymnastics as a younger man of not feeling ashamed of what I liked."

Her brow furrows.

I nod. "You're confused."

"I am. I just can't imagine you being ashamed," she says in a soft voice I'd rather have right in my ear as my cock is inside her than across the table.

I knew her as an innocent young girl. I postured myself to be her intimidating older *stepbrother* to keep her away from me.

She wasn't supposed to know anything about me. To

keep everything safe and sanctified. But she needs to understand we all struggle at one point or another. Even Doms.

"In my first sexual encounters, all I wanted was to control, to dominate, to make sure everything went *my* way. But I had to yield to vanilla encounters. I knew what I wanted but didn't know how to express it. Wasn't finding the right kind of women to express myself with."

The server comes over with the champagne, pouring the Dom Perignon into two glasses and then letting the bottle rest in an icy bucket tableside.

We freeze in our conversation, a beating heart between us.

The wonderful thing about servers at luxury establishments is that they make it a part of their job to be able to read a table. Our server disappears without trying to rush us to order our food, allowing us to pick up where we left off.

"*Then*, since I was old enough to try the Underground, I did. I watched scenes, much like you did. Only a few, though. Because I knew what I wanted. What I *needed*. And unlike you, I didn't have the desire to wait for the perfect sub." I let my eyes fall to the bubbles in my glass of champagne. "Didn't have the restraint to wait for you."

Bridget smiles.

I rest my forearms on the table and look her in the eye. "What I'm trying to say is, I have done my time feeling ashamed and when I'm with you, I don't want to be reminded of *them*." The people who won't understand. Will never understand. "Clear?"

Bridget nods, eyes dipping low, the submission clear in her posture. "Clear."

I take my glass of champagne off the table. "Another rule," I change the subject with grateful ease. "You will always wait for me to do anything first. Except sit, of course. I will drink first, take my first bite of food."

"Yes, Seth."

I sip my champagne. Then, I look to her. She takes her glass, sips it too. A half-smile creeps onto my face, and I realize my pulse is racing.

I've exerted my dominance in the privacy of the Underground, but never out in the real world. Never thought I'd find someone I could do that with. And while I am keeping my composure, I am afraid I'll fall into cracks here and there.

"And Bridget?"

"Yes, Seth."

So good. *So good for me.* "If you break any rules out in public with me..." I let my words trail off and hang in the air.

Bridget squirms in her seat just a bit.

"I *will* keep track. And you can count on those punishments later."

Her pupils dilate.

Dirty girl.

I eye her champagne glass. Her lipstick has transferred.

Once again, I am thinking about her mouth on my cock.

I grab my champagne, knock it back fast, then push myself out of my chair.

Bridget's brow furrows.

I step next to her, place a hand on her shoulder, my fingers following the line of her collarbone.

My body concealing her from sight should anyone be looking at me, I slide my hand so the tips of my fingers are placed at the base of her throat, reminding her of her collar. Of her promise. "Follow me."

She does a double take to the table. "But lunch–"

I raise my eyebrow.

Bridget rises to her feet, her expression needy and intent on being the best girl she can.

I lead her through the restaurant to the black, marble-floored hallway leading to the single occupancy bathrooms. I open one of the doors and gesture for Bridget to step inside.

She is flushing all the way down her neck but does not question.

As she slips inside, I keep lookout to make sure we won't be spotted, and no one will come knocking. And once we are in the clear, I get into the bathroom after her, closing and locking the door.

When I turn, Bridget is leaned up against the bathroom vanity, her fingers clinging to the black marble countertop, bright bulbs haloing her.

She is an angel. My angel.

Though I have come here with a different intent, I can't resist her.

I close the space between us, cupping her head in my hand and kissing her as deep as I can.

Bridget gasps as I press her against the vanity. Hard. Not to hurt. But to show her my need.

I slide my tongue into her mouth, let it roll with hers.

For someone so inexperienced, her kisses indicate otherwise. Graceful and passionate.

The act of oral service is a lesson.

But sometimes a man cannot wait for a lesson to present itself.

Sometimes, he must act because the woman before him is so beautiful and so submissive and so *eager* to please him.

And he has waited so many years to have her.

No woman has ever made me lose control.

Bridget is the one exception.

I rip my mouth from hers, my hand gripping her hair tight.

Our noses are smashed together, we breathe as if trapped.

"Get on your knees." A demand. A plea.

"Yes, Sir."

Oh, fuck.

I didn't account for that. But we are behind a closed door...

Bridget falls to her knees before me, her hands folded in her lap, patient.

I undo my belt and pants, then pull them down to release my cock and, fuck, it's harder than I realized.

Bridget's green eyes widen.

I wrap my hand around my member and stroke it. Slow and gentle. "You do this to me. I want you to remember that *you* do this to me."

She nods.

"You've never had someone in your mouth." I am not fully confident that is the truth. Virginity is one thing. All the elements surrounding it...

Bridget shakes her head.

"But you're eager to have me, aren't you?"

"Yes, Sir."

I push away a smile.

With two fingers, I guide her chin up.

Our eyes meet.

I push my cock against her lips, slide it across her mouth, letting my precum coat her lips like gloss. Then, I sneak my thumb up to her lower lip, pull on her lower jaw. Her lips part, skimming the head of my cock.

"I will not force my cock in your mouth." That's an

unnecessary exercise of power. Besides, for it to be enjoyable for us both when I fuck her mouth, it requires training. A lot of it. It will happen one day, but not today. "I just want you to enjoy it. Explore."

Bridget nods.

Her tongue darts out, and she swirls it around the head.

I brace every muscle in my body to keep from losing it.

Her pink tongue against my reddened member is more beautiful than I could have imagined.

For a moment, she adjusts to the feeling of me on her tongue. The corners of her mouth adjust.

"Want you to know how I taste." I sigh. "How it feels... Take your–"

My eyes flutter shut, pleasure coursing through me. "Take your time."

Bridget follows my instructions to a tee. She runs her tongue down my length, using her fingers to pull and prod. And though her touch is clumsy at first, it feels amazing.

Just to have me in her palm is such a beautiful feeling.

"You're doing so good."

She kisses the tip of my dick.

"Take it in your mouth, baby. And look at me while you do."

Bridget adjusts her gaze to meet mine.

"Oh, fuck..." I murmur.

Her mouth parts and engulfs the head of my cock. Tight lips.

Almost as good as her pussy.

Almost.

But this is not about pretending or replacing what I could feel between her legs. It's an act of surrender.

On one hand, she is surrendering to me. To pleasing me.

And I am surrendering to the pleasure she wants to give me.

I reach out and press a hand against the wall, the other hand stroking her hair as she works the head and next few inches with her mouth.

Do not thrust. Do not buck.

It feels so good I just want to fuck her face, but I need to be strong. I need to let her do it in her own time.

Funny enough, I'm training Bridget, but I'm training myself too.

My cock throbs, skewering me with pleasure.

"Yes, good girl. You're such a good girl."

Bridget moans around me.

"Christ, fucking hell," I mutter.

Her lips vibrating around me adds another level of pleasure that makes it even more difficult to hold onto my composure.

Bridget's speed increases. She takes me deeper. Deeper.

My hand clenches against the tiled wall, my fingernails threatening to rip out the grout with how hard I'm trying to keep control.

Her excitement reaches a boiling point, and she moves to take me all in.

"Wait—"

Bridget gags, her body convulsing, a beautiful fucking sight.

But it surprises her, and she releases me from her mouth to cough, to try to steady herself. "I'm sorry, Sir."

"No, baby, don't be sorry."

Baby is not in our lexicon. But it's familiar and endearing. I wouldn't mind Bridget being my baby.

I am so taken by Bridget. Her beauty. Her intelligence. Her elegance. *Her need.*

"That's normal. I'm big, and taking me all in will require some training," I explain. "You did nothing wrong, okay?"

"Thank you, Sir."

I wrap my hand around my cock that is now stained with her lipstick, just as I wanted. It aches for release. "Look at me and open your mouth."

Bridget does so.

"Tongue out."

Her tongue lolls onto her lower lip.

I start pumping my cock.

Shit, it's not going to take much. "You want me on your tongue?"

She nods.

I nudge my cock onto the cradle of her tongue and continue. "I'm going to come into your pretty mouth." I try to remain measured. "And you'll swallow every bit of me."

Bridget can't speak, but she nods once.

Her glimmering eyes look up at me. Like I am somehow her everything...

I ride the thought.

My hand moves faster and faster until my insides heave, and the orgasm arrives, harsh and unyielding. I bite down my cry as my cock spurts into her mouth.

And knowing my come is landing on her tongue, that she is accepting me into her, makes me come even more until my cock has jerked and tremored to completion.

Her eyes flutter shut. She swallows. She smiles.

She's mine.

"Lick me clean, baby."

Bridget does not hesitate, wrapping her hand around the base of my ebbing cock, lapping up the little bit of cum on the tip. She is precise and detailed.

She doesn't want to be done.

My good, *good* girl.

Without speaking, we return to the table as if nothing happened.

The server returns and, just as I explained, I order Bridget's food for her.

No salads for my girl. Only the best. Filet mignon, broccoli rabe, risotto, not to mention an appetizer of caviar for us to share.

She deserves it.

Neither of us can stop fucking smiling.

For Bridget, it makes sense. She is always sweet to everyone, always willing to face the world with optimism.

I'm not a person who smiles. I've had too much taken away from me to smile much.

With Bridget in my life, though, I think I'm going to find reasons to smile again.

16

BRIDGET

My life for the past month is blurry. The work I do, the appointments I have to run to, the dinners with friends or family, all the errands and chores. It all blends together.

The only thing that sticks out is my training. Of course.

I can replay almost every encounter I have had with Seth since the very beginning. Though our meetings are not as frequent as I would like, there have been many to help me learn life as a sub. It's when I'm at my most alive.

And in-between sessions, I have never begged to see Seth, though my body aches for him always.

That's probably why I don't remember much. Because my brain throbs with Seth. I walk around the world aching for the next time I can see him.

I'm different. And apparently, it shows.

Sonia, upon returning from her honeymoon, told me that I was glowing and seemed more relaxed. Amelia remarked that I don't seem like I have as much on my mind. And Deborah Angelise said I had more confidence in our second meeting.

I don't feel like I'm trying to be confident.

I guess now that I have someone taking care of me, I can just be me.

I have Seth to thank for that.

After a month, I have learned so much. And I am loving this process every step of the way.

There is something so empowering about walking through my everyday life knowing that when I'm around Seth, I give him the reins. And when it is just the two of us...

All bets are off.

The more we do, the deeper we get.

It's thrilling.

And terrifying.

No one knows why I'm a different woman. But I do. And Seth does.

I wonder if we can keep it this way forever. However, every time I go too far off track, I remind myself I need to get through training first.

He texted me from the office at almost midnight that he needed to see me. And though his text woke me up, I didn't hesitate to leap out of bed and run to him.

As I walk through the club, there are no nerves. I'm used to navigating to the Underground, to the room Seth always has reserved for us.

When I arrive, Seth is sitting on the chaise.

I close the door behind me as swift as possible and get to my knees.

"Good girl," he says.

His voice is edged with exhaustion. I am not surprised given that he was at the office so late. He's been a workaholic as long as I've known him.

I want to tell him not to work so hard. But I must save

that for an appropriate time, for when I am allowed to speak without permission.

"Let me see you."

I realize I haven't removed my hood. I push it back, toss my hair out of my face.

"All of you, Bridget."

My breath catches in my throat.

I have done something that might surprise him. Something that he might like. Something he might think challenges his control.

Either way, I am either rewarded for my goodness or punished for my indiscretion.

And I like both. I deserve either.

I unbutton my coat and shrug it down my shoulders, revealing what I'm wearing underneath.

Seth breathes in sharply. "*Stop.*"

I hold back a smile.

It is my duty as his sub to be naked.

But the surprise under my coat might change his mind for a bit.

I have designed a new lingerie set with Seth in mind.

Blue, as seems to be the color he likes me best in. Seemingly simple. A silk bra with soft cups and a pair of panties that create a vee down to my pelvis. However, the kicker with both are the metal cords that cris cross, uniting the two pieces. They can be reconfigured in any whichever way the wearer likes.

Or in whichever way pleases the viewer.

It is another step in my attempt to integrate BDSM into my elegant artistic vision.

The closest thing to how I feel inside I've ever designed.

All because of Seth.

With my eyes downcast, I'm not able to get a read on Seth.

He is silent, though. And does not move.

We remain like this for a long time. And I mean a *long* time. Maybe twenty minutes.

Patience is a virtue I am supposed to have as a sub. And I appreciate Seth teaching it to me. I will remain still as long as he likes because all of this is for him.

All of me. His.

"I...don't know what to say," he says after the endless silence.

I do not speak.

"I have half a mind to reward you for looking so fucking beautiful and half a mind to punish you for throwing me off."

Why not both?

"You're smiling."

Am I?

I try to relax my lips.

Seth's breathing is hard.

I can hear it all the way across the room.

His arousal is sexy and now so obvious to me.

His breathing grows heavy and strained, and he attempts to maintain control by pausing and taking the time before his next moves.

I adore my Dom. I know him so well.

"Punishment first. Reward after," he says. "Now put your hair up."

I pull my hair into a ponytail in a hurry.

"Crawl to me."

I move onto my hands and knees and begin to crawl toward him. The scene started as soon as I set foot in this room. But even if it hadn't he is still my Dom. I will follow his instruction. The more of his domination in my day-to-day life, the better. So, I will crawl whenever he desires.

I stop beside his legs.

"Lift your chin."

I do so, avoiding eye contact.

He withdraws my training collar form his pocket, wraps it carefully around my neck, locks it.

Seth rubs his jaw. I can hear he's unshaven. I bet that would burn so good between my legs if he were to...

"How should I punish you today, pet?"

Seth gets to his feet, leaving me on my hands and knees. He goes to the closet. The sounds of all the familiar toys start to clatter. Paddle, riding crop, flogger.

But there are other ways he can punish me. He can bind me in strange contortions, tie me up, edge me without letting me orgasm.

"None of them are speaking to me." He sighs. "Pet, come choose your punishment."

I crawl across the room.

Seth watches me, his smirk in my periphery.

The fact that I can please him by doing such simple things feels unreal.

Crawling, kneeling, bending over and taking a hand to my ass over and over...and those simple things make me perfect in his eyes. I am good by being the simplest and truest form of myself.

"What do you think? What kind of punishment should you get for distracting your Master?" Seth asks, stepping beside the armoire.

None of the punishments look good to me either. Not because they aren't delicious-feeling. But none of them feel as personal as I'd like.

"Speak, pet."

"I would like your hand, Sir."

Seth chuckles and crouches down to be eye level with me. "You want me to spank you with my hand?"

"I want…" I am not used to communicating my want. The only time I've been able to do so was choosing my collar. But training, Seth has said, is about learning the rules so we can learn to feel each other without speaking.

I can't explain my desire.

Seth remains quiet.

"Yes, Sir."

Seth nods. "Very well."

I have been punished before. By the hand, the paddle, the flogger.

My heart palpitates.

Seth reaches out and grabs my ponytail. He stands and goes toward the bed, using my ponytail like a leash. Not pulling hard, but enough that if I resisted it would cause significant pain.

"You know the position." He sits down.

I follow his instruction and bend over his legs.

Seth's hand caresses my ass cheeks, warming me up. "You have ruined your training tonight, pet. Ruined my concentration with this fucking stunt you've pulled."

I bite down on my lower lip.

"What do you have to say for yourself?"

"I'm sorry, Sir," I say, my voice light and airy.

"Louder. Like you fucking mean it," Seth growls.

"I'm sorry, Sir," I say, this time more insistent and clearer.

Seth shakes his head. "Not fucking good enough."

That's when his hand lifts and connects for the first time. It is a mere tap, but I know he's just getting started.

"Were you trying to get punished on purpose?" His hand is back to caressing.

"No, Sir."

Another spank. This time it smarts a little bit more.

"How fucking dare you come in here wearing something like that?" His hand connects again, each word punctuated by a spank. "Are you trying to disrespect me?"

"No, Sir. I was trying to please you. I'm sorry, Sir."

"You wore this for me?"

"I made it for you, Sir," I say in small voice.

"God fucking dammit, Bridget."

He caresses my burning, and surely red, ass.

I remain still. Frozen.

"Why the fuck do you have to do this to me?"

I'm not sure if it's a rhetorical question.

"I'm sorry, Sir," I say, unsure what else to say.

"You've already received your punishment. All is forgiven, pet," he says in a soft voice.

That's it?

Seth lifts me up and sits me on his lap. His expression is unreadable except for his eyelids which are low and, I swear, wanting.

"You look fucking amazing." He bites down on his lower lip.

I perk up.

He smiles. "You made this?"

"Yes, Sir."

"For me?"

"Yes, Sir. I made it just for you."

He closes his eyes for a second, before opening them and looking into mine, but I lower my gaze to his chest. "It's beautiful, Bridget."

He tilts my chin up so we can enjoy each other's gazes. "You're beautiful."

I bat my eyes.

A grin spreads across Seth's face, tongue sliding along his lower lip.

My cheeks flush, and my eyes fall from his.

"Now. I want to take advantage of this gift you've given me."

"Yes, Sir."

Seth smooths a hand back over my hair, guiding me back down onto the bed. His other hand glides down my neck, my breasts, my belly, to my hip, then diverts between my legs and–

I gasp as his fingers enter me.

"Crotchless…" he mutters. "I should have known."

Seth's fingers pump inside me. His other hand finds my neck, right above my chain-link collar.

As his hand works, he presses down on my windpipe, diverting more blood to my pussy, intensifying my sensitivity.

His expression makes my pleasure even more intense. His brow is hardened, almost like he's studying me.

"So wet."

I nestle my hips lower, trying to swallow up his fingers.

Seth chuckles and tightens the grip on the front of my neck, squeezing until my breath is barely sneaking out from between my lips.

"You're going to come on my hand, pet."

If this is my reward, then I am a very grateful girl.

I will please him by offering my mouth for his cock. Or my ass, somewhere we have yet to go, but I am eager to try.

Seth buries four fingers into my pussy and circles my clit with his thumb.

My g-spot is on fire, boiling, ready to blow its top.

"Ready, pet?"

I nod.

Seth's hand tightens on my neck until I can't breathe, and his hand works at a merciless pace.

I press my heels to the edge of the bed, my body bucking wriggling for release as I am suffocated until I burst, contracting around his fingers.

"Yes, ride it out. Keep going. You can do it," he encourages.

I'm still coming. Feels so good I barely care that my chest is in pain from not taking a breath.

My hands fly up to his around my neck. Black creeping in at the corners of my vision.

17

BRIDGET

Seth releases my neck and removes his fingers from me.

My mouth drops open as I gasp for breath, but my mouth is filled right away with his fingers.

"Suck," he demands.

I do so, heaving breaths through my nose.

My sweet and sour taste drips from his fingers onto my tongue.

"Yes, good girl. Very good girl," he coos.

I suck and suck, our eyes locked.

Then, he taps my cheek and I release his fingers.

My chest still heaves as I attempt to regulate after one of the most powerful orgasms of my life and not breathing for god knows how long.

Seth departs as my body unfurls, goes to the armoire to retrieve something.

When he returns, he demands I sit up at the head of the bed, which I do without question. Pinched in his fingers is a ball gag.

I eye it, shyness blooming inside me.

I've had a fabric gag before. The clinical look of the ball gag scares me a little.

However, I've learned the things that scare me are often the most rewarding.

"Spread your legs," he says. "Always spread your legs."

I wriggle my legs into a straddle.

Seth climbs onto the bed. "Sit up."

I obey.

"Open your mouth."

I drop my jaw.

He smiles warmly. "Pretty pink mouth."

Seth inserts the ball of the gag into my mouth, then buckles it around my head. He is careful to make sure it's not too tight, just right.

"I am going to fuck you." He leans over me. "And I'm going to relish every one of your muffled cries."

He presses a kiss to my ear lobe, then drags his mouth down to my neck until his lips land against my collar where he lingers for a moment.

Then, Seth begins his exploration.

His hands slip up my body to my rib cage, tips of his fingers teasing the underside of the silk bra. "My favorite color on you," he whispers. "You know why?"

I shake my head because the gag makes talking impossible.

Seth kisses the insides of each of my breasts. "Because blue things are infinite. The sky. The ocean. And you, Bridget."

My eyes widen.

"You are my infinity."

I want to touch him, to kiss him, to tell him how much he means to me. But I can't. I need to be his good girl. To behave. Besides, my mouth is otherwise occupied.

I sigh, but it goes away fast as Seth languishes kisses across my breasts, then drops his mouth to my belly where the metal cords weave together.

His tongue follows the line of each one as they zigzag down to my panties, leaving warm tracks across my skin.

His teeth raze at the skin of my belly, grabbing, pinching.

I huff.

Seth runs his fingers along my pussy lips.

My hips stutter.

"My plan was to start preparing you for anal tonight," he groans. "But I changed my mind."

Anal, Seth has said, will take time. Because it requires preparation. It's not something I ever considered before Seth became my Dom and we talked about limits.

I trust him with all my heart, but all of this is still so new, so I'm a little nervous.

I'm still marveling at how he fits into my pussy. Not sure how he'll fit into my ass.

"I want to be inside you, pet. And I want it now," he growls.

I expect him to throw me down on the bed, pin me down, and use me until he's had his fill, until I'm practically one with the mattress.

Of course, Seth never fails to surprise me.

He slides his arms around me and pulls me on top of him, my legs straddling his hips. He's throbbing through his slacks, pressing against me.

Grabbing me by the jaw, Seth turns my face in profile to him. He presses the flat of his tongue against my jaw and licks all the way up to my ear before whispering, "Want to watch you...in this outfit you made for me. I want the best fucking view."

I whimper through the gag, spit building up at the corners of my lips.

"Are you comfortable?"

I nod.

"Good."

I love that even through his need, his desperation to have me, I'm still his number one concern.

Seth releases me, dropping back onto the bed. "Give me what I want, Bridget."

I reach down to the closure on his pants, touch the button.

My hands are close to shaking.

Any time Seth gives me permission to touch him, it feels like a bit of a test. To see if I'm handling myself well.

"Go on."

I unbutton and unzip and release and *holy fuck...*

"Stroke me."

I grab his dick.

It is hot, the head red and throbbing.

I move my hand up and down the shaft, slow at first.

He grows impossibly harder with each movement.

His thighs tighten too.

He's loving it. And so am I.

I wish I could have him in my mouth.

A dribble of saliva streams down my chin. I go to wipe it away, but Seth stops me.

"You're salivating over my cock, pet?"

I smile around the gag and nod.

"God, you're such a good girl, aren't you?" His voice sounds almost... pained.

I would like to check his expression, but that might cross a line.

Seth's fingers hook into the cords across my belly. He pulls on them. "Inside. Put me inside. Now."

I position him straight into the air and lift myself onto my knees, letting the head of his cock brush against the fabric of my underwear, then poke into the open crotch, nudging my wetness.

Fuck, I need him.

"Bridget."

When the end of my name glides up in his voice, just like that, he's bidding me to look at him.

I'm learning him just as he has learned me.

Our eyes meet.

The circles under his eyes have lightened the tiniest bit. Perhaps it's just the lighting. But maybe it has something to do with me.

Seth puts his hands on my hips. Grip tightens. Tightens. Tightens until it stings.

The pain translates to need in my brain, sends signals to my core to get wetter.

"Take me all in one go."

My chest lifts.

"You can do it. I know you can."

I put the head of his cock against my opening.

I moan through my gag. I'm nervous.

He's big, and all at once... Will hurt so good.

"Do it, baby."

Something flares in my brain, setting off a chain reaction in my muscles, guiding me to fall over the edge and force my pussy down onto Seth, to take him all at once.

The stretch, it burns, but all of that is eclipsed by the way Seth's body convulses, seizing upward, his head dipping back, neck revealing his bobbing Adam's apple.

And I get even wetter at the sound that tears form his mouth followed by, "*Christ.*"

I relax around him, circling my hips to warm my walls to him.

"Fucking shit, that feels good…"

I giggle through my gag, more saliva dripping onto my chin.

Seth lifts both his hands, slaps them down against my thighs, sending tingling shocks through me. "Come on, show me what you got."

He begins the rhythm for me, pushing my hips forward and back, delicious friction beginning between us.

Once I catch on, I place my hands against his chest, wrinkling the fabric of his dress shirt.

I bounce on his cock, showing off the tight bustier of the piece I created for him.

Seth's eyes are glued to my breasts. "You look fucking perfect, Bridget."

I flush, groan around the gag as Seth's cock jams deep into me, skidding against my g-spot.

My fingers toy with the buttons on his shirt.

I want to see him naked. And I haven't gotten that chance yet. He's always been clothed.

I've never said anything about it, nor has he explained. But in the heat of the moment, it can't hurt to get a little peek.

Except, before I can get one button open, he breaks them away from his chest.

His hands engulf my breasts through the fabric of my lingerie, fondling their fullness and growling to himself. "Fucking beautiful…"

His hands slide to my rib cage, then down to my ass.

He squeezes, half of his hand on fabric, the other on skin. "You are my good girl, aren't you?"

"Uh-huh." I nod, continuing the ride him, my jaw stretched by the gag.

"Tell me, Bridget, tell me you're my good girl."

I can't talk, not with the gag around my mouth, but I try to anyway.

The sounds that come out are not words at all. I huff.

Tears bristle in my eyes.

I want to tell him so bad.

"Oh, you poor thing, you're trying so hard, aren't you?"

I nod with a defeated groan.

"That's okay." Seth's arms encircle my waist.

He pulls me down so my chest is flush to him. "I know you're mine."

His fingers dance across the back of my neck, touching my chain-link collar.

"I know you're mine," he repeats in a ragged voice.

Suddenly, Seth's hips push me aloft, hitting me deep, causing a beautiful burn inside me.

The new angle gives him room to pull out more, increasing the fiction.

"Let it all out," he grunts. "I want to hear it all."

Despite the gag, I allow every sound to pour out of me from the deepest corners of my soul. Every single bit of pleasure.

Seth is moving at top speed.

I start coming. It's not a fall, just a fire that's become uncontained. I scream out, though my gag mutes me somewhat.

The vibrations quake my insides, increasing the pleasure.

Seth forces his hand against my chest and pushes me far enough away so he can watch as my eyes roll back.

Fuck, it feels so good.

So good, I try to tell him through my words are stifled.

"Look at me, Bridget."

Though my body is blazing with pleasure, taking me into another realm of consciousness, I move my eyes to meet his.

Seth is a fucking vision. His jaw is tense, teeth clenched, but his eyes aren't full of power. They're desperate. For release.

And I'm going to be the one to give it to him.

With our eyes locked and an orgasm still unfurling inside me, I cup his chin in my hand.

Let it go…give it to me…

The tension in his face releases, and his eyes widen before he releases inside me.

I whine and whimper. Why does it feel so good to have him cum inside me?

Before we can ride out the orgasm together, Seth lunches for me, grabbing the buckle of the gag and fumbling to release. He's still pulsing inside me, but he's eager to free me.

"*Off,*" he demands. "*Off, now.*"

I help him release the shackle of my mouth.

The second I am free, I am tugged into his embrace and his mouth is against mine.

The explosive kiss sends shivers all the way through me. My body contracts and expands, ecstasy sweeping through me. How is it that sex with Seth just gets better and better? I'm always waiting for it to fall short of the last time…except it never does.

Seth releases his mouth from mine, panting deep breaths. "Holy shit..."

"Yeah, what you said." I roll off him. Then, I jolt upward. "*Sir*. What you said, *Sir*."

Seth looks over at me, blue returning to his eyes. I'm ready for him to say that I need to be punished for that.

Instead, he laughs. A long, uproarious laugh.

And I laugh too.

Our connection is only getting stronger. Not just as Dom and sub.

But as full-on lovers.

As people.

What happens when my training comes to an end? Do we remain in our arrangement? And if so, how do we live lives separate from our commitment?

Because I don't think we can.

18

SETH

Bᴀɪᴅɢᴇᴛ ᴀɴᴅ I ꜱɪᴛ ᴀᴄʀᴏꜱꜱ ꜰʀᴏᴍ ᴏɴᴇ ᴀɴᴏᴛʜᴇʀ ᴀᴛ ᴛʜᴇ long table.

We're out celebrating Nate's birthday, the whole crew.

The dinner table is separated into three factions: those who are in relationships, those who are not, and those who are in a secret relationship that might not be called a relationship but sure as hell feels like one.

I'll give you one guess at the people who are in that last category.

"I feel a little out of place," Edwin grumbles.

Sonia giggles, then leans into Edwin's shoulder. "You're young in spirit," she says with a sweet smile.

"Gag," Abigail mutters on my right.

I give her a humored smile.

Jack keeps his eyes on his cocktail menu. "One day, when you're older, Abigail, you'll understand."

Abigail takes her napkin and chucks it across the table at Jack. Talk about sibling rivalry.

I glance back at the taken end of the table. Nate, Mason, and Laney are all fawning over each other. As per usual.

Leaving only one person I haven't attended to.

Bridget. Straight across from me.

I know I'm in control of the situation, but I'd be lying if I said I wasn't nervous about going out with our friends.

The few times we've been around others, it's been casual. Sure, we've had family dinner with our parents. Other than that, though, it's run-ins at the club. Her with her friends, me with mine, a little bit of light chatting.

Nothing so formal as this.

I worry my lower lip with my teeth. I want to get this right. Don't want Bridget to feel nervous or worried at all.

I've got this.

More importantly, I've got *her*.

Except it's hard when she's looking so fucking beautiful in a violet sweetheart neckline dress, her neck glaringly bare. Would look even better with a delicate chain around it, locked by a lock. A lock only I hold the key too. A collar marking her as mine.

Her long-lashed green eyes cast shadows over her cheeks as she looks over her cocktail menu.

Out of the corner of my eye, the server approaches Nate at the end of the table to start taking drinks.

It's do or die. "What do you want, Bridget?"

Her eyes shoot up.

"To drink, what do you want to drink?" I press.

Bridget glances back at the menu, then to me. "Um..."

"Why do you care?" Abigail asks with a tone that makes me uneasy. "You want to copy whatever sugary drink she gets?"

Bridget furrows her brow. It's endlessly cute. "I don't get sugary drinks!"

"Sure, Miss Pina Colada, extra Pina." Abigail leans her chin in her hand, smiling like an imp.

I ignore Abigail, eyes hardening on Bridget. If she wants a choice, it's now or never.

Bridget drops her cocktail menu and sighs. "Gimlet."

"Not too sweet." I nudge Abigail's arm.

Abigail rolls her eyes. "Whatever."

Bridget wraps her arms around herself. She's holding back. Not the usual firecracker she can be at events like this. Not letting it all fly off the handle. Trying to be controlled. For me...and perhaps because she's scared.

I still adore her just the way she was before we began our...dynamic. While she was always so free, I was withholding. We balanced each other out that way.

I remind myself that we have time to develop our understanding of our arrangement.

Although I'm tired of calling it an arrangement. It's a relationship the same as anyone else's. Not one that can see the light of day, but...

I look at the rest of the table and feel my blood wanting to boil.

Why *can't* our relationship see the light of day? Edwin was Sonia's boss. And Sonia was the ex-girlfriend of Edwin's son. Meanwhile, Laney was Mason's ex-girlfriend before Nate fell for her. Mason couldn't let go either and now the three of them are in their own little love bubble.

Look at how well they all get along now.

We're fucking adults. Things were weird at first in every case and then we built a bridge and got over it because... because they're happy.

And Bridget makes me happy. She has since I met her, though I wasn't always clear about that.

She lights up a room. Her not-so-innocent glimmering eyes always have been filled with curiosity and vitality that's scared me.

She made me so happy I didn't know what to do with myself.

After everything that happened to me, I wasn't ready to accept that there would ever be a bright side again. So, I kept her at arm's length...all the while fending off the interest of any other guy.

I wanted her to be mine because she was beautiful, yes, and I knew somewhere inside we were meant for each other. A perfect match.

But I've been working for ten years to be closer to her sunshine.

Now I'm not afraid to burn.

Fuck, I might love this girl.

"Sir?"

The voice calling me that is wrong.

I snap to attention, look at the server now at my shoulder, her face bent so close to me I can smell the suffocating scent of her spicy perfume.

"What would you like to drink?"

"Bourbon. Rocks."

"Do you have a pref–"

"Most expensive." I point at Edwin. "It's on him, anyway. "

Edwin chuckles, nonplussed by my sticking him with the bill.

The server lifts her eyes to Bridget, her mouth about to form the question.

I interject before she can utter a single word. "And she'll have a gimlet. Extra splash of simple syrup, she likes it on the sweet side."

The server moves on to Abigail and Jack, but I hear none of their exchange. My eyes gravitate to Bridget.

I drink in the soft smile on her lips, the warmth of her cheeks, and the way she's looking at me.

It's not with lust. It's not in submission.

Could that be love too?

After the server saunters off to put in our drink orders, Abigail's fiery eyes shoot to me. "Okay, what the hell is going on?"

"Abigail, relax..." Bridget says.

"He's being nice to you. He's never nice to you," Abigail retorts.

My heart sinks to my stomach.

I know that's the truth, and yet hearing my reputation out loud isn't a good feeling.

"I'm turning over a new leaf." I force a smile. "Is that so hard to believe?"

Abigail's jaw drops, her freckled forehead creased with wrinkles.

Jack shakes his head. "Jeez, Abigail. Why do you always have to get involved in other people's business?"

I glance at the other half of the table. They're all caught in their coupley bliss, not paying any mind to us.

"Well, I just—I'm just confused! Did you know about this, B?"

Bridget opens her mouth to respond, then closes it, unsure what to say.

"I mean, did he even apologize for the hell he's put you through?"

I choke on a sip of water. "H-hell?"

Abigail's eyes narrow, a minxy smile appear on her lips. "Do you know how much Bridget has fretted over your liking her since, well, since forever?"

Jack narrows his eyes at his sister. "You were like eleven when they met, you knew nothing about it."

"I was *thirteen*, asshole," Abigail hisses.

I splay my hands out. "Okay, okay, let's relax, let's..."

Abigail takes a deep breath. Her temper has gotten wilder lately.

Sometimes, her face matches her deep scarlet hair. "I just want to know if you apologized to her. Because she deserves that for all the time she spent fretting that you didn't like her and all the times she tried."

Have I apologized? I don't...I don't know.

Jack rolls his eyes. "Why are you sticking your nose in *their* business?"

Abigail crosses her arms over her chest. "It's all our business because we've all put up with their fighting for years, haven't we?"

I fix my eyes on Bridget.

Her silence is speaking volumes. She's trying to be good.

I don't doubt getting ready for this event was stressful. Because she wants to get it right.

My sweet sub. Wanting to make things right for me always.

"Fine." I cut Abigail off from her next tirade. "You're right. I owe Bridget an apology."

Bridget shakes her head, unable to speak.

"Bridget," I say. "I haven't apologized, have I?"

Her green eyes tremble, her pink-painted lips contorting with nervousness. "No, S-Seth."

I can sense the hesitation before she calls me Seth. If only she knew my name causes just as much pleasure as when she calls me Sir.

"Well, I obviously owe you one after all this time." I glance at Abigail and Jack, then refocus on Bridget. "I was selfish and...misguided. I didn't realize the way I was treating you was having a ripple effect. But none of that matters because I was hurting you." There's a hitch in the back of my throat.

I hurt Bridget all the time. The way I've treated her was wrong and neither of us deserved to hurt that much for the past ten years, but she deserved it even less.

I realize now I've hurt in ways I need to atone for. And that goes further than making her come and telling her sweet things. It entails accountability and strength in a way that I've never been very good at.

I'm ready to be good at it now.

"I'm deeply sorry for the trouble I've caused you," I say. "I've never disliked you...I just..." *Didn't like myself very much...*

Still don't.

But I like myself with you.

"You're just shit with emotions," Abigail says.

Jack must kick Abigail under the table because she growls at him.

I nod. "You could say that."

Ever so innocently, I slide my hand across the table, palm facing upward. "Forgive me?"

Bridget smiles, a soft smile like the flicker of a candle in the dark.

She places her hand in mine, and I have a hot flash from the top of my head to the tips of my toes.

"Yes, Seth. I forgive you."

I squeeze, run my thumb over the back of her hand and then release it.

That's probably as much intimacy as we can get away with in public. Because even if we never really had that kind of relationship, in the eyes of everyone around us, we are...stepsiblings after all.

AFTER THAT LITTLE AWKWARD BUT NECESSARY moment, both Bridget and I get more at ease.

I can read Bridget like a book. It's my job. My *responsibility*. I know when she is scared.

Now, after two, going on three, extra gimlets, she is relaxed. Posture melting, smile effervescent, and easeful with conversation.

She only speaks to me when addressed, but I sense she is getting used to the give and take of our dynamic out in the world.

After Nate disallows us from singing happy birthday, we are all given dishes of tiramisu.

However, it becomes painfully obvious not everyone needed their own dish since the crew at the left side of the table is all *sharing*. Dipping their spoons into each other's dishes, sliding them into each other's mouths.

"Ick," Abigail mutters before grabbing a huge spoonful of her dessert.

"*That* I agree with you on." Though there is a small part of me that would love to dip my spoon into Bridget's perfect mouth, hold her chin delicately in my hand, watch the sweetness titillate all of her senses.

"It all happened so fast, didn't it?" Jack leans on his elbow. His spoon sticks straight up in his tiramisu, his expression downturned.

I feel for my friend.

Up until Bridget, the two of us were in the same boat. He works too hard in finance, and I work too hard in tech. The difference is, I know what I like, and he doesn't even have the wherewithal to guess at what he likes.

I can see the Dom in him. We've talked some about the

lifestyle and I've tried to take him to the Underground on a few occasions, but he gets too nervous.

It is okay. Everyone must come into their own at their own pace.

"Yeah, it was like a domino effect after Dad met Sonia," Abigail says, her usual brashness eclipsed by discontent. "It's just the four of us left."

Bridget's eyes flash to mine for the briefest second.

"We need to be going out and wingmanning each other!" Abigail says with a bright smile. "Then we don't have to sit at the kids' table!"

Jack grunts. "This isn't the kids' table. We are literally all at the same table."

She waves him off. "Oh, hush, you."

I laugh.

"What do you think, Bridget?" Abigail asks. "We should come up with a plan. We all know each others' types, it would be perfect, right?"

"I–I–" She shakes her head. "I don't know, I wouldn't even know where to begin. What do you think, Seth?"

I don't know what to say either.

"Could work." I knock back the rest of my bourbon.

"Please, what happened to my party animal?!" Abigail teases Bridget. "You turned twenty-six and started having to pay for your own health insurance and got boring?"

"No, nothing like that..." Bridget says, eyes downcast into her drink.

Thankfully, Abigail is a little tipsy too. She slams her hands on the table and cries out, "I know! We should go on a trip."

"Here we go," Jack mutters.

"I'm serious!" Abgail scoops up another bite of dessert. "We all go on a trip. We relax, we go–a beach! We're all hot.

We hang around, make it clear we aren't coupled up, and we go have fun. An experiment. Let's see if we can do it in the best circumstances, not just a crappy New York winter night at a club."

Jack hesitates. "Well, I guess that's not the worst idea."

No, no, noooo. I don't need Jack agreeing.

Abigail stares eagerly at Bridget. "Well, what do you think?"

Bridget's anxiety buds to the surface again, a grimace on her lips.

Abigail whips out a hand, flat-palmed. "And don't ask Seth. You're your own person."

Inside, I glower.

Of course, she is her own person. She's just consented to giving me the reins.

I can't punish her for other people's actions. But I can flounder in frustration.

"I...think it's a good idea," Bridget says. "Seth, what do you think?"

Her agreement makes me uneasy.

I have to wonder if that's what she wants. To go meet other men that she can have out in the world.

Am I not enough behind closed doors?

I'm not an insecure person. Except when it comes to Bridget. And since my life has revolved around her for ten years, perhaps I am a *very* insecure person.

Fuck.

Most of the time, I'm able to read Bridget's expression, get an idea of what she's thinking from a tiny look. But right now, I can't. It's all muddied, clouded over with the crack in my heart growing more intense.

I won't survive if Bridget wants to be with another man.

I can't hold her back either.

I'm jumping to conclusions.

Bridget is polite and sweet to a fault. She's probably just being agreeable.

Guess I'll take a page out of her book.

"Sounds like a great idea," I say. "In fact, my family has a place in Key West that just sits empty. We can head out whenever we want."

Abigail's eyes brighten. "Key *West*?! That's perfect!"

"I didn't know you had a place in Key West, Seth." Jack furrows a brow.

"I..." I lick my lips, then look into my plate of mostly untouched tiramisu. I'm suddenly not very hungry. "It was my dad's place. Don't go much." Haven't gone ever since he died.

Jack exchanges a look with Bridget. "We can go somewhere else. We can find a place, no problem."

Bridget nods.

"Are you kidding? Don't look a gift horse in the mouth, Jackie boy." Abigail is far gone with her old fashioneds...and she's supposed to be half-Irish. Her tolerance is blasphemous.

"It's fine, guys." I force a smile. "It'll be nice to go back there. Been a while."

Abigail starts raving about all of the things we'll do. The bars we'll go to, the days lounging on the beach, the shopping, the outings.

And I retreat into myself. Wish I could be anywhere but here right now.

Until I feel Bridget's foot against mine under the table.

I look up at her, find her beautiful, sympathetic smile. Her fingers touching the dip of her clavicle reminding me of her collar. The one I wish she could wear out in the world.

She belongs to me. And she fucking knows it. The whole world should know it too.

And I...belong to her. My heart aches for her. I want a life with her. I want to be a part of the coupley end of the table, want to be able to smile at each other, knowing that we will go home together, that the other side of the bed won't be empty.

If I could tell her tonight, I would.

But there are parts of me she doesn't know yet.

Key West will be perfect for that. Or it might wreck me.

19

BRIDGET

ABIGAIL'S VOICE INTERRUPTS MY CONCENTRATION. "Put that phone away! You're on vacation!"

I look up from the text I'm trying to send. "I can't just leave Deborah Angelise on read, Abigail."

My friend crosses her arms, leaning into her hip.

She's already in her bikini and sarong, a sun hat the size of a sombrero, and is slathered in a white cast of sunscreen because without it she'll burn like a hot dog left on the grill too long. "Fine, I'll make an exception for Ms. Angelise."

I smile.

Abigail saunters past me, sliding her hand over my shoulder. "I'm going out on the beach. Seth and Jack are already out there. Come out when you're done, yeah?"

I nod. "You got it."

Abigail leaves through the sliding glass doors and heads down the wooden slatted boardwalk to the private beach.

The ocean is mesmerizing. Gorgeous, endless blue.

I need to get out there asap.

But first, Deborah.

Her text was surprising.

I've got some interest in your sketches, what's your schedule like this week?

The Deobrah Angelise got interest in *my* sketches. I have half a mind to tell her I'm free whenever she wishes and head straight back to New York.

But no, I've already committed to being here, already put in the mental labor to figure out how to make this trip work.

Out of town until Sunday. Any time next week will do. Let me know what you need from me.

I resist adding a, "You're the best!" to the end of that.

Trying to keep it professional and level-headed, tame my enthusiasm, isn't always easy, though, especially when I'm losing my mind that *Deborah Angelise* got someone interested in my designs.

Who knows who it might be? A fellow designer. A merchandiser. A fashion house.

I don't fucking care! I'm over the moon.

For now, though, I click my phone screen off and head up to my room to change into my bikini. I've picked out something... 'modest' isn't the right word for a bikini, but simple.

Seth and I agreed to keep our distance during the four-day trip, and I am trying to make that as easy as possible by making myself as plain as possible.

Who knows, maybe a girl will catch his eye as is Abigail's plan?

Jealousy flares inside me. I try to tamp it down, but it's hard when I've allowed myself to be his for over a month now, committed my body to him.

And in committing my body, I've also committed my soul, whether he knows it or not.

I glance out the window of my room. It's got an ocean

view, which means I'm able to spy Abigail, Jack, and Seth on the beach.

Seth and Jack are chilling on some lounge chairs with morning beers. When in Key West, right?

And Abigail is standing with her hands on her hips, giving them a talking to, as she is wont to do.

The flight here was hard enough, just the four of us.

Seth arranged for his company jet to take us down, which meant the four of us were in tight quarters for a few hours.

Despite our agreement, I wanted nothing more than to lay myself at Seth's feet, be his perfect little sub as I've been trained to be.

Instead, we all quietly drank champagne and played Scrabble.

On more than one occasion, my fingers brushed Seth's and it sent tremors of need through me.

I'm worried it won't get easier the longer we keep our distance. In fact, I think it's only going to get harder.

Once I'm dressed, I head down to the beach.

Abigail waves at me when she sees me, grinning ear to ear. "There you are!"

Jack glances back at me. Seth keeps his head down.

I keep a smile on my face though my insides droop. Feels like old times when he was ignoring me in what I thought was dislike. Turned out it was suppressed want.

Seth might be a master of restraint and withdrawnness. But how long can he keep that up now that we know what's on the other side?

"Look at you! Back in black, huh?" Abigail shimmies her hips.

Why is she calling attention to it?! This is supposed to be an understated bikini.

Damn her.

"I'm trying to get them to come in the water, but they're too busy *reading*." Abigail sticks her tongue out at Jack and Seth.

I give the boys a once over.

Jack has some self-help book in hand. Classic for him.

And Seth got a willowy copy of an old James Patterson. More notable than either of the books is Seth's t-shirt and trunks combo.

I want to ask him if that's even comfortable. I've asked him about it in the past, whenever we've been at a pool party or the like.

Come to think of it, I've never seen him with his shirt off. Surely, a trip to Key West would call for that, right?

Guess not.

Shirt on or off, though, no man holds a candle to Seth. His stubble is freshly trimmed, highlighting his hard jawline. And the sunlight makes his blue eyes sparkle in a way I've never noticed before. Never *let* myself notice.

"Party poopers," I say to Abigail.

She scoffs. "That's about right." She whips her hat off and sighs, stroking her fingers through her hair. "You come with me, Bridge."

"I still need to put on sunscreen." I take a tube out of my bag.

"Oh, well. Jack can help with that." Abigail grins.

Jack's kneejerk reaction comes in the form of "Ew." Then he looks at me apologetically. "Sorry, Bridget. Nothing personal."

I laugh. "Trust me, I don't take it that way."

I grew up with all the Lyons kids. I've seen them all at their worst, including Jack. He's an attractive guy, but I can't shake the memory of him saving his chewing gum in an Altoids tin so he could chew it later. That was middle school. Far too old for crap like that.

"I'll do it," Seth offers.

The blood rushes to my pussy at the thought of him touching me. Not the best idea.

"Double ew!" Abigail interjects. "You two are siblings!"

"*Step*siblings. Not like you and Jack," I clarify.

"That's worse."

"Why?" I scoff.

"I don't know. It just–" She shivers in a dramatic fashion. "*Is.*"

Further proof that whatever happens between Seth and me has to remain a secret. And my chest hurts more than it should at the thought.

Abigail snatches the sunscreen from me. "Jack will do it." She tosses it at her brother, and it lands right in the gutter of his book.

"*Fine,*" he growls, dropping his legs off the side of the lounge and patting the free spot. "Sit. I'll do your back."

I have no choice unless I want to go against the grain of being agreeable. "Thanks, I know it's a big sacrifice for you." I attempt at a joke.

Jack smiles. "You're so welcome."

I sit at the end of the lounge chair and let Jack slather sunscreen onto my back, all the while feeling Seth's energy shift.

I don't think he's looking at me. That would be too obvious. But there is tension in his legs, a darkness to his aura.

He doesn't like this.

I don't either.

I should have said no, but I didn't want to cause a scene.

I'm sure he'll keep a tally of my punishments to be

served once we return to the Lyons Club. Although if we're on a hiatus through this trip, does it even count?

I still want to be a good girl for him. But this weekend I'm not his.

My brain is in knots.

After I'm all lubed up with sunscreen, Abigail and I go down to the shoreline and comb the beach for shells and beach glass.

The tide is cold, lapping at our toes and stinging every time it grabs us.

"I dare you to go in the water," Abigail says with a devilish grin.

I shrug one shoulder. "I'll go in if you do."

She grabs my hand, announcing, "Deal!" as loud as she can as she drags me into the surf.

Though it's cold, the ocean water is lush and salty, swallowing us and our laughter up as if we've always been a part of it.

This is the natural order of things. In a way.

No matter how much fun I have, though, the memory of Seth tugs at my belly.

"Put your head under, put your head under!" Abigail begs.

"Wait, wait, wait–" I pull a hair tie off my wrist and wrap my hair aloft on my head. Don't want to get it all mucked up. Then I dive into the water.

It's like we're kids again, playing mermaids, laughing our tails off, both imaginary and real.

However, unlike when we were children, we get waterlogged much faster.

Abigail and I emerge from the water and rush to grab our towels. We dry off mere feet away from the guys.

"Ugh, okay, enough of that." Abigail falls into her own lounge chair. "Shall we drink, Bridget?"

"What time is it?" I look up at the sun in the sky.

"Five o'clock somewhere," Seth mutters.

I eye him. Well, his knees. I'm too scared to look in his eyes in case that's not welcomed. "Fine. Sure. I'll go grab us something. What do you want, Abs?"

"Mm...need a beach drink. Like a pina colada, extra pina," she says, grinning.

My mouth salivates for the first time in a while for something other than Seth's cock. "Oh damn, that sounds good. Okay, be back in ten."

I head back up the boardwalk, towel around my waist, squeezing my ponytail out as I go.

A pina colada is *just* what I need to take the edge off my nerves. If I remain semi-drunk the entire trip, maybe I will be so concentrated on not making a fool out of myself that Seth will fade into the background.

Once inside, I head into the gorgeous kitchen.

Marble countertops, light blue cabinets, and a fridge stocked fully with everything one would need for a Key West getaway including precut pineapple, rum, coconut milk, and Coco Real.

Perfect.

I get to work on throwing everything in the blender. Extra pina, an extra squeeze of Coco Real for my sweet tooth.

Before I press blend, I realize I've forgotten the limes. What kind of pina colada doesn't have lime juice? I go back to the fridge and bend down to reach the fruit drawer, sorting through for the fresh limes.

Until two hands wrap around my hips and pull my ass up against a hardened ridge. A dick.

Seth's dick. I know it well by now.

I gasp and straighten up. "What are you *doing?*" I whisper.

One of his hands slides up from my hip, gliding across my bare stomach, all over my breasts, up my neck, to my jaw.

He jerks my face to his and kisses me.

"*Seth!*" I try to cry into his mouth, though it comes out muffled and unrecognizable.

He jerks my face away.

I get a good look at his eyes and, oh god, he's mad.

"What the hell was that?"

"What was *what?*!" I squeak.

Seth's jaw tightens.

Without warning, he pushes me away from the fridge, up against the corner, pinning his hips with mine. "You know playing dumb doesn't get you anywhere with me."

My heart is racing, blood pounding, and...I'm getting wet. This wasn't supposed to happen. "Seth, we agreed–"

"*Fuck* the agreement." He presses harder against me, so hard the counter digs into my back. "First, you wear this poor excuse for a bathing suit..." He grabs the back of my top and yanks at the string bow I tied around my neck.

The cups tumble down, exposing my breasts.

I suck in a breath, glancing at the doorway to the kitchen. "Seth, we can't. Not here."

"Then–" he ignores me.

And I love it.

He needs me so bad he doesn't *care*, doesn't care that we might be caught. He's willing to let it all fall apart for me. "You let Jack touch you like that when you know you're mine."

"I didn't know what to say, I didn't–"

Seth grabs my ponytail and yanks it back so my neck is exposed to him. He ghosts his lips up and down my neck. If this is how I learn Seth is a vampire, that's fine with me. Bleed me dry, baby.

"And then you put your hair in this...when you know that *this*–"

He tugs again, and I cry out, the sting spiking through my scalp, sending electricity through my body.

"This is mine. This is for me." Seth presses his face against my jaw. "For *us*."

"I'm sorry."

"You've been *teasing* me," he mutters.

"I didn't mean to," I reply in earnest.

Seth is quiet for a few moments. "I know," he finally croaks, a dark and pained sound. "I can't do this. I can't pretend like everything is as it was between us, Bridget."

"Me either," I exhale.

Well, we made it less than twenty-four hours pretending we aren't anything more than begrudging stepsiblings. "We can...we just have to be secret about it, okay? We can do that. We've done it so far."

Seth looks me in the eye, expression unreadable. Not the same composure he has in the Underground. There's a brokenness in his eyes I don't know how to repair. Because I don't know where it comes from.

Two of his fingers slide between the towel and my skin.

He pulls until the towel loosens and falls to the ground. "Yes, we are good at keeping a secret."

The world stills. Our eyes locked, his fingers now toying with the string of my bikini bottoms.

"Kiss me," he says, as easy as a breath.

I touch his cheek with tenderness. Though he's rough with me, that's what I sense he requires.

I let my fingers toy with his chestnut hair before pressing an insistent kiss to his lips.

Seth undoes the bikini fully as our lips and tongues dance. It falls to the floor at my feet.

And with suddenness, just the way this encounter began, he spins me around so my ass is pressed against his cock again.

His hand presses against my collarbone. "I'm gonna fuck you right here."

"Yes, Sir."

The sound of fabric shuffling aside. The weight of his bare cock against my ass.

"I'm going to make you come *right here.*"

"Yes, Sir."

His teeth graze my earlobe. "And I don't care if anybody hears or sees. Because you're mine."

"Yes, Sir."

Seth slides his cock between my thighs, coating himself in my essence. "Say it. That you're mine."

"I'm yours, Sir."

"Damn fucking *right.*"

The head of his cock pops into my wet center.

We both sigh, as if it erases all the struggles of resisting each other in such close proximity the past however many hours.

I grip the edge of the counter.

I'm in for a fucking ride. Need something to hold onto.

Seth pulls no punches. Though he seems to have no fear of anyone walking in, it takes only seconds for him to gain enough momentum to fuck me at a ruthless pace.

Each of his thrusts elicits a ragged breath from me.

His cock hits all the right nerves inside me. If he

released his hold on my body, I'd crumple to the floor, melting with delicious pleasure.

"You like my cock, baby?" Seth murmurs in my ear, snaking a hand up my front to fondle my breasts.

"I love your cock, Sir."

He lets out a warm laugh. "You're such a good girl, Bridget." He pulls his cock all the way out. "Such a good *girl*."

His last word is punctuated by his return, thrusting himself as deep as he will go.

I scream as torrent of warmth shudders through me, bending further forward so he can get that deep each and every time.

"Tell me how much you need me," he says.

"I need you so bad, Sir."

His hand moves up from my breast to splay across my chest. "Say my name."

"Sir…"

Then, his hand moves to the lower part of my neck. His fingers act as a collar, reminding me of who I belong to. "My *name*, Bridget."

Through a haze of impending orgasm, I muster his name, his *real* name, on my lips. "Seth, oh my *god*, Seth."

"Tell me you need me."

My eyes blur, tears of pleasure pricking as heat threatens to annihilate me. "Oh! I need you! I need you, Seth. I've always needed you."

Seth's other hand finds the button of my clit without fumbling and presses *hard*. "Come for me."

He doesn't have to demand. It would be impossible to avoid.

My body bucks, head thrown back as an orgasm runs through me. A screech comes from my mouth, a sound I've never made, even in the throes of pleasure.

"Yes, *yes*. Let them know you're mine."

My body trembles and shakes.

I can't see the end of the orgasm and that keeps me going as every spasm of pleasure echoes through me as if there are a million more to come.

Seth drops his mouth to my shoulder and groans.

His hips slam into me.

One. Two. Three.

Release.

As he fills me, his body slackens, yet loses no strength, holds me in his arms almost like he's afraid he'll lose me or that I might turn into a million grains of sand sliding through his fingers.

I slide my hand around the back of his head, press my forehead to his cheek, trying to catch my breath.

The duality between the ferocity of our fucking and softness of this moment fills me with joy. Makes me think more might exist beyond the commitment to our lifestyle.

However, I shouldn't let the post-coital fog dictate what might be between us.

Our reverie is interrupted by the sound of the sliding glass door.

How did I miss that sound earlier?

"Did y'all get lost?" Abigail's voice echoes through the house.

I shudder away from Seth, struggling with my top. "Couldn't find–"

Seth puts his dick back in his shorts and grabs my bottom from the floor, tying it in place faster than I thought possible.

"Couldn't find the limes, but I–" When I'm properly covered, I run back to the fridge and fish out the bag of limes to hold up in triumph, just as Abigail walks in. "Found 'em!"

Abigail leans into her hip, sassy as always. "And what's your excuse?" she asks Seth. "You were just supposed to be getting beers."

Seth tucks in beside me, grabbing two beers from the fridge. "Helping Bridget, of course."

"Damn, you have turned a new leaf," Abigail says.

Seth rolls his eyes and leaves, just as silent as he came.

As he leaves, the bliss leaves my body.

He didn't want everyone to hear or know.

And I guess I didn't either.

"Come on, I'll help you. I need a pina colada, stat." Abigail shuffles into the kitchen and sets to cutting the limes.

I wash my hands with the pungent lemon verbena soap to wash away the smell of sex and pull the towel back around my waist so she can't see the way Seth's seed has leaked onto my upper thigh.

As soon as that's hidden away, it's like nothing happened between us.

Like nothing has ever happened between us.

20

SETH

THE PLACE MIGHT BE CROWDED, BUT MY EYES ARE glued to Bridget. She's standing at the bar with Abigail, waiting for the next round of drinks.

Her outfit is...fucking perfect. As usual.

It shouldn't be surprising a woman in the fashion industry knows how to dress, but ever since her training began, she's been dressing for me. Lots of blues, dresses that hug all her curves, makeup that highlights her full lips and big green eyes.

Tonight, she's all about the tropical vacation wear of Key West, wearing a halter top dress decorated with palm fronds and fruits.

No corny pattern could detract from her beauty. If anything, one of the printed fronds accentuates the curve of her ass just so...

Jack's voice infiltrates my focus. "What do you think about her?"

I follow his gaze across the bar.

His eyes are focused on an icy blonde pixie cut across

the room. She's wearing a crop top and tiny shorts. Cute. Not my type, but cute.

She's standing at the lip of the karaoke stage, cheering on someone, maybe a friend, who is doing a rendition of *The Stranger* by Billy Joel. "Not a fan of short hair."

"God, how antiquated of you." Jack rolls his eyes.

"Do *you* like her?"

Jack bites his lip and leans back on our table, ticking the fingers on one hand. "She's hot."

"There you go. So, why didn't you just *say* that?"

"I don't know, Seth. Don't you think this whole trip is kinda stupid?" Jack's brown eyes look sad.

I gulp. "W-what do you mean?"

Jack looks over at the bar where Abigail and Bridget are still waiting for their drinks. "You know Abigail doesn't just want to fuck around and find out. This isn't just some hurrah for her. She wants to settle down the way everyone else has."

I frown. "Doesn't sound like Abigail…"

"Okay, she hasn't told me that outright, but–"

"She's still so young. She's got so much time. We all do." I don't say I don't want more time. I already know what I want.

"I just know it's kinda getting annoying for her that everyone is coupled or *throupled* up and–"

"Are you sure you're not projecting, Jack?" I raise an eyebrow.

My friend hesitates. "Well–"

"I understand, buddy." I smile.

He sighs. "Okay, fine. *Fine.* I would like to meet a woman to have a long-term relationship with. True. But I'm not going to find her in Key West! People here are from all over. Including Florida. And lord knows I'm not dating a Floridian."

I laugh. "You're ridiculous. What's wrong with Floridians?"

Jack shakes his head, eyes widening. "They're crazy, man. They've got a death wish."

"You want me to go talk to her?" I nod toward the blonde.

Jack sighs. "I don't know. I think this whole thing is–"

I notice Bridget moving through the crowd again out of the corner of my eye and all my attention is drawn back to her. I don't hear a thing Jac says. The universe pinpricks a spotlight on Bridget. She is the one and the only.

Since our session in the kitchen yesterday, the truth has become clearer every second. The thought I try to push away is refusing to be put swept aside.

I don't know if she realized this the way I did, but that was the first time we just...fucked. Not in scene. Not after a scene.

Just us out in the world, two people with pent up desperation, tearing each other to ribbons of pleasure.

That could be our life. Out of the Underground. Out in the world.

I know a life isn't made up of only sexual encounters.

That's somewhere we can start, though, right?

Here is the truth: if I don't make her mine, I'm afraid I'll be lost.

I've made the past ten years of my life all Bridget, all the time. I've come so far. To lose her now would...it would just kill me. And I'm not sure that's an exaggeration.

"Where's Abs?" Jack calls out as Bridget gets closer.

Bridget takes a sip of her strawberry daquiri, no doubt extra strawberry included. She smiles at the taste, then offers Jack an answer. "I don't know. She had to go do something."

"That sounds suspicious..."

Bridget giggles.

Oh, that giggle. Want it to be my ring tone.

She shrugs. "You know how she is."

"I do. Sneaky," Jack replies.

She laughs again before her eyes snap to me for a mere moment before traveling away. "Anyway..."

"See anything you like?" Jack asks Bridget.

My body bristles, every nerve pricking, goosebumps spreading across my skin.

Bridget scans the bar, then shakes her head. "'Fraid not. Everyone's a little too Jimmy Buffet-coded for me."

I try not to breathe an audible, obvious sigh of relief.

Jack raises his glass. "Rest in peace."

Bridget raises her daquiri too, and they clink glasses.

I feel like an audience member to my own life.

In the Underground, I always know what to say. But out in the real world, Bridget leaves me tongue-tied. I guess I've never been a man of too many words. Lots of thoughts, lots of action, but words have never been my specialty.

Especially not when it comes to my stepfather's daughter.

Even worse now that she's my lover.

Some jaunty piano starts up, and a voice blares through the microphone. "Jackieeeeeee!"

All three of us turn to the karaoke stage.

Abigail is standing center stage, one microphone to her mouth, another in her hand. She's waving our hands in our direction.

"Oh *no*," Jack groans.

I'm getting secondhand embarrassment for him.

"Come sing with m–" The first lyric to *Thank You For Being a Friend*, the opening theme song to *The Golden Girls* starts, and she just goes for it.

"Big *Golden Girls* fan, Jack?"

Jack's head dips lower. "She's butchering it."

Bridget and I exchange a look and then both laugh.

"Hold my beer." He forces it into my hand before barging through the crowd to join Abigail and save her from her poor performance.

Bridget and I watch for a few moments, neither willing to speak or acknowledge that we're alone, even in this sea of people.

"You should sit," I say in a soft voice and place my hand on Jack's stool.

"Alright."

I hold her daquiri as she shimmies onto the stool, trying not to stare at the beautiful profile of her cleavage as she does so.

I've seen her naked more times than I can count now and yet eyeing her in public feels taboo. Like someone might see and point at me, announce to the world that I'm sexualizing someone who in the eyes of society is my stepsister.

Except I said fuck you to that identifier since the moment we met.

As soon as Bridget is on her stool...we are silent again. Watching as Jack and Abigail fight over who has the next line on stage.

I clear my throat. "You having a good night?"

"Yeah. Are you?"

I nod and tap my fingers against my beer bottle. "Yeah, I am."

Bridget scans the room. "See anyone you like?"

My insides balk. "Don't insult me like that."

Her green eyes widen. "I–I'm sorry."

I scan our surroundings.

No one seems concerned with the two New Yorkers on the corner.

So, I dare. In a delicate fashion, I place my fingertips against her knee, clock her expression to see if my touch is welcomed.

Bridget's back straightens. She's not good at the subtle card. But she isn't saying no.

I increase my touch.

My fingers, my palm, splayed out on her knee.

"You know I'm only looking at you." I rub my thumb across the fabric of her dress.

Her skin heats through the fabric.

"May I say something? I don't want to upset you by speaking out of turn."

"We're not in the Underground, Bridget. There are rules, but not like that."

"Sometimes, I don't know what's allowed or not and that..." She bites her lower lip.

Fuck. I might be a good Dom behind closed doors but out in the world, our relationship has always been too complicated for me to treat her like this is something easy. "I don't want you to be scared of me, Bridget. That's not the point of any of this."

Her eyes are downcast into the daquiri. "I want to please you."

"You do. All the time. You always have." I smile and lean closer. Perhaps too close for people who are supposed to be siblings, but fuck that.

Jack and Abigail are the only people who know us here, and they're in the midst of a rousing, off-tune chorus.

"I didn't know that until we started training, though," Bridget says.

My heart is starting to race. The edges of a rejection fray her voice. Or maybe I'm imagining it.

"I still am not used to you...liking me..." Her blush is apparent even in the darkened tiki bar.

I swallow. "I guess we haven't had a lot of opportunities for me to show you out in the world how I feel about you."

"No, we haven't," she says in her soft, Bridget way.

I nibble on my lower lip for a few moments. What to say? How to say it?

"I know you're my Dom. I know that complicates things. But sometimes, I remember how things used to be, and while it feels so far away from what we have now, it's confusing." She tries to keep a smile on her face.

I squeeze her knee. "I was a jackass."

"Seth." She giggles.

"No, really, I was." I lean closer.

She leans away. As she should. We're not alone after all.

"I was a fucking emotionless robot, and I didn't know how to be normal around you because I wasn't supposed to feel the things I was feeling. So, I decided to push you away."

"And yet, try and keep men from me," she adds.

I start to respond, to defend myself, but stop in my track.

I want to tell her I was trying to protect her, but that doesn't measure up. There aren't good excuses.

I wasn't kind. I've confused her for ten years. That's not something I can erase in the matter of a month. Especially not when behind closed doors, I'm the Dom I've always wanted to be for her.

Out in the world, there are still so many questions for

us. Ones I want to answer with my mouth and my hands and three words I've never said to any woman except my mother and certainly not in the way I'd like to.

I need to give her more than my dominance.

But I don't know if I'm anything more than that.

"Then let's be..." Lovers. Out in the open. For everyone to see. "Let's be friends. It's what my mom and Solomon have always wanted. Who cares if it's confusing to people? We can get to know each other in the light and in the dark."

Bridget's smile relaxes. "I'd like that."

It's a start. Not the what I want or need. But a start.

"I want to touch you so bad," I say in a low voice. "Want to stroke the backs of my fingers against your cheek and watch your eyes flutter shut."

Her head leans to the side almost like she's feeling the ghost of my hand.

"Want to kiss you," I mutter.

Bridget laughs, then pulls her knee out from under my hand, sipping her daquiri, which has become her nervous tick.

We're interrupted by cheering and clapping. Seems like Abigail and Jack's song has ended.

"Thank you! Thank you, you've been a great crowd," Abigail yells from the stage. She knows how to work a room even if her voice isn't up to snuff.

Jack is also eating up the applause from the crowd. He's blowing kisses across the room, one meant for Blonde Pixie cut who is only a short distance away from the stage with her friends.

She giggles.

Guess this trip isn't totally wasted.

Abigail's eyes search the room and land on me. "Your turn!"

"Oh, fuck no," I mutter.

"Please welcome to the stage, Seth and Bridget!" Abigail yells, then gestures to whoever is in charge of the karaoke to play the next song, her finger circling through the air.

Bridget and I look at each other, fear matching fear in our eyes.

I stand up, puff my chest, start to wave my hands. "No, we're not, we're–"

"Come on, get up there!" someone yelps and pushes on my shoulder.

"No, I can't sing, I really can't–" I begin but am drowned out by the opening notes of *Under Pressure* throbbing through the speakers.

Damn. That's a good song. I do know the words.

Before Bridget and I can get our footing, we're being borne through the crowd by encouraging words and hands until we're at the edge of the stage.

Abigail grins and holds her mic out to me. "I think you're the David Bowie."

"What's that supposed to–"

She shoves the mic toward my mouth. "Sing!"

I'm usually very in control of everything. It's why I'm a dominant. It's why my life has been all work and very limited play the past ten years.

Something about the power of Queen and Bowie combined, complemented by the tiki bar full of drunken vacationers, and the fact Bridget is beside me, grinning ear to ear as she accepts the mic from Jack hits me, and I start singing. Immediately. I can't explain it.

We both get on stage, lights blaring down on us.

There isn't a moment to collect or decide, we're already in the middle of the song, and we do it. We fucking do it.

We blow them out of the water because even though I say I can't sing, I can carry a tune, and Bridget has a voice like an angel.

I don't care if that's not objectively true, it's true to me.

We have fun, singing together, the world drifting away.

I want thousands of moments like this with her. A lifetime-worth of them.

Behind closed doors, in the Underground of my dreams, she will submit to me. Be my good girl, the one I always wanted.

And out in the world...

We can have *fun*. All the time. *Together*.

I realize as we sing and laugh and the crowd eggs us on that I truly haven't had fun in years.

Not until Bridget. Not until I let my heart go.

I'm totally lost for her.

21

BRIDGET

I step out of the shower and squeeze out my hair before looking at my form in the fogged-up mirror.

It's our last night in Key West. We're headed back tomorrow afternoon, and while I know Abigail wanted to go out *yet again*, the rest of us couldn't muster up the energy.

It's been one drunken day after another.

Tonight, we're keeping it low key which, in Seth's mind, means hiring a private chef for the evening and some help as well, so that we don't have to lift a finger.

While I've always known Seth is wealthy, he doesn't seem to flaunt it most of the time. Maybe he's working too much to have time to really enjoy it.

However, I got a taste of the private jet the other night, the luxuries of a black card, and tonight, a meal at home that's going to be more like a meal at a Michelin-star restaurant.

I guess that's the Carlton way. I don't mind that one bit.

Once I'm dried off, I head into my room to start beautifying for the evening.

Just because we're staying in doesn't mean I don't want

to look my best. For Seth. Always. As is my duty as his sub. To please him, always. Although the lines are getting muddier and muddier since our encounter in the kitchen, and then last night at the tiki bar.

Revelations. I'm not used to them. Things have been the same for so long.

Sure, I've pushed myself to be successful in my career, but I have been sweet Bridget Vance for many years.

To hear that Seth, the man I've wanted in secret for a decade, wants to make amends beyond our sexual dynamic is...hard to believe.

I toss my towel on the bed and grab my bottle of moisturizer but before I start to slather it on, something catches my eye.

A flat jewelry box on my pillow on top of a box that is bit bigger.

I go for the jewelry box first with trepidation, as if it might disappear if it sees I'm too eager. Once it's in my hands, my heart begins to pulse in my throat.

I think I know what this is. What this means.

I pop the box open.

My jaw falls at the sight of a necklace. Two hands pulling on two linked rings, a chain binding the rings. The metal cord the necklace is made of is short. The hands would probably rest against my throat.

My collar.

It's not time. Not our agreed upon closing date.

Seth explained there would be a ceremony where I would graduate from the training collar to my permanent one that I could wear out in public if we wanted to continue after my training was over. If we became a committed pairing as Dom and sub.

In the community, these ceremonies are often public.

But *we* don't have a community where anyone knows about us, so we were planning to do it in private.

Could this be it? My forever collar? Or is this just another placeholder?

Has he decided the time is now?

My cheeks fill with warmth. My core pulses.

I wish he was here now, putting it on me.

There is a note nestled in the lid.

I take it, unfold it carefully.

It's Seth's writing.

I smile.

You're my good girl. The best girl. You deserve this. Please wear both items to dinner tonight.

Both items? There's only one in the jewelry box.

That's when I remember the other box.

Is it lingerie? A dress? What could it be?

I set the jewelry box aside and grab the other one.

I lift the lid and have to blink my eyes clear to make sense of what's inside.

It's a purple wand item. Phallic looking. Except not like a dildo that is all one shape.

Whatever this is, it has three wide points.

My jaw drops when I realize what it is.

It's a toy...for my ass.

Could this be the last part of my training? Is he trying to tell me something or just start the ball rolling for when we are back at the Underground?

I stare at the toy and sit on the edge of the bed.

Well, it's way smaller than Seth's dick. But I never had anything up there. Can I even handle it?

Is he expecting me to wear this for dinner? While we are with Jack and Abigail?

What if I can't? I will fail him.

And oh, my god. What if I can? Will they be able to tell?

It will probably be written all over my face. I can't do this!

But I have to.

This is Seth.

I look at it again trying to understand it better and maybe looking to see if I'm wrong. Because I have to be, right?

There are two buttons on the toy. One makes a small light flicker. The other makes it vibrate. Am I just supposed to let it vibrate in me all night?

I grab the note once more, read it over.

I missed a line.

Remember. I'm in control.

I look between the note and the toy as my throat threatens to close around the giant knot forming there.

This cannot mean what I think it means, can it?

SITTING IS NOT THE MOST COMFORTABLE THING WITH the toy in my ass. Not to mention I'm on edge because we've already made it through the first two courses of dinner, and Seth hasn't done anything. Not one vibration. Not one pulse.

I'm grateful he hasn't because I'm not sure I'd be able to hide what is happening. But I know it is coming, and I have no idea what to expect.

It is hard enough having to wear it. And it was awkward having to put it in myself, the stretch was difficult at first.

Not that it is easy now. It isn't. It is a foreign object stuck where nothing should ever be stuck.

It's shameful, it's torturous, and weirdly enough, it is confusing, because wires are being crossed inside me making me feel like this is sort of pleasurable too.

I have no idea what to do or how to even deal with how I'm feeling.

Seth and I are across from one another at the long table. Abigail and Jack face each other.

I know he's been purposeful about keeping our distance. I know he wants to watch. Any other time or if we were alone, I'd love to give him a show, but here? Now? With our friends watching? I can't.

"When did you get that necklace, Bridget?" Abigail asks after we're served dish number three.

A salad which is three leaves of some overly expensive green leaf topped with a delicious smelling sauce and some multi-colored tomatoes and fresh mozzarella that apparently arrived from Italy today.

I place my fingers against it. "You like it?"

"Love it. It's very..." She furrows her brow. "I don't know, it's unique."

Seth's blue eyes are like lasers on me. They burn.

I *love* that feeling. That with only a look, he can consume me in such a complete way.

"I..." I rub my finger up and down the chain. I won't lie, but I won't disclose the whole truth either. "It was a gift."

Abigail frowns, which is miraculous considering yesterday she was so burnt she said it hurt to move her face. "Oh? Who gave it to you?"

Though I have no idea what to say, I open my mouth to respond but am cut off when the toy comes to life inside me.

I gasp and push my chin to my chest.

"You good?" Jack asks.

Oh god. No. I mean. Yes, but not in a way I can say.

The toy is rotating inside me, a feeling so foreign, yet not unpleasant. Actually, it's kind of good.

It's taken my breath away as it rolls and massages parts of myself I've never had even considered in a sexual way. And though it's an alien feeling, it's almost familiar, like if I was touching my clit, except it's...my ass.

"Yeah, I'm fine." I manage a flash of a smile. "I was just thinking I might want to keep a few of my secrets, that's all."

My eyes land on Seth.

He looks, as usual, nonplussed. Except I know him better now, so I notice the micromovement in his bicep.

Abigail scoffs. "You? Secrets?"

"Why is that so hard to believe?"

Seth punctuates the way I say hard by increasing the vibration the tiniest bit.

"You're just not the type." She takes a sip of her fancy, purple cocktail.

I'm tensing inside, trying not to clench my teeth as the plug tortures me so good. Trying to go for nonchalant, I shrug one shoulder. "Maybe I'm growing up. Turning over a new leaf."

Another notch of vibration. The toy rotates the other way, refreshing the feeling of newness. I hate that I have to pretend that nothing is happening when I'm so close to losing control. But I'm starting to love how it stretches me. How it presses up against one particular spot that has my insides singing. Even as my mind still rebels against the fact that this is so unnatural.

"So, you're telling me you have a secret admirer? Someone you don't want me to know about? Wow...so secretive." Abigail narrows her eyes at me.

I tuck my thumb under the hands at my neck. "Not secretive. Just... appreciative, Abigail."

Seth ramps up the intensity for a few seconds.

I dig my fingers into my thighs, roll my lips together, and ride out the burst of pleasure until it settles to an idling roll and ache.

I make it through the salad course, onto the fourth course, the fifth.

Throughout, the vibration goes on and off at uneven intervals. It is on long enough to drive me crazy, but not long enough for me to actually come. It is almost annoying.

I am so worked up. I just need to come already.

I shift in place, trying to move my hips back and forth as if I can somehow relieve the tension or give myself the final push to finally explode.

The trick about anal stimulation, I'm learning, is that it alights *everything* down there. My pussy is swollen and dripping, my clit is begging to be touched.

I haven't masturbated since Seth demanded all my orgasms. I have been such a good girl.

If I come, is this *his* orgasm? He is in control still, after all.

I have so many questions I'd like to ask. But then again if I get it wrong, that will mean a punishment.

And while I'm not a brat, I have to say, I have enjoyed a couple of his spankings here and there.

After the main course, Seth turns it back on and ramps up the intensity.

I'm sweating, and not just from the warm Florida night. I focus on the sounds of the waves in the distance, the cool breeze tickling my skin, and the color of the melting sky.

They are pitiful distractions from the fireworks threatening to go off inside me.

It's so funny that anal has ever scared me…And remembering how big Seth is, it still scares me.

But if this is the kind of pleasure it can elicit, boy oh boy, I'm going to be begging for it.

Can only imagine what it would feel like with Seth's hot cock inside me–

Seth demands my attention. "Bridget."

I snap my eyes to him. "Yes?"

"You're somewhere else."

I try to steady myself, but the toy is revving harder inside me. "Am I...?"

"Your eyes *are* kind of glassy..." Abigail says.

Of course they are. I've been close to coming so many times.

"I thought those oysters tasted weird." Jack places a hand to his stomach.

Seth scoffs. "The oysters are fine. I think her mind is somewhere else."

Abigail says something to Seth. Something admonishing. But I can't hear it because he cranks up the intensity.

All I hear is blood rushing in my ears as the toy roves in a circle around and around, skimming up against that delicious pressure point.

I bite down on my lower lip, furrow my brow, concentrating all too hard on not coming. Or coming. I'm not even sure which I'm going for anymore.

"Jesus, something's wrong," Jack says.

That's when Seth pushes me all the way over the edge.

The toy must be working as hard as it can, rumbling and rolling.

I snap.

My insides explode with a torrent of pleasure. It is almost like someone has been playing with me clit, except this comes from deeper inside and *holy fuck I don't know what to do.*

I squeak, pressing my chin to my chest, feel my new collar dig into my skin which makes the pleasure double.

I'm his.

I'm his, I'm his.

There's a hand on my shoulder.

Abigail.

"Oh my god, Bridget, are you okay?"

Seth pulls back on the intensity of the vibrator, thank god, which gives me a moment to recalibrate myself.

I need to go somewhere private. Breathe. Splash cold water on my face.

I can't take a second longer of this torture. I need to go. Now.

I push myself away from the table. "Sorry. I..."

Jack and Abigail look horrified.

Seth gloats from the end of the table, a smirk on his lips and a darkness in his eyes.

I touch my forehead. "Migraine. Suddenly. I need to go take something."

"You sit, Jack will get it for you," Abigail offers.

Jack doesn't hesitate and starts to rise from his chair.

"No!" I shoot up to standing and wave my hands. "I got it. You don't know where anything is in my room and–"

Their faces are all blurring through my tears of pleasure welling in my eyes.

Need to get out of here.

Need to be alone.

I turn on my heel and rush back inside, weaving around the two servers who are coming to collect dishes.

They both nearly drop their trays.

I mutter a quick apology, not bothering to look back as I head upstairs to my room.

Once in my private sanctum, I can't think. I can hardly breathe.

I need to take this out of me. Now. I can't...

I reach under my dress, grab hold of the toy, and ease it out of me.

I have to keep my breath measured. Everything is swollen and tight down there.

I drop the released toy on the bed and let out a heavy sigh.

Seth's voice swoons from the doorway. "Did I tell you to take that out?"

I start to turn. "Seth–"

"Hands on the bed."

My body feels lighter all of a sudden.

"You know what happens when you break my rules, pet."

Warmth pricks my cheeks.

"Yes, Sir."

Seth comes up behind me, touches my shoulders. His fingers skim down my arms.

Every hair on my body stands on end.

"You liked that, pet?"

I smile, let my eyes flutter shut. "Yes, Sir."

"I reward you with your collar," Seth begins, snaring the metal chain between his fingers. "And this is how you repay me? By disobeying me? Disrespecting me?"

"I'm sorry, Sir."

His fingers tighten. The metal digs into my skin. Then, he releases it.

Silence fills the room as he drags the skirt of my dress up until my ass is bare to him. He pinches a handful of my backside in his hand before withdrawing his hand and letting it crack against my skin.

My body balks forward.

I take in a sharp breath.

"I gave you two gifts tonight, and you repay me by giving up?"

"No, Sir. I'm sorry. I didn't mean to—"

He slaps my ass again. "Say it. Say you gave up."

I tilt my head back, open my mouth, almost like I'm praying at an altar. "I-I'm sorry, Sir, I gave up."

In a way, accepting my punishments, my delicious, stinging spanks, is praying. I am praying at the temple of Seth. My Dom. The man I...

The man I love. Because it is true. I do love him.

But that feels silly when I still have so much to learn about him. And there is no way this could ever lead to anything other than what we are right now.

He doles out my punishment. It is not too much, nor too little. Just enough to get my clit buzzing.

And remind me how good it felt to have that toy...

Seth touches the rawness of my ass. I bite the inside of my mouth. Feels like rugburn.

"Let me get you some cream..."

"I'm fine. I don't need it," I say in a hurry, then add a quick, "Sir."

A moment passes.

Seth wraps his hands around the fronts of my thighs and presses me to his front. He tucks his mouth against my ear. A kiss to the lobe. A nuzzle of his nose.

So soft on me.

His scent is intoxicating. Fresh, clean. Musk.

I tilt my face closer to his.

His stubble rubs up against my cheek. More intoxicating burn.

"I just want you to be good, Bridget. You understand,

right?"

"Yes, Sir, I understand. I promise I'll try to do better next time."

He places his hand to my collarbone, tips of his fingers skimming the collar. "You like it?" There is a genuine concern in his voice. A quiet hope.

I turn in his arms, tuck my hands against his chest and dare to look in his eyes.

How normal a moment like this feels. Like we're two people getting ready before a party. A couple. And I'm supposed to smooth out the wrinkles of his army green linen shirt. Give him a final smile to remind him that no matter what happens tonight, I'll be here when it comes to an end.

"Love it, Seth."

The corners of his eyes are crimped with an emotion I can't identify. Like there's something he'd like to say.

Though it's a risk, I lean in and press a kiss to his cheek. I whisper, "Thank you, Sir," with as much meaning as I can. I want him to hear all the things I'm thinking with just that kiss.

That my training has meant the world to me. That I feel complete by knowing what kind of sub I am now. That I'm so, so happy *he* is my Dom.

"Come." He steps back from me. "Downstairs. Play your part."

He walks out of the room first. And before I follow, I clutch the collar to my throat.

We chose each other.

What happens next, though, has yet to be decided or discussed.

And though I do everything in my power to understand his mind, stoic Seth is going to need to give me something to work with.

22

SETH

The sun set a while ago. Jack, Abigail, and I are out on the beach surrounding a dying fire.

Bridget retired an hour ago. She was spent.

Jack and Abigail think it's because of her migraine, but I know the truth.

I brought her pleasure she'd never dreamed of. I'm smug over that, I'll admit it.

"I could sleep out here." Abigail leans back in her chair, pulling her sweater tight around her.

"You'd freeze to death," Jack says.

She scoffs. "It's not the desert. I just need a few blankets. That's all."

Jack rolls his eyes. "Okay, here we go."

He goes to Abigail and hauls her out of the chair and over his shoulder, not paying any mind to her playful kicking and screaming.

"Let me go, let me go!"

"Nope, you're going up to bed. Now. None of this sleepin' on the beach talk."

"I am one with naturrrreee." Abigail's red hair swings as she hangs over her brother's shoulder.

Jack chuckles. "You good out here, Seth?"

"Yeah. I'm good."

"Say goodnight." Jack heaves Abigail further onto his shoulder.

Abigail lifts her head. Eyes mere slits. "Goodnight."

I watch as Jack carries her down the boardwalk and into the house.

Then, I look through the dying fire back at the ocean.

The godforsaken ocean.

It's no wonder I crossed the boundary Bridget and I discussed as soon as I did. The second I set eyes on the beautiful terror of the ocean, I needed something to ground me.

Not *something*.

I needed *her*.

Needed something to tether me to this moment and time, not send me back all those years ago. Over a decade.

It's been over a decade since I lost my dad.

Nearly fifteen years, actually.

And being down here, I am reminded of him at every turn. The cabinet of fishing gear that hasn't been used all this time, his favorite anchor-printed napkins.

The ocean.

I thought I had gotten good at dealing with the grief, but being here has made me realize I never really *dealt* with the grief. I just put duct tape over its mouth and told it to shut the fuck up.

I never anticipated it would wriggle free of its binding and start yelling all the things I've needed to deal with since losing him.

I should have known that coming back here would dredge up all these feelings. But I thought maybe by being here with Bridget, I could rewrite the memories of the last time I was in Key West. Rewrite what this place means to me.

However, I haven't been here *with* Bridget. Bridget is mine, yes. But if no one knows except me and her, is it even real?

I drop my head, clasp my hands together, and try to breathe.

We missed so much of life together, my dad and me. Missed out on making so many memories. Never saw the success of my company, will never see me fall in love, or have kids, or anything like that. And if I keep up my life of secrets, no one will ever know anything. No one will ever see how happy I am. Because for the first time in so long, I'm happy.

With Bridget in my life this way, I'm so goddamn happy.

And I'm tired of keeping secrets.

I'm not sure how long I sit outside listening to the surf cascading across the shore. Long enough to get my wits about me. Long enough to know what I have to do.

I LET MYSELF INTO BRIDGET'S ROOM. SHE IS MY SUB, but over the time we have spent together, she also became more. And I need her now.

Thankfully, she is awake, and I don't scare her. She's ready for bed, tucked under the covers, an e-reader in her hand.

"Seth..." she says in a soft voice upon my arrival.

Her collar is around her neck.

My insides warm to know she hasn't taken it off.

I shut the door behind me. Tight. Lock it.

Bridget lifts herself onto her elbows.

Her thin nightgown hugs her breast so tight I can see her nipples pricking through the fabric.

"Do you need something?"

I came here to talk. Didn't come here to dominate or to have her. I came here to *tell her*. Tell her what I need from her. Although this need is not related to our training. This need is so much more than that.

"Are you okay?" Her dark brows furrow.

I can't do it. Can't say it. I don't know how to use my words, only know how to use my body to communicate with her.

She was right at the bar the other night. We don't know each other. Not really. But if that's true, how come I feel closer to her than anyone else in the world?

I don't answer her question. Instead, I go to the bed and grab the edge of the covers.

Bridget's eyes dip down to my hand, then rise to look at me. Breath shallow in her chest. She can tell what's coming.

I rip the covers back, exposing her whole body to me. Her beautiful, luscious body.

Her skin looks luminescent against her lace-trimmed, black nightgown.

And her curves laid out on the bed before me swoop and swerve in such a tempting way.

There is no way I'll be able to resist her.

Maybe she will understand me without my words. A foolish thought. But...

"On your stomach." My throat is constricting my words because it knows that's not what I came here to say. What I wanted. What I *needed*.

It doesn't feel safe to do anything else, though.

Bridget follows my instruction.

Her dark hair drapes across her back.

"Ass up." I pull a tiny tube of lube from my sweatpants pockets.

She pushes her ass toward her heels, the thin fabric taut against her backside.

"Show it to me," I say.

As she pulls the nightgown over her ass, I realize she isn't wearing underwear. Her ass cheeks spread apart to reveal her glistening pussy and the puckering hole I pleasured earlier today from across the table.

I touch her ass cheek. "You know what I want, right?" Not what I need. But it might be enough to ground me.

"Yes, Sir."

Sir...I love it, but this time it falls flat.

I want to be Seth to her today. I don't know how to say that to her, so I keep my mouth shut, and squeeze a squirt of lube into my palm.

I coat her hole and surrounding areas liberally to make sure there's no threat of injury.

I coat my fingers too and begin to glide them across her opening until she relaxes enough for me to slide them inside.

Bridget's body tightens.

"Relax around me..."

The way she clenches on my fingers is enough to get my cock hard to a raging degree. I'm already imagining how it would feel to be inside her tightness.

"Touch yourself," I say with a ragged breath.

Bridget reaches a hand under herself to start toying with her clit. Relaxes her even more.

We go on like this for a bit as I scissor my fingers inside her to prepare her for my girth until Bridget starts to moan.

I withdraw my fingers. "Don't stop...touching yourself." I hurry to yank my sweats down my thighs.

Bridget doesn't, begins rocking into her hand, moaning.

Fuck, I need her, I need her so bad.

I grab my cock, stroke it with a squirt of lube to make sure I'm as slippery as I can be.

I kneel on the edge of the bed, press the head to her last virgin hole.

I pop in more easily than I expect. The toy and my fingers must have loosened her enough.

Her head flicks back, dark hair flying. "Oh, fuck."

"Easy..." I press a hand to her upper back. Not harsh, but insistent. "I'll go slow."

The tightness is incredible, the way my cock squeezes into her.

And though the pleasure is sublime, it meets a different feeling in my stomach.

Betrayal. Of myself.

I didn't come here to fuck her. At least not first. I came here to tell her what I feel. What I need her to know.

I'm a coward. I can posture and dominate her all I want.

But when the rubber hits the road. I'm a fucking coward.

"Please, more, Sir."

I snap back into reality.

Have to maintain composure. Have to hold on.

I inch further in, thrusting slow and shallow inside her, letting her body guide me in deeper when it's ready.

"Oh fuck, yes," she groans, pressing her face into the bed, her muscles relaxing.

Bridget's making sounds I've never heard before.

Bringing her pleasure means the world to me. So, I keep going. Try to lose myself in controlling her. In claiming her.

However, it becomes clear with every building block of pleasure inside me that I'm not losing myself in the control.

I'm losing *control*.

Not of my body, god no. It would never be that bad. I'm good with the control of my body.

No, it's the emotions and thoughts fluttering through my brain. Confusing me. sending tears pricking into my eyes. My head is starting to hurt with the loud cries of the past. The empty and brittle vacuum of my future.

If I continue to hold everything in, I'll never get anywhere in life. Who cares about the money and the power without anything to show for it? Without any world to go home to.

"Yes, Sir. Thank you, Sir," Bridget moans.

I'm not saying anything, not giving her anywhere to pour her affection for me.

I keep trying to form words, but nothing comes out. I just...fuck her.

She feels amazing. And yet, I feel nothing. So lost in my own head that the euphoria inside me pales in comparison to the chaos of my mind.

Bridget begins to thrust her hips back to meet mine, taking me as deep as I'll go. "Yes, yes, yes, please, Sir. Please make me come, Sir."

I place my hands on her shoulders to press my cock as deep as I'll go over and over until she cries out, a sound unlike anything that has ever come out of her mouth.

Her body trembles and quakes so much it's impossible for me not to come too.

Except I'm so numb I don't even feel like I've come. I

know I've released into her, know that I've given her all of me.

And yet...

My head falls forward. And I break.

Or... I don't break.

Breaking is dangerous. I need to be in control.

She is my sub. She depends on me to be in control and know what's best for her. For both of us.

I don't know if I've ever known what's good for me, though.

Despite trying to suppress it, I let out a sob and a few tears fall from my eyes.

I try to catch them, but they land against Bridget's back.

I retreat from her body as fast as I can without hurting her. I pull my sweatpants back on, hiding my face in my hand as I take a step toward the door.

"Seth, oh my god, did I hurt you?"

"No, I have to–I have to go, this is–"

Bridget's hand lands against my waist.

I have no power against her.

I let her hand guide me back to the bed.

The backs of my knees hit the edge of the mattress. I sit down. Collapse more like it.

I have no strength to make any other choice. A torrent of weeping thrums from me. I press my face into my hands and cry.

What Bridget doesn't know as she cradles me, leans herself against my back, is that her closeness is making me cry even harder.

I cry for so many things. For my father, for the person I was before he died and the person I was for the past ten years, intimidating Bridget, making her think I hated her.

I weep for everything I want and don't know how to ask for.

All the while, Bridget remains beside me. Unafraid that her Dom has lost control.

Her arms and legs loop around me. She presses her lips to the side of my head. "It's okay. It's all okay. I'm here, Seth."

And the second my name leaves her mouth, I lift my head and let it fall against her shoulder. My heart has been expanding all this time, and I am just now feeling how big it's gotten in my chest.

I've tried to fill up the hole my father left inside me with concrete. It has weighed me down, kept me from letting anyone in.

All it has taken is a single chink to ruin the infrastructure I laid down as an act of desperation.

Bridget has broken me open.

And I can no longer pretend.

I want her in every way a man can want a woman. Everything be damned.

23

———————

BRIDGET

It might sound silly, but I never knew Seth was even capable of weeping. Didn't know he even felt this much.

But of course, he does. He's human.

I've never thought of Seth as human. The way he kept me at arm's length, then became the measured, precise Dom I've always wanted.

As he weeps in my arms, I feel like weeping too.

For one, I've realized I care for him in such a way that his emotions are becoming my emotions. My insides mirror his pain. And for another, I know this must be coming from somewhere so deep and painful that Seth doesn't even know what to do with himself. I hope he doesn't turn away from me.

The only thing I can control is not turning away from him.

So, I let him sob his eyes out for lord knows how long. I hold him.

And he doesn't push away.

I bestow soft kisses to his shoulders and neck, say his

name in a low and soft way to remind him I am here. And I will not be going anywhere unless he physically pushes me away.

He never does.

When Seth's tears begin to abate and his breath steadies, he turns his head just slight enough to look at me. Not eye contact. No, too embarrassed for that, maybe.

"I'm sorry," he says.

I squeeze his biceps. "What? Don't be sorry."

"I lost control, I wasn't supposed to–"

"Seth, I won't let you apologize for feeling." I tuck my chin on his shoulder and tighten my arms around his chest.

He tucks his fingers on my wrists. Thumb strokes the back of my arm. "Thank you," he whispers.

I have learned from the best what good aftercare looks like. And I am more than happy to give it in return. "Lay down with me."

"Bridget, I should–"

I have learned when I can press back on my Dom. When to cross the line. And I won't allow him to walk away from me now. "Please lay down with me," I repeat in a voice that I would give to no one else.

Seth does not refuse. He allows me to pull him down into the pillows, allows me to pull the covers up over our shoulders.

We face each other now but our bodies don't dare touch.

I'm able to get a good look at him in the warm lamplight and...

Oh, my poor baby.

His face is sticky with tears, face blotched with red, eyes catatonic from how hard he was crying.

I'd hazard a guess that it's been a long, long time since he's cried.

Years, maybe.

I grab his hands and pull them to my mouth, kiss his knuckles.

Again, he doesn't pull away.

I will do everything he has ever done for me. Even if he doesn't tell me what's going on. I will be his comfort, his care.

I feel too deeply for him to pretend like his pain is not my own.

I won't go as far to tell him I love him because...

That's too scary. Too much.

However, my heart screams at me just go for it. To use the words appropriate to the situation. My brain says, "Hush, not yet."

Seth opens his mouth so slowly that I can see each minute movement.

I wait. Do not press. Do not look with expectation.

"My dad..." he says, his voice pained and strangled. "He died here."

My eyes widen, brows jumping. "Oh my god."

"Not in the house," he amends. His eyes flutter shut. He swallows. "On the ocean."

Dad never told me about how Seth's father passed away. I just knew it was an accident. And of course, I've never asked Amelia about it. I haven't wanted to spoil her happiness.

I've never wanted to spoil anything. Which makes lying here with Seth...

"We were fishing. We did that a lot down here. We were way out on the ocean. Storm rolled in. Sudden. That's how it is in Florida." He squints his eyes. They are fixed on our clasped hands.

He worries his lips together for a few moments. "The waves became huge. Dad did all he could but eventually, the boat capsized."

My organs start twisting in knots. I think I know where this is heading.

"We started trying to swim. Dad started losing strength, I pulled him along with me as long as I–" His voice breaks, and he presses his chin to his chest, another sob escapes.

I release Seth's hands and pull my body to his, sliding my fingers through his hair.

I need to be close. Need to let him know I am receiving each and every word. I won't look away.

"He told me to let him go."

Tears threaten my eyes. I push them back. I won't upend his moment with my own sadness.

"I didn't want to," Seth cries. "But if I was going to survive, I–"

"He knew that, Seth. He was trying to save you."

Seth's lips contort. A combination of distress and anger. "I should've been able to save him too, I should've..."

"He wanted you to live, Seth." I'm not sure the words are even coming out of my mouth.

I'm discussing his father's death with him, something I never thought would happen. And I never in a million years would have anticipated how truly horrible his death was.

Seth's lower lip trembles. "But I wanted my dad," he says. "I *want* my dad."

For all his strength and posturing, Seth still has his inner child trembling inside him in need of love and attention. Just like anyone else.

I've never gotten a chance to glimpse it. And now that I see it, my heart is screaming at me louder to love this man.

I cradle Seth's head to my shoulder. His arms slide around me, clinging to me. "I'm so sorry, Seth. I am so sorry you had to go through that."

He buries his face into my neck, tries to catch his breath. His tears tickle my skin. "I thought coming here..." he says between heavy breaths. "I thought coming here with you would help me move on, but I can't."

I try not to freeze up.

What does getting over his dad's death have to do with me?

Still, I press on. "You'll never get over it, Seth. He's your dad. And you loved him. You'll always miss him. I mean...I lost my mom so long ago I barely remember her." I look at pictures. I have videos. Recordings. Her writing. Things she left for me so I'd remember her, cards she wrote for all important moments of my life. She spent the last months of her life as breast cancer destroyed her writing to the woman she hoped her three-year-old would become.

I miss her. It hurts.

But I've never questioned the grief I have for a life without my mother.

Seth has pushed it all down for too long. Now his grief is looking for reparations.

He swallows thickly and retreats again so that he can look in my eyes. "That's why I'm like this, Bridget. Why I don't like to lose control."

"I understand."

"BDSM, it gives me the power over my life I didn't, well, I guess never had."

I nod. Submission gives me the freedom I don't feel I

have in my day-to-day life. "You're answering a part of yourself."

The corners of his lips creep up. Thank god, a little smile. "Yes, that's exactly it."

"I love that smile." I touch my thumb to his lower lip.

His face is still blotched with tears, but if it wasn't so red, he'd probably be blushing.

He kisses the pad of my thumb. "You've turned everything upside down."

"Oh?"

Seth's eyes drop to my collar. He skims it with the tips of his fingers. "What I thought I wanted and what I need are more different than I ever expected, Bridget."

I hold my breath.

"Do you...do you know what I mean?" He seems unsure.

Seth is never unsure.

I open my mouth to respond but shake my head instead.

Seth wraps his hands around the side of my head, pulls my face closer to his so we are only an inch or so apart.

He could kiss me. But instead, his breath caresses my lips. Then his words. "My feelings. I can't control them."

Oh no.

"I don't just want your submission. Not just your body. Bridget..." Seth tips his forehead against mine. "I want all of you."

I'm not sure how long the silence lasts.

I want to respond in kind because I know my feelings are the same as his. I want more. Want everything.

But for all intents and purposes, Seth Carlton is my stepbrother. Perhaps he's forgotten it amidst all the fucking and the punishments and avoiding eye contact. Perhaps everything has gotten too messy, misconstrued, and–

"I want to be with you, Bridget."

My body reflexes away from his touch, I roll away from him, leap off the bed, and back away until I'm pressed up against the window. "Seth, you know we can't do that."

Seth moves languidly, his hand sliding across the bed to the spot I once was. His expression is calm, lips turned into a smile like I'm a child who needs to be convinced to jump off the high diving board.

"I know it will be complicated. But it can't be more complicated than punishing ourselves for feeling this way."

I stare at him. My forehead hurts from how it's wrinkled.

"Unless..." His smile fades. "Unless you don't feel the same."

"I–I feel–" I can't confirm. That will make it harder when I let him down, won't it? "It would be selfish of us."

Seth sits up. "Selfish?" he echoes with an angry tone. "How would it be *selfish*?"

"My dad and your mom both deserve what they have, you know?"

"Of course, they do. But what does that have to do with us deciding to–"

"They deserve their happy family."

Seth licks his lower lip. "I agree."

"And if we–" I wave a hand between us. "If we ruined that, it would be selfish. We'd spoil everything."

"And what we've done so far hasn't?" The coldness is creeping back into his voice.

I've been familiar with his stoic self for so many years, been party to the way he can stare right through somebody. I don't want our lives to go back to the way they were.

But we can't have our cake and eat it too, can we?

I'm asking.

Can we?

"You think having me as a Dom in secret somehow exempts you from betraying this 'happy family' dynamic you're talking about?" Seth presses further.

I chew on the inside of my cheek.

"God." Seth throws off the covers and climbs out of the bed. "You're so fucking naïve, Bridget."

I grip my hands into fists. "Don't be *mean* to me."

Seth stops. Takes a measured breath. "Fine. You're right. I'm sorry."

I lean on the window frame.

Outside is the ocean, the devil of an ocean, the one that swallowed Seth's father whole. If it hadn't, Seth and I probably never would have met. And maybe that would have been for the best.

Or maybe our paths would have crossed and...it wouldn't be complicated. We could have each other.

It's useless thinking in what ifs.

"Does it matter to you? How I feel about you?" Seth says in a defeated tone.

I wait too long to respond. I know I do. But I don't know what to say.

Then I whisper, "Can't we just...can you give me some time? We can keep things how they've been, and I can think about it. Get used to the idea."

Seth looks away, tucks his tongue against his cheek. And when his eyes return to me–*oh god*–It's exactly how it used to be. Cold. Dark. Threatening to turn me to ice.

"I don't have any more time to give, Bridget."

My heart cracks. "Seth, please, just because I'm not saying yes doesn't mean I'm not–"

I grab my chest. I'm throbbing for him. I have never felt full before him. I need him. He's a part of me.

My hand slides up to my collar. "I'm yours, Seth. This doesn't change that I'm yours."

He shakes his head softly. "No, you're right. That doesn't change."

Without another word, he leaves my room and leaves a haze of confusion in his wake.

I slide down to the floor and sit there for a long time.

I do not release my collar. The collar I earned by being his. The one I just fucking earned *today* for being a good sub, for giving into all his desires.

Except the one that actually meant something.

I blink. Tears run down my face.

God. I wish I could have said yes. So bad. But I can't.

I can't hurt my dad.

He can't know that I'm not his good little girl. He doesn't deserve that.

And neither does Amelia.

They've wanted us to get along for years. Not *fuck* each other.

Not fall in love.

Seth is right. I ruined everything.

24

SETH

I busy myself on the return trip with work. Lots of work. Headphones in, eyes glued to my computer screen work. I ignore Bridget to the best of my ability, so much so that Abigail pinches me at one point and tells me I'm being as asshole.

Yes. She's correct. I'm an asshole.

Back in New York, I throw myself into my work even deeper. Long nights at the office, not a single visit to the club. Just work, eat, and sleep.

Well, not eat. Not really. My grief has taken up residency in both my chest and my stomach, making it impossible for me to eat more than a few bites of anything.

I do have plenty of room for alcohol, though. It is not a good habit to get into, drinking every night. Drinking sometimes as early as noon too.

I just want to forget. Want to forget I felt a fucking thing *ever*.

Bridget has every right to the way she feels, but I'll be damned if I don't hold her accountable for ripping my heart into a million pieces and throwing them around like confetti.

Every phone call from a number I don't recognize I pray will be her on the end of the line, saying in her sweet voice, "Seth? Can we talk?"

It never is. Of course, it isn't.

I have half a mind to pull a Nate.

Years ago now, Nate up and left New York after a falling out with Edwin, abandoned us all for LA.

In the nighttime hours, when heartbreak has been keeping me awake, I daydream of where I could go to escape it all.

Every time I settle on a location, though, Bridget shows up in my fantasy.

In Barcelona, she poses on the steps of the Sagrada Familia. In Cambodia, she walks the halls of Angkor Wat. Even when I give up on beautiful locations, I still see her on the streets of Topeka, Kansas.

She is in every corner of my mind. Which means I will never be able to escape her.

Bridget will follow me everywhere. Unless I get over her.

But I can't just get over her. Not after all of these years carrying a torch for her in pained silence. And not when she's still my sub.

God, I hope she's still wearing her collar for me.

On top of all of this, the ghost of my father has been following me. I have been having scores of memories of him. Ones that haven't crossed my mind in years.

I want to talk to my mom about him, but I'm afraid it will hurt her. She was devastated after the accident. As was I. And though she's never blamed me, not outwardly or even implicitly, I can't help but feel there's a part of her that wonders what actually happened out there.

Or even wishes it was me who didn't make it instead of him.

So, I bury myself in codes and algorithms, fixing problems and trying to get myself out of every meeting I possibly can.

I'm distracted only when my phone starts buzzing repeatedly.

Jack: *Hey man. We're going out tonight.*

Jack: *Hate to say it but Abigail was right. Think it's time I put myself out there.*

Jack: *Wanna come?*

I drop my phone and rub my hands over my face.

Fuck.

I start to type out my response. A short, "No, but thank you."

But Jack beats me to the punch.

Jack: *Don't be a hermit, dude.*

Well, fuck it. Fine.

I'll tell Bridget. I'll cut things off. And then tonight, I'll be available to whomever crosses my path. And if I can't pick someone up at the club, I'll go find a sub in the Underground. That's the way to get over somebody. Get under someone else, right? Or in my case, very much on top of.

Except the mere thought of having a sub other than Bridget sends a wave of nausea through me.

How will I possibly move on? How could I even suggest that to myself?

I text him back quickly.

I'll wing for you, dude.

Hopefully, a night out might get my mind off things. At

least I won't be drinking alone. Don't have to make any moves on anyone. Even if I wanted to, I don't think I could.

The second I press send, another text rolls in. Except, it's in a different thread.

I back out into my list of contacts and feel the nausea return. A good nausea, though.

Because Bridget just texted me.

I open up the thread with the utmost caution, afraid I might tap on something I don't mean to and screw everything up. Need to treat this situation with the utmost care.

Hope you're having a good week. <3 I Just wanted to say...I'm still here for you. I know it's not the way you want, but I don't want things to end just because we can't–

I don't even finish reading the message. I take the phone and whip it across the room before dropping my head onto my desk.

I don't need more excuses from her.

Why doesn't she understand if I can't have her in the deepest way a man can, I can't be around her? It will be too hard, too painful to know that I am not worth the leap.

I understand she's scared. I'm scared too. But doesn't the possibility of what lies on the other side of the fear intrigue her enough to at least *try?*

I love her.

Why didn't I say *that?*

Before I understand what's happening, I rise to my feet, grab my jacket, and walk out of my office.

My brain doesn't know where I'm going. But my body does. And when my brain links up with my body, I realize what's happening.

I'm going to my mother's house.

I'm going to tell her.

And that way, Bridget won't have to worry.

I'll take the heat. I'll bear the burden.

And then I can love her out loud.

My mother pours hot water into my cup.

I watch the tea bag erupt with redness through the water.

Who knew raspberry tea could look so violent?

"I'm so glad you stopped by today, honey." She sits in the chair next to me at the kitchen table. She touches my wrist in such a tender way it makes me want to cry. "I haven't seen you since your trip. I want to hear all about it."

I take the string of my tea bag and bob it up and down, dispersing the redness more and more until the tea is all a beautiful ruby color. "It was good."

"Yeah?"

I nod. I glance around the house. "Solomon is out, you said?"

"Yes, he's at the office today. Just you and me," she says with a gleeful bounce. "I'm so happy you showed up!"

My heart breaks, knowing I'm about to totally ruin her day.

She smiles down into her cup of tea, twists the cup on her saucer. She's more patient than me, allowing the tea to steep before bobbing it up and down. "Was it nice to visit the old house?"

"Yeah, it was good."

"Yeah?"

"Mhm."

We are quiet for a few moments. Me bobbing the tea bag, her watching her tea.

"Was it difficult at all?" she asks.

"Mom."

She bites her lower lip before finding the next thing to say. "I was surprised you wanted to go down there. I mean, I haven't been ready, and it's been–"

"Well, if we're not going to sell it, someone should enjoy it, right?"

My mother sighs. "Right. No. You're right about that. I mean, we rent it out, it's an investment. Not a burden."

I know the property as a rental narrowly breaks even. We're holding onto it because we don't know how to let go of it.

"Well, you had your friends. I hope that they were able to support you if you were feeling...down."

I laugh under my breath in a wry way.

Yes. Down. That's a word for it.

My mom reaches out and strokes her fingernails through my hair. I'm taken aback, lifting my eyes from my tea to look at her.

There comes a point in life where you suddenly realize that your parents have gotten older. I've only had the privilege of that experience with my mother. All the thin wrinkles on her cheeks and the silvery strands of hair amidst her curls. Her kind blue eyes are the same. Her smile is the same.

The look on her face could break my heart if I let it.

"You know, you never visit me during the workday?"

I blink. "I don't?"

"Don't act surprised," she says with a light laugh. "You're busy. I know that. I just like when you go out of your way to see me. When it's not family dinner. That feels like the only time I see you these days."

Is that really true? Am I such a shitty son that not only

am I disregarding my mother, but I also haven't even realized it? "I'm sorry I haven't been around."

"I don't need an apology, honey." Her nails softly slide down my neck in a comforting motion. "I'm just so happy to see you."

Her expression is so earnest.

The truth pounds at the seal of my lips. The desire to let it all go.

"Did Bridget enjoy it? I've always wanted to take her down there. I thought she'd like it."

And there it is. She just walked right into the reason I'm here.

A reason for me. Not for her.

Dammit. I'm a shitty son.

My mother furrows her brow, removes her hand from my neck, and sits back in her chair. "Have a sip of tea, honey, you're looking faint. Have you been eating?"

I watch her as she blows on her teacup.

I can't hold the truth in a second longer. "I'm in love with Bridget."

She freezes with the cup a centimeter from her lips. Her big, blue eyes turn to me. Her stare is not scathing or angered. It's confused. Majorly confused. Which is more than reasonable. "Come again?"

"I'm...we're..." I stare into the cup of red. "I love her."

Mom puts her cup down into the saucer. "Wait, let's think through this, honey. I know you're close, I mean, we're family." She lets out an awkward laugh. "Are you sure you're feeling alright these days?"

"It's the truth," I say. "I can't stop thinking about her."

"Well, uh, that's different," she says. "That we can talk about. But love? Are you sure, Seth?"

Fuck it. Lay it all out there. "We've been sleeping together."

Now it's my mother's turn to go pale. She stares at me.

"More than...that. But that's not the point." I don't need my mother knowing my preferences behind closed doors.

"You can't mean...you don't mean Bridget. *Bridget* Bridget. Solomon's Bridget. Must be a different..." She stops when she realizes I'm nodding. "Oh my god, you're serious."

"Why would I lie about that?"

She places her hands against her cheeks. "How did... how did this happen?"

"It just...did." I shrug. "I've always been interested in her."

"You have?"

I don't bother beating around the bush. All I can do is give her the truth. The facts. "It's true. And she's always been interested in me."

She places her head in her hand. "Oh my god. This is..."

"I know it's a lot."

"Seth, this is...well," she says with another uncomfortable laugh. "You know I'm married to her father, so you two are–"

I lay my hands out on the table. "Don't you think I know that? Of course, I know that. That's why I'm telling you that, why I'm trying to explain to you why I'm...why it's..."

"So, you two are together now? Is that what you're trying to tell me?"

"No, she–" A lump grows in my throat. "She won't take me like that."

My mother frowns, her head bouncing back. "I'm confused."

I swallow. "We were just keeping things...physical." That's not *not* the truth.

My mother plays with her wedding ring.

We don't talk about this kind of thing for obvious reasons.

"A secret. Because we knew…we know it's wrong. Or strange. Or–" I bite down on my lower lip. "Mom, being down there and remembering everything…" My voice warbles, and I know I'm not long for keeping it together.

She puts her hand on my knee. "I should've told you not to go down there, I should've known it would–"

"No, Mom. I've been keeping down all the hurt for so many years. I haven't dealt with any of it. I miss him so much." A few tears slide down my cheeks. Thankfully, nothing like the torrent I experienced with Bridget.

My mom wicks the tears away. "I know you do, honey. I do too."

"But you have Solomon. I can't replace my dad."

Her brow furrows. "Solomon has never been a replacement for your dad, honey."

"But you…you fell in love with him. And he's trying to be all buddy buddy with me and–"

"You and I are allowed to have people in our lives that love us and care about us the way your father did," she says. "That doesn't mean we're replacing him or moving on. The grief will always be there."

I tilt my head back as more tears pour down my face. "I want to feel complete again."

"That will never…be the case after you've lost someone."

"I want to try!" I burst without thinking.

My mother sits a bit straighter, stunned at my outburst.

"I want…I need…" I try to steady my breath. "Bridget… fills something in me I didn't know needed filling until I went down there, and I realized how hollow I've been all these years."

When our eyes meet again, I see my mother is crying too.

"Don't cry, Mom. That's going to make me cry more..." Crying after over a decade of not crying is painful. The tension in my jaw and the front of my neck is shattering.

"I didn't realize you were in so much pain," she says. "I'm such an idiot."

I have never held it against her for meeting Solomon. For falling in love with him. But it did happen fast. Only a couple of years after Dad died.

And then they were getting married.

She went from an era of darkness to an era of light. In the blink of an eye.

But I remained in the darkness. Just tried to smile so she didn't worry.

"You're not an idiot, Mom."

She says nothing. And I say nothing.

The truth is still out there. Undealt with and unclaimed.

"I know it's not convenient," I say in a soft tone. "But I fell in love with Bridget."

"Did you tell her?"

"Not that I love her."

My mom waves her hand. "Oh, Seth."

"What?! That's a scary thing to say!"

She tsks. "I know, I know, But you have to let people know how you feel."

"Well, she knows I want to be with her."

"And she doesn't feel the same?"

I shrug. "She doesn't want to ruin things for you and

Solomon. Maybe that's her way of sparing my feelings but... I don't know."

My mom's lips spread into a wide smile. "And you're telling me because you want to clear the pathway so you two can have a shot. Is that right?"

I look down. "Yeah. I know it's not an easy thing to accept. And I'm sorry for going behind your back, but–"

"You two are adults. And you're not...it's not like you were kids together. I'm sure this isn't the first time something like this has happened. If anything, this explains so many of the quarrels you two have had over the years."

I chuckle. "Well, I suppose."

"All I need to know as your mother is that she makes you happy. Does she make you happy, Seth?"

I make sure to look her in her eyes. "I didn't know that I could feel like this again, Mom. After Dad died, I thought my life would pale in comparison to one spent *with* him. But Bridget has made me see that's not true."

"Then, I see nothing wrong with it. I'll do whatever you can to help."

"Really?"

"Of course. My baby is in love. I've always wondered why you haven't brought a girl home, and it turns out it's because she's been here the whole time."

I groan. "Moooommm."

She pats my hand. "I'm teasing you. Drink some tea."

We sip our tea quietly for a few moments, and I relish that the world has not imploded around me.

"Don't tell Solomon," I say. "Just. Not yet."

She puts her fingers to her lips and twists like a key in a lock. "Secret safe with me. And Seth?"

"Hm."

Her eyes crinkle.

My mother's entire being is love to me. And I think I've forgotten that over the years.

I don't think I've really seen the world for all its beauty before Bridget.

"You two will look so cute together," she says.

Gotta admit...didn't know I wanted to hear that. I beam. "Thanks, Mom."

Now the question is, will Bridget think the same?

25

BRIDGET

I NEED A NIGHT OUT AT THE BAR LIKE I NEED A HOLE IN the head. I'm surprised my liver is still intact after Key West.

Not to mention, I haven't felt like doing much of anything since things went haywire with Seth.

I look down at my phone one more time, check our thread of messages to see if I missed a text.

Still, nothing.

It took everything in me to text him today after my meeting with Deborah Angelise. I was on cloud nine, felt as powerful as I ever have, and thought, "*Fuck it*. I'll text him."

He said I'm still his, right?

So, we should be able to have scenes in the Underground, still spend time together, in secret, the way we always have.

I know that pales in comparison to the real thing, but...

We've waited so many years to have each other like this. He won't throw it all away just because it doesn't look the way he wanted it to, right?

"Stop staring at your phone." Sonia waves her hand over the screen.

I look at my friend sitting beside me at the bar. "Sorry, I'm distracted."

"Yeah, we all can tell." She glances over at Laney and Abigail who are collecting a round of shots from the bartender. "Everything okay?"

I click my phone off and drop it back in my clutch. "Yeah. Fine."

She narrows her eyes. "Are you sure?"

"Why are you on my ass, Sonia?" It's supposed to be an attempt to be funny, but it just comes out edgy.

Sonia's eyes widen. "Sorry. Didn't realize I was *on your ass*."

I sigh. "I didn't mean...sorry, I'm just. I have things on my mind."

"Clearly. Which is why I, your best friend, am asking you if there's anything you want to talk about."

In the club lighting, Sonia's brown eyes illuminate like the flames of candles. Threatening to burn me.

"I'm just feeling a little low tonight. I shouldn't have come out." But when Sonia asked, I immediately agreed. I haven't seen her one on one since the honeymoon. She's been wrapped up with Edwin, and I've been wrapped with Seth, and other than group activities, our paths don't seem to cross, so...

"Well, I'm glad you're here," Sonia says. "And if you want to talk about what's going through your mind, you should talk to *me*."

I smile. "Thanks, So."

"Okay, tequila!" Abigail cries out, four shots between her fingers. Laney flanks her with a glass of limes and a saltshaker.

Sonia holds up a hand. "None for me, thanks."

Everyone goes silent. We stare at her.

"You all...good?" Sonia asks.

"Holy shit," Laney says. "You're–are you–"

Sonia doesn't say anything, just smiles.

"Oh, my god, are you serious?" I ask. "You're pregnant?"

Sonia's small smile grows.

Abigail squeals and grabs Sonia's arm. "Stop it! You're lying!"

Sonia flushes, looking away. "I mean, it's still early, but–"

Laney, Abigail, and I all titter over Sonia's news, almost loud enough to break through the din of the club sounds.

"When did you find out?" I ask.

"Just yesterday. I thought I should keep it a secret given how early, but..." She smiles at all of us, her eyes glimmering with tears. "You're all family, so..."

A twinge in my chest.

I'm not technically Sonia's family. Abigail is her step-daughter. And Laney is engaged to her stepson. I'm an extra, squeaky wheel. Knowing that Sonia doesn't see me that way, though, means the world.

However, a baby...that's going to take my friend further away from me than a marriage.

I think of my unanswered text I sent to Seth.

I don't want to be alone. On an Island of Bridget with just my designs to keep me company. Sure, I have my dad. I have my friends. But I'm not anyone's first choice. Not like I was his before I screwed things up. But that's how it has to be, right?

"I'm so happy for you." I wrap my arms around her, trying to make myself push past the threat of disappointment at the back of my throat.

Sonia hugs me back, so tight and loving. She's going to be a good mom. And she deserves it.

Abigail grins. "I've never been so happy over the thought of my father having..." Her whole body shudders. "Okay, never mind, I don't want to think about it."

We all laugh. It's exciting. The first baby in the friend group.

We're getting older. And that's exciting.

Except Laney's getting married and Sonia's having a baby and I'm...

I lost my virginity and broke Seth's heart. Now he won't even talk to me. How pathetic is that?

Abigail lifts her head and shakes out her hair, resetting. "Now, who's having Sonia's shot, then?"

"Me," I say without thinking. I take one of the tequila shots and knock it back, then another. I pay no mind to the burn, ignore Laney when she offers me limes and salt. "Come on!" I grab Sonia's hand and pull her toward the dance floor. "Let's dance!"

They're all looking at me like I've just flipped personalities, and maybe I have.

I need a release. I need a release so bad. And I can't have the release Seth gives me. I don't know if I'll ever get it again.

I tried to avoid this, tried to plan ahead, tried to make sure I didn't give myself to a Dom who would chew me up and spit me out.

Seth didn't do that. I did that to him. And now I'm paying the price...

I lost him.

Maybe that's what I deserve. Maybe I've never been a very good sub at all.

Sonia doesn't resist my pull, though I see her looking at Abigail and Laney out of the corner of my eye.

Whatever. Who cares.

I need to dance.

We fold into the crush of nightclub goers all swinging their hips and waving their arms to the sound of the music.

I pull Sonia close. She's my bodyguard with her wedding ring. Plus, if we keep close enough, maybe people will think we're together. That's the way I want it. Don't want any man thinking he can put his hands on me right now.

In my heart and my mind, I still belong to Seth. The collar around my neck proves it. If he can't understand my position, that's alright. But until he says no more, I am still his through and through.

Laney and Abigail follow us, their heels clicking quickly across the floor.

Laney glowers at a fratty-looking guy who pulls on her hand as she winds through the crowd. She flashes him her hand and shouts out at him. He waves a hand toward her.

"You want me to get security on him?" Abigail shouts over the music as Laney joins our circle of safety.

"Forget about it." Laney brushes her blonde ponytail over her shoulder. "Nate and Mason are dropping by the club later. If he wants a fight, he'll get it."

I get lost in the music. The DJ is playing some top forty remixes, and I have my hands in the air like I don't care. I let the rest of the world drop away, just me, my girls, and the music.

Tequila shots course through me, my muscles loosen. I can actually breathe.

If I want this feeling to last, I'm going to have to drink way more than this. Lucky for me, the night is young yet.

"Go, Bridget! Woo!" Abigail gases me up as I bounce down to the floor into a squat.

"I can't do that, my knees." Sonia takes my hand and yanks me back to standing.

We laugh and dance.

Abigail gets us more shots. I take two again, the second glass I hold into the air, tip my chin back, and let the disco ball scatter little lights across my face, smiling ear to ear.

My eyes catch on a familiar face in the second level of the club, the balcony shaped like a horseshoe around us.

Seth.

Our eyes meet. Doesn't matter that the lighting is low, or the music is pounding. Everything freezes.

What's he doing here?

I should have known when Laney said Mason and Nate were coming by that it was some sort of guys' night. I should have *known*.

I drop my arms.

Should I go upstairs? Should I say something?

Before I can make a decision, Seth looks away. Like he didn't even see me.

It doesn't feel like a part of our Dom and sub dynamic. It hurts to the deepest part of my soul.

And I know I deserve all the pain I get. I broke his heart.

Yet, while I know all of this in the logical sense, my chest aches. And a fire is brewing inside me.

I want him to watch.

I'm going to put on a show for him. A show so good he can't look away.

I toss the shot glass over my shoulder and dance again. Harder. More unfettered. The straps of my dress are desperate to stay on my shoulders as I twirl and undulate and shimmy. My friends egg me on, and soon other people on the dance floor do too.

From the outside, I might look like I'm having the time of my life.

On the inside, I hurt like I never have before.

Look at me, I want to scream. *Look at me. I belong to you. Why won't you look at me?*

As my hips roll and my head turns to gelatin, I lose myself, yes, but I lose my balance too. I trip over my high heels and attempt to steady myself. But gravity pulls me backward.

If I am writhing in pain on the floor, will he look?

Except I don't fall to the floor. I land against a hard mass of body.

Hands engulf my hips. And there is a hardness forming at my lower back.

Someone's *dick.*

"Long time no see, Bridget," a voice from my past growls in my ear.

I want to run. But I am locked in his grip.

"Don't run away." He grips my hips harder, locks me to him. "Let's *talk.*"

It takes everything in me to turn and look at the face of the man restraining me.

And when our eyes meet, the past slaps me in the face.

26

SETH

"Stop staring at my sister," Jack says.

I glare at my friend across the high top we're crowded around. "*What?*"

"You keep looking at the dance floor," Jack goes on. "Doesn't he?"

Mason and Nate exchange a look with each other. Their stupid telepathy. Wonder if it's gotten stronger once they started a relationship with the same woman.

Nate cocks his head to the side. "Did something happen between Seth and Abigail in Key West?"

"Oh, my god, no. Nothing happened with *Abigail*." I pinch the bridge of my nose. Me and my stupid *eyes*. The second I realized Bridget was at the club, it's been impossible not to stare at her. Her beauty is captivating, always, but the way she seems so free tonight. On top of the world. Untethered.

I have to wonder if I should let her go. Let her find someone she can bring home to Mom and Solomon that isn't her fucking stepbrother that's been sitting with her at family dinners since she was sixteen.

But she's still wearing the collar. That has to mean something.

"God, why did I even come tonight?" I ask to no one in particular.

Jack shrugs, "I don't know, dude. You *were* acting really strange the whole trip. And like the whole point was to try and go out and meet people, and he didn't even try."

"Did *you* even try?" I growl.

Jack balks. "You know I did. And succeeded." He dips a straw into his old fashioned. "But she's a Florida girl."

I roll my eyes and start to look back at the dance floor but stop myself for fear I'm going to add to the suspicions that I am lusting after Abigail. "I'm not looking at Abigail, alright?" I look Nate dead in the eye. "I've never seen her that way, and you know it."

"I mean, it's cool man, you're both adults," Nate replies.

I gape at him. "I'm telling you the truth!"

"Okay!" Nate says, lifting his hands in defense. "I'm just saying *if–*"

"There's no *if!*" I cry out over the music.

Mason touches Nate's arm. "I think what Nate is trying to say is that we'd rather be told the truth than anyone sneaking around."

I drop my face into my hands. "For god's sake…"

"I totally agree. I'm just giving you shit. She's my sister, so I obviously expect you to treat her well, but–" Jack starts.

"I'm not looking at Abigail, dude."

"Okay, but you're like *really* defensive right now, bro," Mason says.

I slam my fist down on the table. "For the last fucking time, I'm not looking at Abigail!"

My friends stare at me wide-eyed. I know that didn't do

anything but make me look *more* defensive. Fucking great. Fucking fine.

Maybe I've said enough to get them to move on, but I know it will sit like a cloud over all of us the rest of the night, hell for weeks after. And who knows, maybe Jack will say something to Abigal and then she'll say something to me, and god forbid Abigail actually wants anything to do with me and I have to let her down easy…

Fuck this. Fuck it all. I have had enough of everyone being on my ass about my singledom, about who I'm looking at. The most important person in my life has already accepted the truth, someone who should be more scared of it than anyone. Might as well tear off the fucking bandage and let the blood spill.

"I'm not looking at Abigail," I say one more time as calm and composed as possible. "I'm looking at Bridget."

Nate's eyes bulge, and his lips start to form the first letter of her name.

"Like *that.*" A declaration. "I'm looking at Bridget *like that.*"

Like I want her. Like I need her.

Like she's mine.

Because she is. She still wears the collar I gave her. That's as good a sign as any.

She's not ready to give us up.

I'm ready for a barrage of questions. Of clarifications.

Instead, though, Jack grabs my arm. His eyes are pinned to the dance floor. "Dude."

I follow his gaze to the center of the dance floor where only a minute ago Bridget was throwing her body around, living her best life, the most delicious temptation I'd ever seen.

Now, she's in the arms of another man.

Not by her own volition, though.

His hands are digging into her hips, her short skirt riding up, so close to revealing more than her uppermost thighs.

She's squirming. Not dancing.

No one seems to be noticing them.

She's been separated from the girls.

Bridget tries to pry his hands off her, but he's much too big and strong for her. She looks around helplessly until her eyes meet mine.

Her lips form my name.

She screams, but it doesn't make a sound over the music and club sounds.

Her eyes are filled with a fear I've never seen before.

Fear I will *not* let become a reality.

My body reacts first. Seems to be a pattern these days.

I leap out of my chair so fast I knock it to the ground. I push through people, not bothering with excuse me and pardon me.

Someone is in danger. My girl is in danger.

Once I'm down on the floor, it's much harder to gauge where she is.

I force myself onto the dance floor, shouting out her name.

Someone taps me on the shoulder, and I turn my attention for a brief moment to lock eyes with Mason.

All my friends have followed me without me even realizing.

"We're going to split up and cover more ground."

I give him a quick nod and keep wading through the crowd.

I can't find her. I don't see her.

I emerge on the other side at a complete loss.

I run my fingers through my hair, trying to calm myself enough to focus on my surroundings.

I scan the perimeter of the room, looking for any strange activity.

Nothing seems out of place.

People drunk and laughing. No one paid any fucking attention to a girl screaming and trying to get away from a guy.

"Bridget!" I cry out.

Useless. My voice is swallowed by the music.

I spot Lourdes, the head of club security, and rush over to her. "Hey, I just saw a guy on the dance floor grabbing Bridget–Bridget Vance–" As if she doesn't know who Bridget is. But I'm desperate. "–and I don't know where they went, but she needed help and–"

Lourdes's big, brown eyes widen. She lifts her finger to her ear to ready her com to disseminate the information. "What'd he look like?"

"God, I don't remember. Big. Tall. Muscles, she couldn't fight him off. I didn't–I didn't get a good look before I–"

She holds up her hand. "Got it." She tilts her head to the side and speaks into her earpiece. "We need eyes on Bridget Vance. Code *red*."

I abandon Lourdes and continue my own search, stalking around the club.

So much time has passed.

What if he's taken her away from here? Thrown her in a car and driven away? And what if I never see her again? What if he–

My heart beats so hard I think I might cough it up and spit it out.

I can't live without her.

And I can't live with myself if anything bad happens to her.

Security begins to mobilize around the club.

But I can't stop with that. I need to find her.

It has to be me.

My eyes never stop skimming every corner.

In the darkest corners of the club is the back hallway to the bathrooms, the only light that isn't dark and moody.

It's also the way down to the employees' breakroom and a fire exit. And in that spot where the light transitions from dark to light, I see a flurry of movement.

Skeins of dark hair, pale skin, the glint of a necklace.

Bridget being pulled along by that big fucking asshole that had his hands all over her, pulling so hard her feet barely touch the floor.

They disappear down the hallway.

I sprint after them, running smack into a bottle girl on the way over, sending a bottle of Dom to the floor. It shatters.

I don't fucking care, put it on my tab.

Time is running out.

Every obstacle is a second closer to everything going wrong.

I can't have that happen. She's already so scared.

I can't let her down.

I *won't*.

When I enter the hallway, it is empty of people.

But I can hear them. Hear her cries.

The music isn't nearly as loud down here, which means everything is audible.

"Hold the fuck still so I don't have to hurt you... much," the pitiful excuse for a man growls.

I follow the sound of his voice down the hall, follow Bridget's cries.

He has her pinned into a small recess in the wall, a secret spot by the fire exit.

The guy must be fucking off his rocker to think there's any way he's going to get away with assaulting her *here*.

I grab his shoulder and yank him off her. "Hey, fuckhead!"

The man whips around, fiery anger in his eyes.

His teeth are bared. Looks more like a monster than a man. Broad shouldered, dark eyes, buzzed haircut.

Fuck, he's willing to kill for her, isn't he?

But so am I.

I throw a punch, my fist colliding with his jaw.

Pain radiates across my knuckles, and he howls, grabbing onto his cheek.

However, I don't give a shit about the pain.

The split second the man recoils from me, I get a glimpse of Bridget. She's pushed up against the wall, cheeks streaked with mascara, one side of her dress pulled down so far her breast is exposed.

"Oh, god, Bridget..." My body lunges for her, but the man punches me in the gut, sending me up against the opposite wall, knocking the wind out of me.

I grab onto my belly and try to catch my breath.

The man throws himself onto me.

I don't move fast enough.

He pins his forearm against my throat, cutting off my airway. "You want me to fuck you up first, pretty boy? Gladly."

I can practically see my blood dripping off his teeth.

Little does he know the adrenaline coursing through me is unlike anything he's ever experienced.

"She's *mine*," I seethe, then throw my knee upward.

It collides with his junk.

The man yelps and stumbles back, giving me just enough time to throw another punch.

And another. And another.

He does everything he can to push me away, but there's nothing anyone can do.

The strength of another world overcomes me.

When he's too dazed to do anything, I grab him by the collar of his shirt and throw him down on the ground.

I follow him, straddling myself across his stomach so I can punch him some more.

This fucker thinks he can hurt my girl? He thinks he can hurt *anyone* and get away with it? Well, he's never dealt with *me*.

His blood covers the lower half of his face, and the swelling has started.

I think I may have even knocked a tooth out.

My knuckles are black and blue. Might have broken some.

Don't. Fucking. Care.

Someone grabs me from behind.

I leap to my feet, rear my fist back, ready to throw another punch, but I find myself face to face with Lourdes.

She presses her palm to my fist, closes it up, and guides it down to my side. "We got it from here," she says.

A fleet of security guards stampedes down the hallway.

I leap out of the way just before they descend on him.

"Seth." A broken, beautiful voice.

Fuck, I've been so focused on destroying him I forgot...

I turn into the alcove.

Bridget has righted her dress and presses herself into the

corner. Her arms are wrapped around herself, tight and terrified.

I want to grab her, pull her into my arms and carry her away from here. But she's scared and vulnerable. I don't want to scare her any more.

Holding out my hand to her, I try to smile, if one can smile in a situation like this. "It's okay. You're safe."

Bridget's trembling green eyes fall to my hand.

She reaches out to me in slow motion, as if she fears her hand might go right through me, that I'm some sort of hallucination.

The second her hand lands in mine, I pull on her.

She gives in, burying her face in my chest and letting out a sob.

"You're safe. I've got you. I've got you." I make sure my embrace is as protective as it can be.

I scrape my hands through her hair, press a kiss to her temple. "I won't let anything happen to you. I promise. Nothing bad is going to happen."

Lourdes appears at my side. "Carlton, get her out here, huh? Take her upstairs, to the Lyons Club. Police and paramedics are on their way."

"She's fine," I say. "She doesn't need para–"

"I'm talking about for *you*, Carlton," Lourdes interrupts. "That hand of yours will need to be set."

I glance at my hand and realize my ring finger is pointed at an angle it shouldn't be.

Didn't even fucking realize. Didn't even feel the pain. Still don't.

"I'll be fine," I say to myself.

With Bridget tucked in my arms, I guide her away from the commotion of the security guards and that fucking prick, muttering the same thing over and over.

"You're safe with me. You're always safe with me."

Not only a reassurance to Bridget. It's also a promise to myself.

As long as I live, I will be that safe place for Bridget. Even if she doesn't want me anymore.

I will *always* be her safe place to land.

BRIDGET

"Take a deep breath in..." the EMT says to Seth.

Seth inhales, tilting his head back so his eyes are focused on the ceiling.

The whole process makes me queasy, but I can't look away as the EMT adjusts Seth's dislocated finger back into its socket.

"*God* fucking *dammit*," he growls through clenched teeth, his neck roping with tension.

I remain quiet, curled up on the big velvet chaise in the corner of the room.

We've camped up in one of the private rest rooms that are only accessible to club members.

They're equivalent to rooms at a five-star hotel. Great for privacy. Also great as a basecamp for recovering from a traumatic incident.

Security has been coming in and out to check on us. The police have already come and gone. They questioned me privately, took witness statements.

The EMTs tried to insist on taking Seth to the hospital,

and since he wouldn't leave my side, and I couldn't leave the club yet, here we are.

I took a shower to wash off...everything. I threw my dress in the trash. I never want to look at it again. I put on the plush robe left behind for overnight guests.

Seth and I haven't spoken much. What is there to say?

It all happened so fast I barely remember the story.

I told the police what I could, but my mind is already trying to block it out. The same way it blocked out most of my college experience for the same fucking reason.

I watch as the EMT wraps Seth's finger in a splint. He rattles off some directions about making sure his dislocated finger recovers properly, gives him an ice pack.

Seth looks over his shoulder at me. I don't look away, though I've trained myself to. I smile at him, though I don't have much strength for such things.

He smiles back.

We're both so tired.

The EMT stands and gives me a look. "Alright. And you're sure you're all right?"

"Yes," I say as loud as I can muster right now, which isn't very loud at all.

The worst of it are the bruises on my arms. Nothing to be done about them.

He grabbed me hard.

Zack.

"Thanks, doctor." Seth gets to his feet.

He walks the doctor to the door of the suite and gives him a handshake with his good hand before sending him out the door.

Seth turns around, leans up against the door, and looks at me.

We are alone. Finally, alone.

I pull my robe tighter around me.

I want to be alone, but if Seth left, I would need him to come right back.

He walks toward the chaise in a slow manner. "May I sit?"

I nod and draw my legs up under me to leave a spot for him at the end of the lounge.

Seth is careful as he sinks down to sit.

His eyes are on me. I can feel him watching. trying to understand where my head is at. Trying to read me the way he does in a scene.

I touch my collar, cool feeling of metal grounding me in reality.

Seth splits the silence with two words. "I'm sorry."

I frown. "Why are *you* sorry?"

He looks off, his bad hand resting in his good one. "I should have gotten to you faster."

"You got there before anything bad happened," I say.

"That's not true." He frowns. "One moment with that guy was one moment too many. I should have been down there with you."

"Seth–"

"When I saw you, I should have gone down there." His jaw his hardened, tone is cold. But it isn't standoffish. His coldness is to himself, something I've never heard from him. "I was too fucking prideful."

I shake my head. "You couldn't have known."

"But I knew you were mine," he says with such strength I almost fall over.

His mouth is taut. His nostrils flare.

This all hurt him too. Not only the dislocated finger. All of it.

"And I should protect what's mine," he continues.

I want to reach out and touch him. But touching anyone right now sounds hard. "Well, you did," I say. "You protected me."

He looks down. "I wanted to kill him."

"Me too," I say with wryness.

Seth looks at me, eyebrow raised, small smirk on his lips.

I try to smile too, but it must look crooked and strained because Seth's smile fades.

I know I have to tell him the story. The truth. "I knew him," I say in a soft voice.

"...What?"

I chew on my lower lip.

The stitches of the past have been torn open. I can't keep the memories locked in anymore.

No one knows my story. Not even my father. But Seth should know. Because I am his. And he shared so much with me in Key West. Bore it all to me.

Now, it is my turn.

"Zack. His name is Zack," I say. "He's my...ex-boyfriend."

Seth's eyes widen. "Your ex-*boyfriend*?"

"You never knew about it because I made sure you didn't. College," I say.

He continues to stare at me.

"I went all the way to fucking Iowa so you couldn't have eyes on me." Two years in Iowa, two of the longest years of my life away from my beloved New York, all in the name of an independence I found out I hated. An independence that punished me. "Zack and I started dating at the beginning of my sophomore year and he..." I swallow. "You remember how I was in the hospital for a bit? And then I came home?"

Seth forehead pinches at the center. "Solomon said you fell down the stairs at your dorm and–"

"That's what I told him, yes."

We stare at each other.

"Your...ex," he says.

I nod.

"Don't tell me that fucking piece of shit–" Seth begins.

"Please, please, I know you're angry, but please can we just be...can we be quiet about it?" I ask in a soft tone. My eyes burn, but tears do not threaten me. I'm cried out. "The anger makes my heart race."

Seth takes a few breaths. "I'm sorry. I can't help it."

"I know, but please try."

"Of course."

I wait a few moments to determine if Seth will be able to rein in his temper before going on. "Yes. We were drunk and I told him what I liked. That I wanted to be a sub. And he took that as an opportunity to..." I get a flash back to a clump of my hair in Zack's meaty linebacker hand. The taste of blood in my mouth. The pain of the cracked ribs. "Hurting me brought him pleasure. But he wouldn't stop. It went too far."

"Oh my god, Bridget..."

"I didn't want to go to the hospital, but one of my friends made me go, and thank god I did because I had a concussion and... anyway. The only people who know what happened are me, Zack, and that friend." A friend I no longer speak to. Someone I left behind in Iowa after I decided to come back to New York after the accident. "Anyway, you were probably right to be overprotective of me. I didn't know what was good for me. Trusted the wrong person."

"No, Bridget, no. Trusting the wrong person...we all do that. They don't always come with those consequences."

I blink. My throat threatening to close once more.

"I was overprotective because I wanted you for myself. My intentions weren't good. Of course, I never in a million years, whether you were mine or not, would have wanted you to be hurt. Like that or otherwise. You deserve perfection, Bridget."

I sniff with laughter. "No, I don't."

"Yes." Seth places his hand against my knee.

My body swells with warmth.

"You do."

I put my hand on his, tug on him to come closer until I'm able to fall into his chest. I push my face up against his neck. "That's why I've waited for so long. That's why I didn't just go with any Dom and let him have his way with me. I needed someone who would take care of me. Who I could trust."

"You trust me?"

I nod into him. "I do."

"Thank you."

I touch his aching hand with the pads of my fingers. Careful.

"Now I really wish I'd killed him," he says, and I know there's no joke about it.

"He'll get what he deserves now."

"Too many years too late."

I sigh. "Better late than never."

Seth touches my chin, guides my face upward so our eyes meet. "I will never let anyone touch you ever again."

"You can't promise that."

"Bridget. I will *never* let anyone touch you *ever again*," he repeats.

He is so adamant I have no choice but to believe him.

"If something had happened to you, I don't know what I would have done. I would have been so mad at myself."

"More mad than you already are?" I tease.

His eyes flutter shut. "God, I don't even want to imagine–"

I press my hands to his ribs. "So, don't."

He sighs. Shakes his head.

"So, *don't,* Seth. I'm here. And you're here. And we're a little banged up, but we're okay. We're here and we're together and–"

"I love you, Bridget."

I close my mouth tight.

"I love you, and you need to know that." He swallows, a thick, audible gulp. "I don't want to just be with you because that's what people do. I want to be with you because I love you with every fiber of my being, Bridget."

As if my head wasn't already full of so much shit, now Seth has to go and say he loves me. What choice do I have? Ignore the thoughts I've had over and over, for weeks now? "Oh, lord have mercy, but I love you too."

Seth gasps into a grin. "Really? You mean that? You don't just have to say things because I say them."

"I thought that was the whole deal with the Dom and sub thing?" I narrow my eyes.

"Oh, shut your pretty mouth and kiss me," he murmurs before pressing his lips to mine.

I want to say it again. Into his mouth so it slides into his body, so he can feel my love forever and ever. Let it become part of his genetic makeup.

Seth lifts his bad hand, then drops it, tearing away to let out a string of curses. "This stupid fucking hand."

I grab his wrist, pull his broken hand into my lap. "It's okay. There's time."

He raises an eyebrow. "Is there?"

I hesitate. "Well, we should probably try and do things the old-fashioned way. You know. Dating. Not just scening in the Underground."

"That's fair."

The more I think about it, the more nervous I get. "Yeah. And keep it quiet at first. Since it's new."

"Yeah, about that…"

I narrow my eyes at Seth.

"I told my mom."

"What?"

Seth nods.

"You *told* your *mother?!*"

"She thinks we'd make a cute couple," he says with a smug smile.

I burble out a few nonsensical syllables before being able to speak. "You're lying."

"I'm not. I couldn't hold it in. I thought—I thought maybe you'd be more willing to try if I could come to you and tell you that I laid the groundwork and that we already had someone willing to accept…us." He says the word "us" almost like a thirteen-year-old girl giggling at a sleepover. It's so cute for a man who knows how to tie me up and play my body like a fine-tuned instrument.

I smile. Still. There's a pull of fear inside me.

"You know, isn't life too short to be scared?" he asks, a nervous tilt in his voice.

I wasn't able to see it when he told me the story of his dad. That was selfish of me. I hate to think it took this trauma for me to see it. But Seth really cares. He wants this so bad.

And so do I. "And my dad?"

"You've gotta be a crazy person to go to your stepfather and tell him you love his daughter," Seth scoffs. "And I'm a lot of things, but I'm not crazy."

I twist my lips.

"At least, I wouldn't go to him without your consent," he amends, squeezing my hand. "If you want me to, I'll do it. I'll do anything for you."

I never knew people actually say things like that. That men call women perfect. That they say they'll do anything for them.

My man does.

"And our friends might know," Seth mumbles.

"What?!" I shriek.

He jerks back. "I mean, the guys! I had to tell the guys!"

"Why did you have to tell the–"

"They thought I was ogling Abigail! And I'm not going to make up a whole narrative when the truth is I just want to love you and have everyone know it!"

I have no response to that other than a wide smile. "I want to love you and have everyone know it too."

Seth leans in, nudges my nose with his. "You mean it?"

"Yes."

"Say my name."

"Yes, Sir."

"No. Say my name."

I press my chest to his, wishing I could melt into him and become one. "Yes, Seth. I want to love you and have everyone know it."

"That's my good girl."

I giggle and slide my arms around him in a tight embrace. I would remain here the rest of my life if it was a possibility.

Seth holds me as close as he can with one hand, pressing kisses to the crown of my head.

I can't believe how far we've come. To go from disdainful stepsiblings to giving into our love with whole hearts and clear eyes.

All because of a few silks and chains...

I'll leave that part out of the story I tell the grand-children.

There's a knock on the door and, on instinct, the two of us pull apart. "Who is it?" Seth calls out.

"Sonia," she says through the door. "And company."

Seth glances back at me.

Without words, I return my hand to his.

We're doing this.

We are going to love out in the open.

And if someone doesn't like it, well, fuck them.

Seth gives me a reassuring smile. Then, he calls out, "Come in."

Our friends come inside. Sonia and Laney, followed by Jack, Mason, Nate, and Abigail.

"Are you doing okay?" Sonia asks.

I tuck my hand around Seth's bicep. "Yes. I'm okay now."

"How's your hand, dude? Gave that guy what for..." Mason says with a nod toward Seth.

Seth holds up his hand. "Dislocated, but otherwise fine."

"And you're...ya know?" Abigail's eyes flick between us.

I lean my head against Seth's arm, look up at him with tired eyes.

You take this one.

Seth might be able to read my mind. "Yeah, we're, uh,

we're together. I mean, it's new, but we're trying it on for size."

The room is quiet as they stare.

"I know, it's confusing and a little weird, but–"

"Oh, my gosh, was that appointment you had at the Underground with *Seth*?!" Abigail asks in a voice a little too loud for the room.

My jaw falls. "Um..."

"Oh, so this was the whole reason you wanted the Underground rented out!" Nate says, snapping and pointing at Seth.

"It's all coming together!" Laney says with a broad grin.

They all start bickering about the details and clues they've gathered over the past month and a half, leaving Seth and me as passive participants in the reveal of our own relationship.

Except no one is grossed out or concerned. Everyone is smiling. Delighted.

Sonia and I lock eyes. She looks exhausted. Probably didn't expect to be out so late and so newly pregnant too. But she manages a smile. "We need to talk," she mouths.

I grit my teeth, smiling in apology.

Seth leans over, brushing my forehead with his lips. "Not too bad as far as responses go, huh?"

I smile up at him. "Not at all."

Somehow, one of the worst nights of my life has also managed to become one of the best.

28

———

SETH

I haven't been able to eat much. I stare down into my full plate, listening to clinking silverware.

Bridget's foot taps against my ankle.

I look across the table to her. Her eyes are wide.

I shake my head in a subtle way.

It's been a week since we decided we were going to make a go of our relationship.

As promised, I need to talk to Solomon to explain the situation to him and if I am to be honest, I'm terrified.

Solomon has never been anything but nice to me, but I can't imagine he's going to take the news that his stepson has been pursuing his daughter under his nose very well.

Still, I am pressing on.

"Delicious, Amelia," Solomon says before patting his mouth off with his napkin.

My mom rolls her eyes. "You say that like I didn't order in."

"You put it on the plate so perfectly." He squinches his nose.

I glance between the two of them.

They are lovers in a way that Bridget and I have yet to become. Of course, we have an undercurrent of a different kind. But if we are to make a life together, which I hope for more than anything, not everything will be Dom and sub. There will be so much more nuance.

So many things to explore...

But first, I've got to talk to her father.

Fuck.

"Yeah, she's good at that. The plating thing,"

Smooth, Seth.

"Solomon, if you're done, would you be able to chat with me for a few minutes?"

Solomon puts his napkin down and leans his elbow on the table. He looks at me through thin eyes, a cautious smile. "I knew it."

My heart falls. "Kn-knew what?"

He wags a finger in my face. "You haven't been able to stop eyeing my ship in a bottle since I showed it to you!"

Relief floods through me. Sort of. "Yeah, that's it. I'm interested in learning your ways." I glance at Bridget who has her face hidden in her hand. Guess this isn't going to plan so far.

Solomon slaps a hand on the table and pushes himself to standing. "Come on. Let's step into my office."

Solomon gets to his feet and lumbers out of the kitchen and toward the office.

I give Bridget and my mother a final look.

Bridget still looks like a nervous wreck, but my mother is smiling with all the encouragement she can muster. She even touches Bridget on the shoulder as a show of support.

With every step, my anxiety says I can't do this. So, I have to fight it.

I *can* do this. I can fucking do this.

When I get to the office, Solomon gives me a look over his shoulder. "Close the door behind you."

My stomach drops. I didn't realize this was a private showing of his ship in a bottle, but I do as he says.

"Sit, sit, sit." Solomon gestures toward the ugly old couch against the wall.

All the furniture in here feels like it's from the eighties.

Just because it's ugly doesn't mean it's bad, though. There's something comforting about it all.

I take a seat and try to look casual, which proves to be impossible.

Solomon grabs his ship in a bottle off the top shelf and turns back to face me. He looks at the bottle, then at me. "Look, Seth, I owe you many thanks for what happened the other night."

My eyebrows lift. "Oh. Well, no thanks needed. Just doing the right thing."

Solomon is quiet for a moment. "Sure. Sure, of course."

He sits down in the armchair facing the couch, admiring his work. Then, he holds the bottle out to me. "Take a look for yourself. Easier than it looks, I promise."

I take the ship in the bottle and stare at it without seeing. My mind is in knots. "It's...nice."

"Well, thank you. I'm working on a new one. Should be even nicer. This one is kind of sloppy."

I will myself to look back at Solomon and just say it. "Sir, I have to be honest–"

"Sir? You're calling me 'sir' now?" Solomon says with an amused smile, leaning back in his chair.

"I just haven't done something like this before, and I'm not sure how it should go." My mouth is hot and dry. I try to wet my lips and then go for it. "I'm afraid I have been dishonest with you."

"Oh?"

"I didn't want to talk about the boat." *That's not what you were supposed to say, dummy.*

"Is that right?" Solomon asks.

"I have to speak to you about something serious. Something important."

"And that is?"

Solomon's eyes are laser-focused on me.

I've never feared him, but right now I am afraid he could kill me.

Better now than later.

"I know that the circumstances make it strange, but I have feelings for your daughter."

Solomon stares at me. Says nothing.

"Romantic feelings."

Still nothing.

"I love her," I say, shocked it even came out of my mouth. "I've fought it for a long time because of our..."

"Circumstances." Solomon crosses his legs.

"Yes, thank you. Our circumstances. But I'm only human." I smile, lips trembling. "And she's amazing."

"I know that."

"Of course, you do. But I want you to know I think she's just as amazing as you do. If not more so. Not to compete, not to say you're not doing your utmost for her, but..."

I lose ability to speak. I'm scared to ask the question. Scared to be told no.

"Just say it, Seth."

The smile on his face tells me everything. He already knows what I'm going to say.

He probably already fucking knew I was going to talk to him about this tonight.

"I'd like permission to pursue her. Romantically. It's

very important to her that both you and my mother are comfortable with it, and I've already spoken to my mother about it, and she's in support. I know it's strange. Some might say perverse. However, I don't feel anything we've done or anything we feel is wrong."

"So, you know Bridget feels the same?"

I purse my lips. Now I've outed Bridget as a liar too. Fuck. "Yes, we've spoken at length about it." Among other things.

Solomon leans his head in his hand, fingers in an 'L' shape. He watches me for a long time. Then, he says, "I have always liked you, Seth. You know this, I hope."

"I've always liked you too, S-Solomon."

"Your mother has done an amazing job with you. Your father too, of course. I would've loved to meet him, although, then we wouldn't be here."

I shake my head. "No, we wouldn't be."

It is a strange feeling. To wish things were one way and to also be happy the way things are. I hope I am allowed that happiness and contentment. If Solomon would only say yes.

"You would have never met my daughter," he says, followed by a heavy sigh. His fingers trace the arms of his chair, and he fixes his eyes to the wall.

I haven't spent enough time in Solomon's office to know the details. But when I follow his gaze, I find myself looking at a small black and white portrait of a little girl held by her mother.

Bridget and...

"Life is very confusing," Solomon says, through a sad chuckle. He slides his hand across his mouth. "It's incomprehensible, really. One day you're high as a kite on life, the next…" He shakes his head, lips tightening. "You know how it is, Seth."

I do. Because one day you're fourteen and going on a fishing trip with your dad, just like you always do. And the next, you're a shell of yourself.

"What I'm trying to say is, I know what love can do to a person. It is the most devastating feeling, because there is an inherent knowledge that with love comes loss. Whether it be the wrong match or otherwise. However, without it, life is meaningless."

I blink at him. My hands are so slick I fear I'll drop the ship in a bottle.

"I would never keep Bridget from that. I would never keep you from that either. Whether you like it or not, you're a son to me in my heart. Which I know is odd considering I'm approving of you–" Solomon clears his throat, "—dating my daughter. But I love you, and I see what an amazing man you are."

"Thank you, Solomon," I say, a lump in my throat.

"As long as you can promise me that your intentions are pure…"

Pure might not be the best word for it, but–

"That you'll treat her the way she deserves and if you don't already know, Bridget deserves everything," he goes on with a warning look.

"I couldn't agree more."

"And you also deserve the best, Seth. Bridget is the best, so I couldn't think of a better match."

I laugh despite myself. Was I really stressing so hard about this all week for my stepfather just to say everything is hunky dory? "I'm–sorry, I'm just–uh…"

"You were shitting yourself, weren't you?" Solomon rubs his shin with an entertained grin.

"To put it bluntly."

My stepfather laughs, one of his babbling brook giggles.

I've always liked Solomon, but I think I might love him. He will never be *my* father. But he is Bridget's. And as he is an extension of her, I love him. For raising the love of my life. Because I have no doubt she is my one. My only.

"I don't blame you," Solomon says. "I mean, it's a strange situation from the outside, but my priority has always been the happiness of you kids and your mother, so what reason is there to be bothered?"

I smile. "Did my mother say something to you about this?"

Solomon gets to his feet and heads for the door. He claps his hand on my shoulder as he passes my chair. "No, of course she didn't," he says, his tone indicative that he's lying.

I suppose this is a good lesson in loyalties.

"Solomon," I say before he exits the office.

He turns, quirking his bushy eyebrows.

"Thank you. For...I've always known my mother is lucky to have you. But I am very lucky to have you too. I'm sorry it's taken me this long."

Solomon purses his lips into a smile, eyes growing watery. "Now, come on, we almost got out of this without tears, Seth."

I laugh. Together, we return to the kitchen. My mother has drawn her chair closer to Bridget so she can calm her nerves, I'm sure.

Bridget's eyes shoot to me, then to her father, and back to me. "Is...everything okay?"

Solomon sits down in his spot. "You and I are going to have a talk about lying by omission, young lady," he says, a teasing lilt in his voice.

Bridget is too high-strung to catch his meaning at the moment. Still her eyes search for confirmation.

"We're good," is all I muster to quell her nerves.

Those two words send her shooting out of her chair and right into my arms.

Polite, sweet Bridget Vance plants a kiss to my lips right in the kitchen of our parents' home which sounds so fucked up, but by this point I'm so far beyond the optics of it, I can't be bothered.

She pulls away, her eyes swimming with sparkles, and mouth spread into a wide grin.

"So, can I finally take you on a date?" I ask, for some reason still buzzing with nerves.

"Of course." She leans her body into me, wrapping her arms around my waist.

Solomon clears his throat. "*Ahem.*"

Bridget flips around and retreats to her father. "Thank you, Daddy. Thank you so much."

Solomon accepts a kiss to the cheek, patting her back. "I've already warned him if he ever hurts you–"

"*Solomon,*" my mother snaps at him.

He grins. "I have to play the part at least a little, Mimi."

She shakes her head, then holds her hand out to me. "Come sit."

I join them.

We talk late into the night around the table, polishing off a bottle or two of wine. Laughing, reminiscing, hoping.

For the first time at a family dinner, there is never a lull, never a moment of awkwardness or strangeness. Because for the first time, there are no secrets.

Bridget sits across the table from me.

And she is mine.

And everyone who matters knows.

Yes, a first date is in order. Dating in general is in order.

But my hopes are high. Because when our eyes catch across the table and her impulse is to look away, she pauses, then returns to me.

Although we have already exchanged words of love, I don't need them now to feel it in her gaze. Clear and bright.

My only regret is it took this long to get here.

Better than never getting here at all.

My life will not be dedicated to suffering. No.

My life, from here on out, will be dedicated to Bridget.

29

BRIDGET

The restaurant is empty, save a single table at
the center of the floor.

Windows surround the room, including a series of
skylights, casting every inch of space in warm pink and
orange light from the Manhattan sunset.

What takes my breath away, though, is Seth. A vision in
a slim fitting brown, plaid suit, complete with a tie and
matching pocket square. Like he's just stepped off a runway
in Milan, looking the appropriate amount of scruffy and
suave at once, and his hair looks desperate for my hands to
run through.

Damn, he looks so good.

He stands beside the table, holding a bouquet of roses
because, of course, he is. And just because roses are cliché
doesn't mean I'm still not swooning over them.

"Don't just stand there, Bridget," he says with a half-
smile.

I realize I've been frozen in place, captivated by his
presence, his beauty.

I haven't even said hello. But when he calls for me, I go

to him. Try to remain steady and graceful, though excitement roils in my gut.

We haven't seen each other in a week. Since the night Seth told my father we wanted us to be together. Didn't want to give my father a full heart attack by leaving at close to midnight to spend the night with Seth.

It turned out to be good I didn't go home with him. We decided to take the time apart, build the anticipation to see each other, give us the clarity of mind to really determine if we still wanted to do this.

My feelings haven't changed. Not for a single moment.

When I reach Seth, so eager for a kiss, he slides his arm around my waist, the flowers cradled between us, and presses his lips so soft to mine I think I might die from how tender he is with me.

He pulls away first, catches my eyes before I'm able to look away. And he smiles in a way that I only started seeing over the past few weeks.

A smile that allows me to see his unsureness. His excitement. His hope. "These are for you." He lets out an awkward half laugh. "Obviously."

I take the bouquet in my arms, cradling them almost like a baby. "Thank you."

I've never smelled roses like these. The scent is so strong, yet fresh and natural. Not at all nauseating. "They're beautiful."

"Not nearly as beautiful as you."

I flush. Corny as hell. But I love it.

"Step back for me. Let me see you." Seth extends his arms to create my catwalk.

I back up and give him a pose.

He beams and takes a deep inhale.

I wonder if the blood is rushing to his pelvis as we speak.

"Turn for me."

I do so, slow and steady, so he can see every angle.

"My god, you look stunning."

"Deborah gave it to me." Of course, I'm wearing blue. It's his favorite, and I will do anything possible to please him, whether it's as small as a favorite color or as big as bending over right here and...

"Deborah...Angelise? Well, that was nice of her. What's the occasion?"

I bite my lower lip, holding in a smile. "I have news."

Seth's eyebrows jump. "Well, let's sit, and you can tell me everything."

Seth is, as always, a perfect gentleman, leading me to my seat, pulling it out for me. I mutter my thank yous and receive a soft kiss on the crown on my head before he takes his place across from me.

As soon as we sit, we are attended to by two servers. One takes my roses to keep in water while the other pours us both glasses of champagne. Seth's favorite, Dom.

Why am I not surprised?

"So, tell me everything." His demands are not forced, but I can always tell they are demands.

They send shivers down my spine. "Well, she was able to get me an audience with Cora Sherwood who is the current CEO of the Sherwood umbrella of brands. She was very interested in my pieces and by the end of the meeting, I'd signed a contract to be represented under the umbrella. Which means everything is about to change with my business. I'm going to have employees and a studio and marketing and–"

"That's fantastic, Bridget."

"It's…" I let out a long sigh. "Yes, it's fantastic."

"You deserve it."

I flush. "Well…"

"Don't discount it. You've worked hard for it. I know you've worked very hard to get to where you are. And without a degree at that."

I scoff. "Well, no one needs a degree to sew."

"Is that what you call what you're doing? Sewing?"

"No. It's more than that."

"So…" He holds out his hands.

I resist rolling my eyes.

"Say it. Say you're amazing."

Excitement flares in my chest. Who knew domination could come with a lesson in self-compassion? "I'm amazing."

Seth lifts his glass of champagne. "You're damned right you are."

I lift my glass too.

"To you," he says.

Our eyes lock. "May I add something?"

He nods once. "I'll permit it."

I giggle, but once my giggle fades, I lift my chin and breathe in deep. "To us."

Seth grins, then clinks his glass against mine.

Conversation over our luxurious dinner is…well, it's like a first date. There are pauses and blushes and questions we've never asked one another.

Doors have been unlocked the past couple of months, doors neither of us dared peer through.

Seth talks about his childhood, even refers to his dad a few times without getting choked up.

I tell him about life with my dad growing up. All the

adventures we had, how hard he worked to make up for my mom's absence.

We talk about lots of things...but not a lot about us. And for some reason, that feels right. All Seth and I have discussed before is *us*. Our dynamic, our feelings, our wants, our needs.

The seal on our vacuum has been broken. Our friends know we're here tonight. So do our parents. A relationship can't just exist on what's between two people. It has to include the world beyond it as well. That means memories and feelings and plans, hopes, dreams...

By dessert, I am more head over heels in love with him if that is even possible.

To talk...just talk, feels like such a gift.

When after dinner espresso is delivered to our table, Seth makes sure to put several cubes of sugar in mine. It's the little things that make me swoon.

"I'd like the night to continue." He appraises me through the steam of his coffee. "Would you?"

I cock my head to the side. "If you would like the night to continue, I would like the night to continue."

Seth hesitates, then puts his cup down without taking a sip. He slides his hand across the table for me to take.

Though I'm confused, I do so.

"Bridget, listen to me carefully," he says in a low voice he's always saved for the Underground or the bedroom.

Out here, it seems serious. Captures my attention. My unease.

His hand tightens around mine. "We need to talk about what happened at the club."

Time slows. I try to smile. "You were there. You know what happened."

He shakes his head in a curt way. "That's not what I mean."

I swallow. "Th-then what?"

Seth engulfs my one hand with his two.

Blue eyes laser into mine so hard I have to look away. It's too intense.

My heart is starting to race.

"Have you discussed it in therapy?"

"Yes." I've had a standing therapy session every week since I returned to New York when I was twenty years old. I've doubled those sessions since the incident at the club.

"You are my sub," he says with gentleness. "I collared you. You have given me your trust. Your control."

I remain silent, trying to keep my breath steady.

"The last thing I want is to hurt you. You know that, right?"

"Yes, Seth. I know that."

He is quiet for a moment. "I need you to tell me what you need to make you feel safe moving forward. Do you want to pull back? Keep things more...vanilla?"

"Is that what you want?"

"That wasn't the question."

"But your desire matters as much as mine." A sub can go too far, but so can a Dom. We have committed to each other. There is an expectation. And a fear of letting each other down. The less we speak to it, the more the fear will grow. The more possibility there is for hurt.

Seth takes our clasped hands to his forehead. "More than anything in the world, Bridget, I want what will make you happy. It is..." He swallows. Thick and difficult. "It is my greatest desire."

I've spoken with my therapist about Seth. Now. I had been hiding it from everyone, including her. Let's just say she is earning her hefty fee since what happened in the club.

And though fear lives in the corners of my body, though the darkness of night hits different than it used to, though I have withdrawn from the crowded beat of New York to recover, there is one thing that hasn't changed.

"You are my Dom," I say. "And I know with every fiber of my being my body is safe in your hands."

Seth raises his gaze.

Are you sure? his eyes seem to ask.

"You are my safe place."

He kisses the back of my hand. "Promise me you will always tell me if that changes. I never want to be anything but your safe space."

"I promise."

"In the moment. Right when it happens. If you can."

"Always, Seth."

Seth's concerned expression gives way to a smile. "Then I would like to take you to the Underground tonight."

I bow my head.

The collar digs into my neck.

I never take it off and become less and less aware of it every day. It is a part of me.

"Yes, Sir."

I HAVE REALIZED THAT MY DESIRE FOR A DOM, MY desire for Seth, is hand in hand with my desire to restage what happened to me with Zack in college. Though I had dreams of submission before then, that incident has always driven me to seek out the safety of a Dom who wants to control me from a place of love. Who will listen to me when I say the safe word.

I could never have known I would be resetting that clock when I went to the club that night that Zack found me. That the desire for restaging would become so potent again.

I want control. I want choice.

I still have that by choosing to give into Seth.

When we enter the Underground, we enter together. Any lingering stares we ignore.

For the first time, I'm not afraid word will get back to my dad. I already have what I want, and there's no taking that away from me.

We enter our usual room and the second the door shuts, I start the process of removing my clothes.

I reach around to grab the zipper on my dress, but Seth stops me, placing my hand back at my side.

His arms slide around me, his lips graze the lobe of my ear. "Let me," he says, hoarseness already enveloping his voice.

I allow him, though it feels strange after all the encounters we've had down here that *he* is the one removing my clothes. Still, I love the feeling of him unzipping my dress, unclasping my bra, rolling my underwear down my legs until all my clothes are a pile at my feet.

"Sit." He directs me to the settee.

I sit down at his direction.

Seth follows me, takes one of my ankles into his hand and slides the shoe off...then the other.

I try not to stare, but I am rapt by the way he is rapt by me.

When my feet are flat on the floor again, I make a move to put up my hair.

"Please." He opens his palm for the hair tie.

I place the small black loop into his palm.

Seth circles the couch and begins to collect my hair in his hands. The tips of his fingers massage my scalp.

I hold back a moan.

Feels so good the way he touches me. I've missed it.

"Since you now wear your collar permanently...I will put up your hair for you as our opening ritual. Does that satisfy you?"

"Yes, Sir."

It is a miracle Seth doesn't cause my scalp to yelp in pain, like he's practiced doing this so many times. Once my hair is tied back, Seth slides his arms under me and lifts me up, bridal style.

I yelp.

"I've got you," he says in a soft voice.

Seth places me on the bed. "Sit. I want to show you something."

I cross my legs and watch him.

We have been here a thousand times before. Me naked. Him fully clothed.

Seth stands beside the bed, slides off his jacket. Undoes his belt. I expect he's about to release his erection and take me.

It will be the first time we will have just vanilla sex, but I can understand the desire. The inability to resist. To wait until after the scene.

The belt comes off. So does the tie.

And then, he begins to work the buttons of his dress shirt until that comes off too.

A few moments flat, and he's left in an undershirt and briefs.

A view I have not yet known of him.

And then he grabs the hem of his T-shirt.

I suck in a breath, my body tensing.

His body tenses too, and he freezes, only a small patch of skin exposed. "I...uh..." He shakes his head, erases whatever he might have thought about saying. "I'll just do it."

Seth pulls his shirt up over his head and reveals the expanse of his chest.

I've only ever felt it, hard under his shirt.

What I notice first isn't the toned muscles or the dark hair peppering his sternum and pecs.

It's the jagged, purple scar that spans from the left side of his navel, all the way to his ribs. The skin is snarled and angry, looks like it might hurt.

"Is that from..." I speak without thinking, an accident.

But Seth seems nonplussed, his eyelids lowering. "The accident. I didn't notice until I got to shore, I'd been gouged by something. Not sure what it was or how I didn't bleed out completely." Seth touches the wound. He shuts his eyes tight. "I guess he was right to tell me to go on, but it still doesn't feel that way."

"Sir?"

His eyes shoot open, body jolting. "Yes."

"May I touch, please?"

Seth's brow threads together for a moment. His expression is...skeptical. But eventually, he gives a single nod. "Yes. You may."

I lean forward and, as his hand moves away from the scar to make room for mine, I allow my fingertips to slide along his skin.

So, this is why he's always wearing a t-shirt. Even at the beach. Why I've never seen him naked.

"It's ugly," he says, more disgruntled than sad.

I shake my head and kiss the top of the scar. Keep

moving down the line. His skin is warm, and his smell is something I have gotten so used to and yet still manages to drive me crazy.

I trail kisses down the scar, traces of whatever lipstick remain on my mouth transferring onto his skin.

Something between a groan and a whimper emerges from the back of his throat.

I want more of those sounds.

I nuzzle the scar before running my thumb against the ridge. A piece of him. A perfect piece of him.

"Be a good girl, Bridget," Seth huffs.

Already on my mind.

I slide off the bed, onto my knees, and move my mouth to the trail of hair that begins under his belly button, continuing the trail of kisses until my lips meet the waistband of his underwear. "May I–"

"Yes," he grunts before I can finish the question.

I pull the waistband of his underwear down until his cock springs free, before it can arc completely out, my mouth is on it.

I've done this a handful of times. But never had the complete experience.

This time, I'm determined to give my Sir all he deserves with my mouth.

I engulf him just below the ridge of the head of his cock.

My tongue swipes at the bead of precum that has already formed.

Seth grabs my hands and places them against his hips. "*Touch* me."

I moan as I sink him further into my mouth, curling my fingers around his hips.

He presses on my hands hard.

His hand wraps around my ponytail. He tugs, only

enough to cause a twinge in my scalp, to remind me that he is in control. I am here to serve *him*.

And I am more than happy to.

His hand remains on my hair as I explore him, lap him up, tighten my mouth and relax it.

He hardens more and more until he is hard as stone.

I push him as deep as he will go, hollowing out the back of my throat so there is room for all of him.

My body jerks with a gag, but I press on, taking as much as I can.

A "fffff" sound" emerges from between Seth's lips and teeth, extends for a while before he growls, "Fuck."

His belly heaves with breaths. "I'm going to fuck your mouth, pet."

I nod.

Seth's hips start to move toward my mouth each time my lips slide down his shaft.

"Touch yourself," he grunts.

I press one hand against his scar to steady myself as I reach down to my pussy.

My fingers coast through my slickness with more ease than I expect.

My clit is inflamed, angry I've left it unattended to.

"Let me know how you feel."

I moan with him in my mouth.

Vibrations thrum through me and into Seth.

He bucks hard, his cock going deeper.

I balk, but don't stop. I neither want to, nor could I, considering how tight his hand has grown on the back of my head. He's using it for leverage as he fucks my mouth.

As his speed increases, so does mine. My sensitive bundle of nerves is already an inch away from release, so I keep teasing the space around it.

I cannot come until he tells me to.

"*Look at me,*" he says, hard, from the back of his throat, like it is life or death.

I pull my eyes up to his.

Even from this strange angle, Seth is sexy. The hardness of his body, the intensity of his gaze, his piercing blue eyes.

I swallow the head of his cock a bit more, eyes pricking with tears.

His mouth is drawn in a tight line. Controlling himself.

I sometimes wonder how fast he would come if he wasn't in charge like this.

It would be a compliment if it were fast.

His tense, almost angry expression breaks, his eyebrows twitching upward, his jaw loosening. "Bridget…"

I blink and a tear rolls down my cheek.

Seth places his other hand against my cheek, can feel the way his cock presses into the side of my mouth. "I love you."

I moan without thinking.

How is that such a turn on?

"I love you so much," he says once more before his eyes twitch closed and his jaw falls open further.

A shallow gasp bursts from the back of his throat, and his cock twitches once in my mouth.

I grab his thigh, continue sliding my mouth up and down his cock and riding my hand simultaneously.

His fingers tighten on the back of my head. He drags my lips almost to the base of him.

He's shaking as he holds me in place. His hips jolt.

And then I feel the burst of heat in the back of my mouth, saltiness slicking the back of my tongue.

"*Come with me,* Bridget," he growls, nails digging into my scalp.

It only takes a few swipes of my fingers over my clit to send me spiraling too.

I groan around him, my eyes rolling up to meet his again.

His cock tightens a few more times in my mouth, releasing every last drop.

I swallow all of it, relishing the way he becomes a part of me.

Seth slides out of my mouth and lifts me back onto the bed.

I am a mere rag doll, trying to recover from the way he used me.

He spreads my limbs out long on the bed.

I can't help but admire his naked form as he works. I hope he never hides it from me again. At least not in the name of anything but pleasure.

Once I am laid out to his liking, Seth stops. Takes in my body. Every inch. A delicate smile appears on his lips.

He lays himself on top of me and nuzzles his face into my neck. His hands cradle me at my lower back.

I could lay here forever. I will if that's what he wants.

"When I say I love you, you can always say it back without permission."

My lips pinch into a smile.

I would have said it back if I didn't have your cock in my mouth...

"In fact, you can say it first as much as you like too. I'd... like that."

I spread my hands down his shoulders and biceps.

His body loosens with my strokes.

"I love you, Sir," I say, then brush my lips across the crown of his head. "I love you, Seth."

Seth moans into my neck, the sound almost like a combination of relief, pleasure, and contentment.

He kisses the front of my throat, above my collar. "Mine."

Kisses again. Lets his teeth brush my skin as he sucks.

He stays until I'm sure he's made a mark. Then he moves his mouth below the collar. "Mine."

Another kiss, another scrape of teeth.

After the third one at the center of my collarbone, it's clear that Seth is going to continue this pattern until he has marked every part of my body with his teeth.

And I will relish every single mark. Every single time he claims me with the word "mine."

Because it's the truth.

Forever and ever, I am *his*.

30

———————

EPILOGUE

SETH

A YEAR LATER...

I shove my hands into the pockets of my slacks for the umpteenth time today.

Yep. The ring box is still there, right where I put it this morning before leaving the house.

I never thought a proposal would be so fucking nerve wracking. Now I feel bad for making fun of Nate and Mason back when they proposed to Laney.

"Psst, Seth."

I turn to find Solomon leaning toward me from his second-row seat. He taps my empty first-row seat. "Why don't you sit, Seth? Show's going to start soon."

I glance at the empty chair and then back at the catwalk that crosses through the middle of the room. It is empty for now, but still taunting.

Despite most of the front row seats being reserved for celebrities and people in the fashion industry, I've been able to snag a front row seat toward the middle of the catwalk between Deborah Angelise and some woman who introduced herself to me like I should know who she was.

"Sitting just makes me more nervous."

Solomon exchanges a look with Mom beside him.

She pats his knee and then gives me a smile. "Seth, honey, it's going to be great."

I tug on the hem of my suit jacket. "Maybe I shouldn't do this here. Maybe it's a mistake."

"She'll love it," Solomon says.

My mom nods.

It seemed perfect in my head when I started planning this a few months ago.

Bridget's first big runway show as a part of New York Fashion Week. A smaller show, but still a slot on the roster means big things for the future.

I already knew I wanted to propose soon, so why not fucking make it big? Why not make her show the best it could be?

Now I'm questioning it, though. Maybe she'll think I'm stealing her spotlight. Maybe I'm overshadowing her with a proposal.

"I'm going to go take a lap around the room," I say.

Solomon opens his mouth to say something, but my mom grabs him and speaks instead. "Okay, honey. We're here if you need anything."

I again shove my hands in my pockets and head down the length of the catwalk to the section of audience at the end of the runway.

I climb the steps until I catch Sonia's attention.

She sits up, the corners of her eyes folding. Her worried look has gotten even more worried since the twins were born four months ago.

By the time I reach her and the section of our friends, she's on her feet and extending her arms to embrace me. "Everything okay?"

"Just nervous," I say.

She wraps her arms around me tighter. "Oh, it's going to be great. Don't be nervous." She draws away and looks at the line of friends beside her. "Right? It's going to be great, right, everyone?"

Nate, Mason, and Laney are the most vocal with their confirmation, followed by Jack, then Abigail who seems distracted with her phone.

Sonia narrows her eyes at Edwin who seems completely glazed over as he stares out at the empty catwalk. She slaps his shoulder. "Edwin!"

His body snaps to attention. "What?! What?"

"Tell Seth it's going to be okay."

Edwin smiles. The bags under his eyes look like they're full of bricks.

I guess that's what being over fifty with newborn twins back at home does to a person. "Don't sweat it."

It's nice of them, but not helpful.

No one is worried Bridget might not say yes. For them, it's been a given from the second she moved into my apartment about a month and change after our first real date.

Marriage has just been the next logical step.

Sonia beams and squeezes my arm again. "You know she's going to say yes."

"In theory..." *But in practice?*

She rolls her eyes. "Don't be like that. You have the ring?"

My hand shoots into my pocket for the hundred and first time. Once again, I met with relief when I feel the ring inside. "Y-yes. It's still there."

"Oh, you poor thing." Sonia sighs. "Let's see it."

I open the box for her, tucking it behind my jacket in case the light glints off the emerald and blinds everyone.

"Beautiful as the day you bought it. She'll love it," Sonia says.

Sonia and Abigail both went with me to pick the ring out.

I was set on an emerald. I like her in blue, but I wanted the ring to match her eyes. Spared no expense on the size of the emerald or the diamonds inlaid around the band. I was thankful to have the support of her friends.

The music shifts and lights in the audience start to dim.

I shove the ring as deep into my pocket as it will go. "I better go back to my seat."

I turn and walk away before I can acknowledge any more words of comfort. I know I won't feel the comfort. Just have to get it over with.

And I don't want to feel that way. Because this is the most important moment of my life thus far. More important than telling Bridget I wanted her to be my sub, more important than collaring her, more important than telling her I love her.

Now, I'm going to tell her, in front of all these people, not just people we love, but strangers, that I want to be with her forever.

Throughout my life, I've risked more. Grandeur things, more expensive things, my life, even. And yet, this risk is paramount to all of them.

I take my seat just in time for the show to begin. Deborah Angelise gives me an appraising smile, watches the show from behind amber tinted sunglasses.

I'm a fine dresser, but I do *not* get fashion.

The moment the first model walks out, though, my worries fade away.

I'm here for Bridget. To support her and all the work she's done the past year now that her brand isn't just hers, but so many others. There have been nights where she gets into bed after me which is a feat since I spend too many nights working late. Less so since Bridget came into my life.

Now, to see all her work pay off...I've always been proud of her. But I'm overwhelmed by the way my heart swells in my chest as model after model comes out.

Her signature mixing of materials, lingerie playing with elegant lines and classic forms of lace, interspliced with latex, leather. Good girls gone bad. Flouncy skirts and garters paired with silicon ball gags. Leather cut and formed to move like silk, paired with a matching flogger.

The final piece is a model wearing a metal negligee that has been detailed and cut to resemble lace. It is incredible, the craftsmanship and detail.

I grin, remembering the moment Bridget came home and declared she needed to learn how to weld.

It's innovative. It's brilliant. It's *Bridget*. Smart, talented, fucking amazing.

Mine.

However, knowing it's the final piece means...

Solomon grabs my shoulder and squeezes. "You're up, kid."

I look at him and then my mom. The fear in my eyes must be more apparent than I'd like it to be because Mom touches my chin. Our eyes lock.

"There's nothing to be afraid of," she says.

I take a deep breath and return my gaze to the runway. The final model walks off, the music changes again, and one by one the line of models struts down the runway. This time, though, the big reveal is not the final piece in the collection.

The reveal is Bridget. In a blue blazer without a blouse underneath, matching pencil skirt, and tall stilettos. She could have been a model out there with the best of them. She throws a glance in our direction, her long brown ponytail bobbing with her head.

Her collar gleams.

God, the way she teases me with that thing drives me nuts.

Her smile, the flash of her eyes, however brief, is everything to me.

The audience showers her in applause and cheers.

She waves at them, blows kisses, spots our friends in the back and waves to them. I'm almost taken away by the moment, watching her receive her metaphorical flowers. The culmination of all her work.

That is, until the stage manager, the one with whom I cleared all of this, pokes his head out from the wing and snaps at me, points to the catwalk.

I leap out of my chair and rub my sweaty palms down the fronts of my pants before reaching into my pocket and... yep, the box is still there.

The stage manager holds his hand out for me.

I grab it, letting him swing me up onto the stairs.

I find my balance only to be totally overwhelmed by lights and the skyscraper models filing past me, faster than they would during a normal show.

They have been briefed and have already started scurrying backstage faster than they already move on their mile-long legs.

I hurry down the center of the runway.

I can see audience members flabbergasted and concerned that this strange man is wading through a sea of models, but I can't be bothered by them. I have to focus on my prize.

Bridget takes a step back with the intent to turn around and tag onto the train of models.

I wanted to meet her at the end of the runway, but I'm not fast enough so I stop in my tracks and drop to my knee.

The room gasps.

And Bridget turns.

Her beaming smile falters when she sees me. "Seth, what's..."

I can tell she's having trouble computing, the way her eyes flick away like someone else might have an explanation.

She didn't expect it.

"Bridget." I hold my hand out to her. "Come here."

Bridget takes a few steps toward me, absolutely dumbfounded.

And though we are surrounded by not just our loved ones but her fans, her public, cameras, and crew, it's just us.

It has always been just us.

"What are you doing?" A laugh burbles from the back of her throat.

"Take my hand," I say.

As always, Bridget follows my instructions, but her hand is shaking in mine.

Not great considering my body feels moments away from the shakes as well. But I will remain composed. Always. For her.

"You know how much I love you, don't you?"

Bridget nods.

"From the moment I saw you," I go on. "Even though you were supposed to be..." I glance over at our parents in the audience. Our biggest champions since it all came to light.

They normalized it so quickly that anyone who had any

qualms with it couldn't say a damn thing because the only people who mattered didn't care.

That's real love there.

"All I've ever wanted to do is make you happy. Even if I had a crappy way of showing it," I say.

She giggles. A few tears slide down her cheeks. She catches a fat one underneath her palm.

"I'm so proud of you. And honored that you have chosen me to be the person you lean on. It is and will always be my greatest honor."

Her smile grows.

"And what I'd like more than anything..." I hold up the ring box in my free hand, flick it open with my thumb as I practiced because I was nervous I might drop it one-handed. "Is if you'd do me the honor of allowing me to be there for you always and forever."

Bridget's smile is so big, pretty lips bathed in a pretty petal pink, I think it might break her face.

There are so many more things I'd like to say. But the adrenaline is pumping, the energy around us is thrumming, an audience waiting on the edge of their seat to know if I've just made a fool out of myself. I need to know her answer.

"Will you marry me?"

She nods, head bobbing. Takes her a second to get the word out. "Yes, yes, of course."

I try to maintain my composure as I slide the ring onto her finger, but it's hard when everyone has just seen her nodding her head and is celebrating in kind. However, the second my ring is on her finger, I shoot up to my feet, pull her into my arms and give her a long, unflinching kiss.

We bask in the glow. Under the eyes of so many. To think our love was borne from a place of secrecy. Something to be kept behind closed doors.

And now we're being photographed on a runway at New York Fashion Week. Bridget, me, and the promise I've just put on her finger.

I wasted ten years of my life staying away from her. Now, I'm grateful every single day to have her in my arms.

For her to be mine.

As the kiss ebbs, my hand slides from the side of her head to her neck where the metal collar sits.

I stroke the chain link.

Bridget's eyes lingering on me with such profound love it makes my head spin.

"You belong to me for life now," I say.

Her lips curl up, and she ghosts her hand over mine, the one that touches the collar. "I didn't need a ring to know that."